"Did you call th

Theo nodded. "Wh

Jenny's eyes trailed over him. He was the
of man any red-blooded woman would notice
in a crowd. Any woman's heart would beat
faster at the sight of that tall, lean body, that
dark hawklike face, the pale eyes like jewels.
"Where was the knife?" she finally asked.

"In my bed."

Jenny gulped. "Do you have any idea who
gave you that threatening phone call?"

"No, they used a masking device."

Jenny sighed. Such a device had been used
during the call *she'd* overheard. But should she
tell Theo the truth now—that she wasn't just a
dream girl entering his life...but a woman
who'd overheard a plot to murder him?

ABOUT THE AUTHOR

Tina Vasilos has successfully written romantic suspense for many years. She has traveled widely around the world, and she uses her trips to research her novels. Tina and her husband live with their son in Clearbrook, British Columbia.

Books by Tina Vasilos

Don't miss any of our special offers. Write to us at the following address for information on our newest releases.

Harlequin Reader Service
U.S.: 3010 Walden Ave., P.O. Box 1325, Buffalo, NY 14269
Canadian: P.O. Box 609, Fort Erie, Ont. L2A 5X3

No Way Out
Tina Vasilos

Harlequin Books

TORONTO • NEW YORK • LONDON
AMSTERDAM • PARIS • SYDNEY • HAMBURG
STOCKHOLM • ATHENS • TOKYO • MILAN
MADRID • WARSAW • BUDAPEST • AUCKLAND

With love to John and George, as always.
Thanks to Debra and Julianne, my patient editors, for
going with this idea.

ISBN 0-373-22403-6

NO WAY OUT

Copyright © 1997 by Freda Vasilopoulos

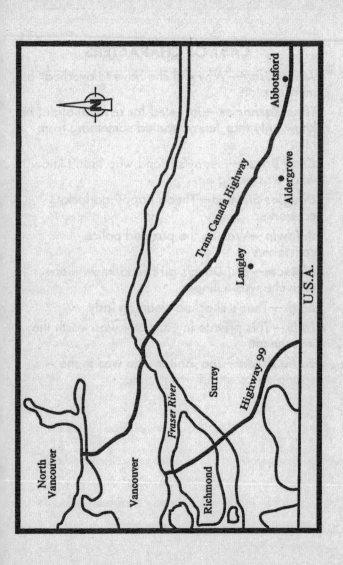

CAST OF CHARACTERS

Jenny Gray—Why did she have to overhear a murder plot?

Theo Zacharias—Targeted for assassination, he knew only that Jenny wanted something from him.

Cindi Brown—Jenny's friend who didn't know what was going on.

Douglas Stevens—Theo's happy-go-lucky co-worker.

Baldwin—Was he the puzzled police constable?

Blossom—Did Doug's girlfriend know more than she was telling?

Edith—Theo's shocked cleaning lady.

Felix—This private investigator was worth the investment.

Eddie Dixon—The janitor who was in the wrong place at the wrong time.

Chapter One

"It just came in. Swift Couriers may be small but they're efficient. The owner herself delivered it. I trust the envelope contains a thousand in cash, the down payment as we agreed?"

"You mean you haven't opened it."

"No, I was away from my desk but I'll get it in the morning. It's safe enough for tonight, as long as the money's in there."

"It is, and you'll get another thousand when the job is over. So you'll do it?"

"Yeah, I'll do it. I'm watching him all the time. So far he doesn't suspect a thing."

"Well, start putting the pressure on. I want him to sweat." The speaker gave a nasty laugh that grated like a rat gnawing a bone. "If you do a good job, you'll get the rest of the money and maybe a way to earn a bonus. And be careful. You've got until April 13. I'll be in touch with further instruction before then."

"Don't worry. I know what to do. By April 13, Theo Zacharias will be glad to have someone put him out of his misery."

JENNY STARED AT THE PHONE in her hand as if she expected green slime to ooze from the little holes in the receiver. Hot and cold flashes chased each other through her body, leaving behind nausea and an overwhelming urge to scream.

She'd picked up the phone in her office, only to encounter an open line and distant voices. Some anomaly of electronics? The building was old, the wiring outdated. She'd heard voices in the background of telephone calls before but only snatches of words had been decipherable. Except for the distortion in the voices that made them metallic and genderless, this conversation had been clear enough for her to understand virtually everything.

Someone on an extension phone?

Letting the receiver clatter to the desktop, she jumped up from her chair. She strode across her office and yanked open the door to the reception area. The room was deserted, the desk bare except for the computer and the empty In basket. Jenny glanced at her watch: 5:26. Cindi Brown, her receptionist, had gone home long ago. As Jenny would have, if she hadn't had a call from a bank at four-fifteen to make a last-minute delivery.

The fateful package destined to ruin or end a man's life.

She crossed over to the little room on the other side, where her employees ate lunch and changed their clothes at the end of the day. It, too, was deserted, as was the washroom beyond. She tested the handle of the door leading to the hall. Locked. No one could have gotten in or out without a key.

She closed her eyes as a new wave of nausea churned in her stomach. Pressing her hand to her waist, she rounded up her scattered wits. Think.

Do something.

Yes, do something. Damage control. Maybe it wasn't too late.

Back in her own office, she snatched up her purse and keys. She slammed the door behind her and headed for the hall. Locking the outer door, she moved stealthily to the next office down the dingy corridor. The warped wooden floors creaked despite her care in placing her sneakered feet. She wrinkled her nose against the familiar smell of old water leaks and decaying linoleum. She should be used to it by now, after three years in the building, but tonight it seemed unusually oppressive.

The next office was locked, as she'd expected, the shiny brass dead bolt gleaming in the dim light, at odds with the ancient oak panels. So was the one across the hall, and the others beyond it. The entire floor was deserted.

Giving up, Jenny stabbed the elevator button with her finger, praying this wasn't one of the days it went on strike. A reassuring wheeze issued from the depths of the shaft visible through the rusting ornamental grill.

Stepping through the opening that parted reluctantly to admit her, she pressed the Down button. As the car jerked downward, she leaned her head on the flimsy panel behind her, closing her eyes to shut out the image of her dead-white face. Diabolical convention, mirrors in elevators. No place to look but at your own mottled reflection, the sickly blue light unflattering and aging, too much a reminder of one's mortality.

The elevator stopped with a jolt. Theo Zacharias. Someone was going to kill him, unless she stopped it. She pulled open the clanking door and escaped the cage.

Theo Zacharias. Who was he? *Where* was he? She had to find out.

Free of the run-down building, she gulped fresh air, swallowing the gentle rain as if it were nectar. Spring—when did it officially start, tomorrow or the next day? It hardly mattered, since it appeared to have arrived on its own. The mild evening enveloped her, softly warm and scented with the tiny purple violets unobtrusively growing in a little pocket of soil next to the building.

I'm watching him all the time. The words played

through her mind, chasing away the brief feeling of well-being. His office, perhaps? Someone who worked with him? That was the logical place to start, the place where she'd delivered the envelope. From the conversation, she knew it had to be the last delivery she'd made, the envelope she'd picked up at the bank and taken to an investment office.

Dodging commuters waiting for buses to convey them to their cozy lives in the suburbs, she ran down the street. The building was only three blocks away, but its marble trimmed elegance appeared a world removed from her dingy office on Hastings Street. She entered the ground floor shopping mall, catching the elevator just as its doors began to close.

More marble and mirrors, plate glass with no pock-marks. Going up, the car was virtually empty. She stepped off on the fifth floor, shouldering her way through the well-dressed brokers and lawyers who waited for the downward trip. Conversation broke off and she felt the hostile stares they sent after her. So she looked a sight, her dark brown hair curling in the damp like the Medusa's snakes. Why should she care what they thought?

The long corridor stretched before her, hushed and empty. Her sneakers fell silently on the thick carpet. She had delivered the envelope at four forty-five. The office, Pacific Rim Investments, had been bustling then, phones discreetly chirping, deals being made. The perfectly coifed receptionist in her pink designer suit had tossed the envelope into a basket along with a stack of documents just dropped off by a UPS driver.

Jenny stopped in front of the double doors, heavy glass elegantly lettered in gold leaf. The place was closed, as she might have expected. The reception area was dimly lit by a single lamp glowing in the corner behind the desk. Her own image appeared as a blurred shadow on the plate glass. She cupped her hands around her eyes and stuck her nose against the cold pane. Nothing moved; the massive desk was clear except for a telephone with an integrated answering machine.

The latch rattled faintly as Jenny tugged on the handle. Locked up as tight as a vault. She'd never get inside unless she smashed the glass. And then she would still have the task of finding and retrieving the envelope she'd delivered, from wherever they'd put it.

The clatter of wheels registered in a distant corner of her mind as she bit her lip, debating her next move. She had to get the envelope back. Somehow. Tonight. She had no doubt that the frighteningly efficient receptionist, Ms. Herrington, would deliver it promptly at nine when the office opened.

"Eh, you there, what are you doing?"

The gravelly voice behind her nearly made her jump out of her skin. She jerked away from the door, spinning around to face a stout, gray-haired woman wearing rose polyester pants and an orange overblouse.

"Uh, I'm looking for someone," Jenny stammered. "I was supposed to meet them here, but it looks as if the office is closed." She knew she was babbling but either that or the scowling woman would hear the loud thump of her heart.

The woman angled a nicotine-yellowed thumb toward the discreet lettering near the bottom of the door. "Closes at five, says here," she stated, unbending slightly. "I've never seen it open a moment longer, and I been cleaning this building for nigh on twenty years."

Twenty years? "Do you clean in there, too?"

"Not me. I just do all the halls and lobbies. The offices hire their own services. If you want in there, come back tomorrow."

"Yes, I'll have to, won't I?" Jenny hastened to make what she hoped was a dignified retreat, but she was acutely conscious of the woman's suspicious gaze on her until she turned the corner near the elevators.

She drove home through the remnants of rush-hour traffic, miserably calling herself a failure. And worse. Even the sight of the North Shore mountains, iridescent pink in the sunset as the clouds parted briefly, didn't cheer her. By the time she crossed the bridge into Surrey, the glow had faded and the clouds were again releasing a dreary drizzle that fogged up her car windows no matter how she adjusted the ventilation.

She parked in front of the anonymous three-story building where she rented an apartment. The building stood behind a shopping mall, which was convenient but sometimes noisy at night when the pub closed and its patrons poured out into the parking lot. Luckily her bedroom window faced the adjacent street.

Glancing over the mail she picked up in the tiny lobby, she trudged down the hall, inhaling the scent of bacon that someone was frying for supper.

Her apartment, a featureless unit probably identical to most of the others in the building, consisted of a living room with a kitchen alcove, a bedroom and a bathroom smaller than the average walk-in closet. Its only virtues were the reasonable rent and the certainty that her neighbors were quiet and fairly law-abiding.

Three years ago, after she'd quit her job with Social Services, she'd given up her pleasant west end apartment. During the early stages of her business, when money had been even tighter than now, she'd lived in a downtown flat where it quickly became apparent her neighbors were drug dealers. After the third late-night police raid, she'd packed up and left without notice, feeling her landlord didn't deserve the courtesy after allowing his property to become a haven for criminals.

This apartment, cheerless as it was, especially on a rainy night, might not feel much like a home but it was a place to sleep and eat. Her business was her life. Even though it was hardly prosperous and sometimes precarious, it gave her the satisfaction of providing employment to young women who would otherwise be earning minimum wages in part-time jobs with no benefits. She could accomplish in a small way what she'd failed to do working for Social Services.

AT THREE IN THE MORNING she lay awake staring at the ceiling. Occasional car headlights strafed briefly along the wall. The scent of rain and blooming hyacinths crept in through the window she'd left open a crack.

Theo Zacharias. What kind of man was he? What had he done to cause someone to hate him enough to pay another person to harass him and perhaps murder him? No matter what, she had to find him and warn him. She only hoped her hunch that he worked at Pacific Rim Investments was right. If he didn't—

She rolled over, moaning and clutching her aching head. If he didn't, where would she start in her search?

A thought struck her. The phone book. She snapped on the lamp, and dragged the heavy book out of the night table drawer. Turning to the Z section, she ran her finger down the row of names. She groaned when she saw how many listings there were for Zacharias, including half a dozen T. Zachariases with or without another initial. It was hopeless; she had no idea where he lived.

Muttering in frustration, she let the book slide to the floor. It landed with a dull thud. Turning off the light, she buried her face in the pillow.

AT TEN TO NINE the elevator whisked her and assorted well-dressed executives up to the fifth floor. Dressed in the cream wool suit, silk stockings and high heels she usually reserved for meetings with bankers or accountants, she walked up to the doors of Pacific Rim Investments. Although Ms. Herrington sat behind the desk, the door remained locked. Jenny rapped on the glass. The woman looked up from filing her perfectly painted nails and pointed to the legend at the bottom of the door.

"It's urgent," Jenny mouthed.

Ms. Herrington pursed her glossy red lips and shook her head.

Fuming, Jenny paced for ten minutes, her toes pinched in the dress shoes she seldom wore anymore. The pain aggravated her anxiety. She had to get back the envelope. She had to.

She heard the mellow chime of a clock toll the hour, and tightened her grip on the handle as Ms. Herrington leisurely strolled across the carpet and unlocked the door.

"About bloody time," Jenny muttered beneath her breath.

The thin brows arched upward. "I beg your pardon?" The young woman blinked. "Oh, you're the bicycle lady."

"Yes," Jenny said, her jaw clenched. "I'm the bicycle lady. That envelope I delivered last night—I need it back. It was a mistake."

"Sorry. I can't do that." Ms. Herrington seated herself behind her desk, crossing her legs. "It was addressed to the company, and once it's in my hands, it becomes company property."

Jenny glanced at the basket, yesterday bulging with mail but now pristinely empty. Her heart sank. "Then do you remember who you delivered it to?"

Ms. Herrington shook her head, her artfully tousled hair not even stirring. "Sorry, you made the delivery so close to closing time last night everything was put in the safe for the night. I just sorted them this morning and put them on the proper people's desks. It's impossible to remember every one. And some people pick up their mail on their way in, sometimes as early as six—that's when the eastern markets open. So I might not have handled it at all."

She put her hand on the telephone as it chirred gently. "If there's nothing else, I'll bid you good morning." She lifted the receiver. "Good morning, Pacific Rim Investments. How may I help you?"

Her tone rivalled the purr of a well-fed cat, Jenny thought uncharitably. She stared at the abstract painting on the wall before her, balancing on one leg to rub the aching toes of the other against her calf. What should she do now? The envelope she'd delivered had had only the company name printed on it. Inside would have been another, smaller envelope containing the money and showing the recipient's name.

"Are you still here?"

The voice, laced with annoyance rather than its mellow purr, jolted her back to the present. Jenny turned. "Yes, I'm still here. Does a Theo Zacharias work here?"

The woman frowned. "Yes, but Mr. Zacharias won't be back until late this afternoon. I can give you an appointment for tomorrow, if you wish one." Her tone said she couldn't imagine what possible business a bicycle courier would have with a financial planner.

"Tomorrow is too late." Jenny turned away, desperation clawing in her stomach.

"Mr. Zacharias likes to take care of his paperwork when he returns from a business trip. Tomorrow afternoon is the earliest appointment I can give you."

She'd see about that, Jenny thought with renewed determination. "All right. I'll call you later after I look at my schedule."

"As you wish." She handed Jenny a glossy brochure. "Here is a list of our services. You might like to look it over."

"Thanks." Jenny rolled it around her clutch purse.

Out in the corridor, instead of heading back toward the

elevator, Jenny walked toward the red exit sign. Sure enough, directly opposite the fire door, a plain wooden door bore the name of Pacific Rim Investments, Employees Only. It was locked, but at that moment a balding man carrying a briefcase emerged from the fire exit, fitted a key into the lock and went inside.

Smiling faintly, she turned toward the elevator. This afternoon she would be waiting outside this door. She would meet Theo Zacharias.

"WHERE HAVE YOU BEEN?" Cindi's husky voice greeted her as Jenny walked into the office. "You're late," she added without looking up from the scattered notes she was transcribing into the computer.

"I had an errand," Jenny said, pleased to see the signs of industry.

Cindi, an attractive woman in her midthirties, raised her gaze from the computer terminal. Her mouth dropped open. "My, my, looks like going-to-the-bank-for-a-loan clothes you're wearing today. And heaven knows, we could use the extra money."

"Sorry. No money. Any messages?" Jenny checked the Out basket.

"None I couldn't take care of. Lots of orders, though, which is good. Bad news is that we've lost one of the bikes. It disappeared while Sandra made a drop-off at the bus depot."

Jenny groaned. Unlike most messenger services who expected their employees to supply their own bikes, Jenny owned the fleet of bikes her couriers used. Most of the young women she employed would not have been able to afford one of their own. All the bikes were equipped with sophisticated locks to secure them during deliveries but, despite that, once in a while a thief managed to steal one. "I suppose she used the lock?"

Cindi ran a hand through her short, sleek blond hair.

"She says so. She's really upset but she said she'd take the nearby deliveries. Walk them."

"Okay. When she comes in, I'd like to talk to her. Have you notified the police, given them the serial number?"

"Of course. I did it first thing."

"Well, maybe we'll be lucky and get it back. Whoever's got it must be feeling pretty conspicuous by now riding a bright pink bike."

Cindi smiled. "Let's hope. Although it'll probably be damaged. That's what happened last time one was ripped off."

"At least it was repairable, only a bent wheel." Jenny moved past the desk to enter her own office, but at the door she paused and turned. "Cindi, you haven't had any problems with the phone lines lately, have you?"

Cindi's brows lifted. "Why, have we been billed for calls we didn't make?"

This had happened before. The phone bill they'd received around Christmas had contained five calls to numbers Jenny had never heard of. The phone company had credited them, no problem, with the unsatisfactory explanation of computer error during a heavy usage period. "No, not lately. But the lines are noisy sometimes."

"I've noticed that, too," Cindi said. "But I haven't had any problems, other than a bit of static."

"What about voices?"

Cindi laughed. "No, not voices. If I start hearing voices, I'll know I've gone over the edge." The phone rang. "Good morning, Swift Couriers."

Frowning, but slightly relieved that the problem with the phones must have been a one-time aberration, Jenny went into her office and sat down behind her desk. She settled down to her own work, going through the basket of neatly organized invoices that Cindi had left for her.

Not for the first time she thought she was lucky to have found a receptionist as efficient as Cindi. She'd worked for Swift Couriers for a year now, and Jenny considered her a friend as well as an employee. Although Cindi sometimes seemed a bit moody, she worked hard and was completely reliable. And, unlike her predecessor, she never mixed up the delivery orders.

JENNY PEEKED around the door of the women's washroom. She'd heard the stair door open, but the man who entered the employee door of Pacific Rim Investments couldn't be Theo Zacharias. Wrong age and coloring. She had an idea what Theo Zacharias looked like, thanks to the glossy company brochure Ms. Herrington had given her that morning.

She glanced at her watch. Twenty after four. She had taken the precaution of calling earlier, and asking in a disguised voice what time Mr. Zacharias would be in. No use taking a chance of missing him, or waiting in the hall when he was already inside. Four o'clock, Ms. Herrington had informed her.

Fortunately she could watch both doors from her vantage point. Standing in the hall would have been too conspicuous but luckily the washroom provided fairly adequate cover. She ducked back inside and checked her hair, patting the springy curls coiled ruthlessly into a knot at the back of her head. She secured a pin, which was working its way loose, and rubbed away a smudge of mascara from beneath her eye. He'd better come soon. Her feet were killing her, and the smooth facade of makeup and dignified hairstyle was beginning to unravel, hinting at the turmoil inside her.

She turned away, leaning against the cool tile wall. What if he didn't show up and her lurking outside the door this afternoon proved to be a big waste of time? What then?

Should she go to the police? In the dark hours of the

night, she'd mentally tallied the pros and cons of reporting what she'd heard. And she'd decided to hold off.

First of all, they probably wouldn't take her seriously enough to launch an investigation. They'd likely dismiss the conversation as a joke or a misunderstanding. They had enough to do with criminals walking out on parole every day and repeating their crimes in endless rotation.

But if they believed her, they might very well consider her an accomplice in the matter. And if she were arrested, she would not be able to warn Theo. She didn't have much faith in the police department's ability to protect him. She had enough experience when she'd been a social worker. They didn't have the manpower to protect a battered woman facing a murderous husband, never mind putting a guard on a man who hadn't been directly threatened except in the vaguest terms.

No, she had to handle it herself, at least for now.

The wheeze of the hydraulic door closer told her someone else had come out of the stairwell. She poked her head cautiously around the door frame. A tall man in a slate gray suit was just inserting a key into the lock. Theo Zacharias. It had to be him.

She'd given plenty of thought to how she could approach him. For obvious reasons a direct confrontation wouldn't do. Hello, Mr. Zacharias. Someone's going to kill you so you should be careful. Get a bodyguard or something until after April 13.

He'd laugh her out of his office. For the same reason, she hadn't told Cindi about the overheard conversation. It was too bizarre.

No, she had almost a month, since today was March 21. She would introduce herself as a potential client and make it up as she went along.

Jenny squared her shoulders and gave her hair a final pat. Here goes nothing, she thought, heart hammering against her ribs. Tucking her purse securely under her arm, she smoothed her wrinkled skirt and walked up to him. "Mr. Zacharias? Mr. Theo Zacharias?"

The man straightened. Awareness and apprehension jolted through her. The small black-and-white photo in the company brochure didn't do him justice. It hadn't prepared her for the impact of silver-gray eyes dominating a lean, dark face. Those eyes bored into her as if she were a particularly loathsome object he'd found on the bottom of his shoe.

She dropped her own gaze, taking note of the perfectly tailored suit, which didn't even show a wrinkle despite the trip he must have just returned from. Beside him, she felt like a poor relative come to beg a handout. Stupid way to feel, she thought, reminding herself of her real purpose.

She bravely looked up. He was handsome without being pretty, the clean planes and angles of his face showing strong character. Early to midthirties, she guessed. His black hair lay close to his head, unruly curls barbered into submission by an expert.

He still watched her, his eyes direct and disconcerting, silver irises outlined in black. The annoyance in them was suddenly gone, replaced by an emotion she could only interpret as shock, mixed with—was it recognition? He blinked, the dense, long lashes fluttering down and then up. The odd expression she'd seen faded—or maybe she had imagined it.

Her gaze slid slower. His mouth, wide and generous in repose, tightened, his lips twisting cynically.

"May I help you?" he said coldly.

"You are Theo Zacharias, aren't you?" she said a little uncertainly. She stiffened her legs, afraid he would hear her knees knocking together.

His eyes narrowed. "Who wants to know?"

Jenny nearly choked on the butterflies creeping up from her stomach. Pasting a wide smile on her face, she stuck out her right hand. "My name is Jenny Gray. I know a cousin of yours who recommended you."

He glanced at her hand as if it held a dead fish. "I have no cousins."

"Oh, come on, everyone has cousins." As soon as the words came out, Jenny clapped her hand over her mouth, wishing she could stuff them back.

His straight brows lifted, his expression becoming more austere if that were possible. "I don't. Good day, Miss Gray."

He'd caught her name. That was something. But he'd opened the door and was halfway through it. She was losing him. "Mr. Zacharias, wait. I've got something very important to discuss with you."

Again the sceptical twist of his mouth. "Oh? Then make an appointment for tomorrow. I've just returned from a business trip and I can't see you now."

She grabbed the door before he could close it in her face. For an instant they were locked in a struggle. She wasn't sure what he saw in her face but suddenly he wrapped his fingers around her wrist and dragged her inside. The lock clicked behind her.

THEO ZACHARIAS stared at the woman who sat on the edge of the chair across from his desk. He'd acted like a jerk, and he was sorry, although he wasn't sure how to let her know that. His business in Japan hadn't gone as well as he'd hoped, customs had searched his suitcase and the taxi had gotten a flat tire on the way in from the airport. All of it had combined to put him in a very bad mood but that didn't give him the right to take it out on her.

But for some reason, the first sight of her, after his initial irritation at being accosted in the hall, had thrown him. Somewhere in the recesses of his soul he'd recognized her. He was sure they'd never met, yet he'd taken

one look at those blue, blue eyes and felt as if he'd fallen
down a well.

He'd quickly pulled himself together. It must be jet lag
clouding his reason, feeding some insidious fantasy.

He looked at her objectively, closing off his emotions.
It took surprising effort to engage the skill he thought he'd
perfected after the debacle of his marriage.

Pretty face, not that he took much stock in outward
appearances, having learned the hard way how beauty
could mask deception. Marvellous hair, thick and dark and
about to burst loose from the knot she'd wound it into.
The escaping strands curled around her face in charming
disarray, practically begging for a man's hands to run
through them. His hands. He clenched them on his knees,
beneath the desk.

A pink flush highlighted her strong cheekbones, be-
traying her uneasiness. Her eyes gazed back at him, as
deeply blue as the sea in his native Greece. A cliché,
perhaps, but they were the exact shade that stained the far
horizon, the edge of the earth as he'd imagined when he
was a child.

She blinked, dark lashes feathering her cheeks, briefly
hiding the smudges beneath her eyes. She looked almost
as tired as he felt, as if she had slept badly last night, or
not at all. Her mouth, naked of lipstick, parted briefly as
if she were about to speak. Wordlessly she snapped it shut
again.

He leaned back, folding his arms over his chest. Outside the closed door of his office, he could hear the usual
bustle of his colleagues packing up and going home. The
back of his neck ached. Too many hours on a plane, and
then the endless line at customs. Well, good thing he
wasn't still in Japan; he'd heard in the taxi coming downtown that they'd had a major earthquake.

"Miss Gray," he said, stifling an exasperated sigh, "I'd

suggest you state your business so we can both go home and get some rest."

She twisted her hands nervously in her lap, setting small white teeth into the lush pink cushion of her bottom lip. A tiny coil of warmth stirred in his gut. With the ease of long practice, he repressed it, reminding himself he still didn't know her reasons for accosting him.

"I—I need some financial advice." The words came out so fast they all slurred together.

This time he let the sigh escape. "Can't it wait until normal office hours?"

"No, it can't. I need to know how I can reduce the amount of income tax I have to pay, and there's less than six weeks until the return is due." She stretched her lips in what should have been a smile but looked more like a grimace. A tiny muscle ticked at the corner of her eye. She rubbed at it, and then pressed her fingers to her brow as if her head hurt.

He found it easy to sympathize. His own temples were beginning to ache. "Miss Gray, if you haven't maximized your pension contributions by now, there's not a lot I can do."

Her bottom lip trembled, and his heart contracted. She looked defenceless, almost as if she were afraid of something. "I still need your advice."

He didn't believe it for a moment. Oh, he knew she wanted something, but it wasn't financial advice and for the life of him he couldn't figure out what it was or why she didn't come right out and say so. He got to his feet, wincing slightly as a muscle cramped in his back. For an instant the room swayed around him. He rubbed his hand over his face. Jet lag catching up. His brain felt stuffed with cotton wool.

Knuckles rapped on the door briefly before it opened and Douglas Stevens looked in. "Oh, sorry, Theo, I didn't know you had company." His eyes lit up appreciatively.

His lips pursed in a silent whistle as he looked the woman up and down. Weary as he was, Theo felt a stab of annoyance. Stevens figured he was Vancouver's stud of the year and he practised on every woman who crossed his path.

"Can I help you, Doug?" Theo said acerbically.

"Just checking if you're going to be here long."

"I'm about to leave," Theo said. "Are you locking up?"

"Yeah, I'll wait for you." Stevens withdrew.

The phone rang. Inside line. Theo picked it up and punched the flashing button. "Yes, Janice?"

"Just checking to make sure you're in, Theo," the receptionist said sweetly. "You wouldn't be interested in going out for a drink, would you?"

Theo clenched his teeth. She never gave up, did she, no matter how many times he rebuffed her subtle and not so subtle advances. "Not tonight," he said in a neutral tone. "Sorry."

"Some other time, then. Good night, Theo."

He barely restrained himself from slamming the phone down. Stuffing the pile of mail into his briefcase, he snapped it closed and walked around the desk. He held out his hand to his visitor. "Tomorrow, Miss Gray. Come and see me at nine tomorrow."

She stared silently up at him, her fingers cool against his. Her eyes looked wide and stricken, and he could have sworn he saw tears swimming in their blue depths. "I'm sorry," he murmured inadequately. "But I can't help you today, especially when I don't know what you want."

Her fingers jerked under his and he let them go. "I said—"

"I know what you said. But it's not what you've come for. When you're ready to level with me, come and see me. Otherwise forget about showing up tomorrow."

THEO JOGGED down the stairs. Not one of his more brilliant ideas, he realized as he stumbled on the bottom step of the parking level landing. He was exhausted. He shouldn't have stopped at the office at all, but he'd wanted to pick up his mail.

His footsteps echoed hollowly among the pillars of the underground garage. A car roared down the ramp from the level above him, its exhaust backfiring. The pistol shot bang reverberated from the concrete walls. Theo closed his eyes for a moment, his head pounding in earnest.

Home, he thought. I have to get home. Beside his car, he fumbled with the keys, missing the lock. They clattered to the floor. He bent and picked them up. The pungency of stale oil swam up his nostrils, swirling nausea in his stomach. He swallowed hard, opened the car door and tossed the briefcase into the back seat.

The Saab started with its usual, reassuring growl. He shifted into reverse, backed out of the slot and headed for the ramp. The exit signs blurred into a red haze. He rubbed his eyes, wishing he'd stopped to take a painkiller. He rarely had headaches but this was shaping up to be a doozy.

The lowering sun hit his eyes like a laser excising cataracts. He reached for his sunglasses, which had slid into the far corner of the dash, pulling the temple pieces open with his teeth. He put on the glasses, closing his eyes in relief as he paused to let the traffic pour by.

A sharp beep behind the car told him he'd loitered too long. He pulled into the line of traffic. The Ford Bronco squealed its tires as it swerved around him, its driver lifting one hand with upraised middle finger as it went by. Theo had the satisfaction of hearing him screech to a stop as the light turned red.

Pulling in behind the Bronco, Theo tapped his fingers on the steering wheel. Sunlight slanted through the windshield, momentarily blinding him when he made the turn heading for the bridge. The gridlock line of vehicles groaned to a stop again. Blinking away the red and yellow spots dancing before his eyes, Theo adjusted the volume on the radio to hear the traffic report.

"Downtown Vancouver is experiencing delays," the announcer said cheerfully. "An accident in the tunnel is being cleared up. The bridges are all clear. Stay tuned…"

He punched a tape into the machine. Mozart rolled out of the speakers. He glanced around the car. Odd, it looked as if a brown rope lay on the gray carpet. Where had that come from—he'd vacuumed the floor just before his trip.

Near the bottom of the seat he saw a flash of yellow— moving toward him. His hands froze on the steering wheel, gripping it in a stranglehold.

Panic blossomed in his chest, forcing out the air until he couldn't breathe. The long body, as thick as his thumb, undulated sinuously up the low console. A tiny forked tongue tested the air as the blunt head aimed straight for his ankle.

JENNY FOUND HERSELF in the elevator heading for the main floor without quite knowing how she'd gotten inside. Zacharias had left her, saying he would take the stairs, that the exercise would wake him enough to drive home. She reached the lobby, and nodded to the security guard who marked something in a ledger, making a note that she'd left the building, no doubt.

She walked down the street toward the parking lot where she left her car. By now Cindi would have locked up the office, and seen that the bikes were secured in the storage area they rented in the basement of the building. There was plenty of paperwork but Jenny didn't feel like going back to shut herself into the dingy office to nurture the incipient headache nagging her temples.

On the next street, a siren wailed, a high-pitched scream

rising and falling in the narrow canyons between high buildings.

She turned the corner, squinting into the westering sun. Near the bridge she saw the red and blue flash of a police cruiser's roof lights. Commuters sat in the motionless traffic, their faces resigned, stoical.

The accident didn't look too bad. One by one the cars inched around the white cruiser, as the policeman directed them. She drew nearer, heels clicking on the concrete sidewalk.

Then she saw him. Theo Zacharias stood beside a dark gray Saab with its fender crushed against a lamp pole. Even from thirty feet away, she could see that his face was drawn and white, except for the trickle of blood from a cut next to his eyebrow.

Fear clenched in her chest and she broke into a run.

Chapter Two

Jenny stumbled and almost fell. These damn shoes. Why did she torture herself? Her pounding heart felt as if it would beat its way out of her chest. Theo looked ill. Was he seriously injured? The cut didn't look deep, nor was it bleeding profusely, but he must have received a severe bump. Sweat beaded his upper lip, clinging to dark beard stubble that formed a stark contrast to his colorless skin.

"You have to stay back, miss." The policeman's stern voice brought her to an abrupt halt.

"Please, let me through," she said recklessly. "I know this man."

He regarded her assessingly, then nodded. "All right. He looks like he's about to fall down."

"Have you called an ambulance?" she asked.

"Said he didn't need one."

"I don't," Theo said, eyeing her with distaste. "What are you doing here?"

"Walking to the parking lot," she said smartly, gesturing with one hand. Her voice softened. "Are you all right?"

"I'll live." He leaned on the side of the car, closing his eyes.

"You don't look all right. Why don't you sit down?" Reaching around him, she pulled at the car door.

"No!" His loud cry had her jerking back her hand as if the metal were hot.

She stared at him, wondering if the head injury were more serious than it looked. Theo appeared on the verge of collapse. His eyes were dull, the skin around them dark and bruised. His lips were pale and compressed into a thin line.

"Then sit on the curb." She grasped his upper arm and helped him around the car.

He sank onto the curb as if his knees had turned to rubber, burying his face in his hands. Heedless of her cream-colored skirt, Jenny sat beside him on the gritty concrete. She twisted her fingers together, itching to touch him, reassure herself that he was all right.

Her fault. The sick certainty lay like a lead ball in her stomach. Whatever had happened to him was the direct result of her delivery of the money, the campaign to "make him sweat."

"What happened?"

Before he could answer her quiet question, another police car pulled up, bouncing its wheels up onto the sidewalk out of the traffic stream. A burly, blue-clad cop got out, clipboard in hand. Theo struggled to his feet, shaking his head. A drop of sweat seeped out of his tousled hair and trickled down his temple.

"Could you tell what happened here?" the policeman said, his pen poised. "Start with your name and address."

Theo scrubbed his hands over his face, raking back his hair, leaving spiky bits sticking up. Jenny stood close to his side, wanting to hold his hand but knowing she couldn't. Not as long as this guilt gnawed within her. Not knowing she was responsible.

He stated the details. Jenny noted that he also lived in Surrey. She didn't recognize the street but thought it was in an area of executive houses.

"Okay," the cop said, busily jotting down phone and

license plate numbers. "How did you manage this?" He pointed the end of the pen at the dented fender.

"There is a snake in my car." Theo's voice rasped hoarsely and he cleared his throat. "It startled me. The next thing I knew, the car hit the post."

The officer blinked in apparent disbelief. "Not many snakes downtown. What kind of snake?"

"How would I know what kind?" Theo said irritably. "It was about a meter long, sort of a dull brown. No, it had yellow on it, too, I think."

"Where is it now?"

"In the car, I imagine. No one's opened the door since I got out."

"Okay. Let's have a look, shall we?"

The cop peered through the car window. "Yes, it's there all right. On the seat."

Theo hung back but Jenny pressed her nose to the window and saw an olive and yellow ribbon lying in an S shape on the gray leather. "It's not brown."

"It looked brown when I first saw it," Theo stated. He remained slumped against the undamaged fender.

Something familiar about the snake nagged at Jenny. She cupped her hands about her face and scanned the floor and the passenger seat. On the gray carpet on the opposite side, she could see an almost transparent brown husk. "It's harmless," she said. "A garter snake. We used to catch them in our garden all the time when I was a kid."

"Better you than me," Theo muttered.

"It's just shed its skin," Jenny added. She turned to the cop. "Do you want me to take it out?"

"Sure." He reached into his cruiser and pulled out a paper bag. "Can you put it in this? I suppose plastic wouldn't be a good idea."

"No." Jenny opened the car door and inched her hand across the seat. The snake quivered, its eyes glittering like black beads. With a quick lunge, she clamped her thumb and forefinger behind its head. The forked tongue darted out as the muscular body flexed against her hold. She deftly stuffed it into the bag and loosely rolled the top. The policeman handed her a couple of paper clips to secure it, and scribbled a number on the bag before taking it from her hand.

She crouched down and retrieved the papery skin. "A souvenir?" she asked, holding it up.

Theo jerked back. "How can you do that?" he bellowed. A shudder ran through his body. His face took on a greenish tinge, and for a moment she thought he would be sick.

"Born and raised in the city, were you?" Jenny asked.

"No, in Greece, where we're taught from our cradles that the only good snake is a dead one."

She digested this, while the traffic swished by. Occasional horns bleated. In the distance, a siren howled. "You don't have any accent."

Faint color crept back into the taut skin over his cheekbones. "My parents came to Canada when I was ten."

Next to them, the policeman cleared his throat. "The tow truck's here, Mr. Zacharias. Call me tomorrow if you have any questions. Here's my card. I'll be on at three."

"Thanks. Will there be charges?"

"I'll let you know tomorrow."

The big red tow truck, amber lights flashing on the roof, backed up to the car. The driver got out and looked at the juxtaposition of fender and steel post. He rolled a toothpick from one side of his mouth to the other and hitched his trousers under an enormous belly. "If I give the fender a pull so it's free of the tire, you should be able to back it away from the pole."

Theo nodded. The man's ham-size hands gripped the crumpled metal and jerked hard. A piece of the plastic sidelight lens clattered to the pavement and the fender reluctantly let go its hold of the tire. Miraculously the heavy rubber was barely scraped. The tow truck driver ran his palm over it. "Tire's okay. Where do you want it?" The toothpick bobbed up and down as he spoke.

Theo dug out his wallet and removed a business card. "Take it to this address."

Within ten minutes the tow truck disappeared across the bridge, the gray Saab ignominiously dragging behind. One police car had already gone. The cop who had taken down the details spoke briefly into his radio. He held it away from his mouth. "Can I call you a taxi, Mr. Zacharias?"

"I'll give you a lift," Jenny said quickly. "I'm going that way."

The cop grinned and winked at her. "All set, then?"

Jenny saw Theo's mouth tighten but he nodded.

The cop touched the visor of his cap. "Okay. Have a good evening."

"A lift?" Theo said.

"Believe it or not, I do have a car, in the lot over there. Can you walk?"

"Of course I can walk," he snapped.

She swallowed her hurt. "Well, you don't look all that well and there's a cut over your eye."

He touched it gingerly with two fingers. Bits of dried blood clung to the skin. He seemed surprised to see it. "Didn't you realize you'd bumped your head?" Jenny asked gently. "It must hurt."

"I already had such a headache, a little more pain didn't make much difference."

"How does it feel now?"

"Sore." A ghost of a smile touched his lips. "But I can walk. Lead the way."

Jenny picked up the briefcase he'd retrieved from the car. "Hey, I can get that," he said.

Theo made a grab for it. Their hands brushed. Jenny felt the heat of his skin in a way she hadn't noticed when

he'd grasped her wrist to drag her into the office. She held
the case out of his reach, steadying him with her other
hand. He bit his lip, leaning against the lamppost until he
regained his equilibrium.

"See?" Jenny said, tucking her hand into the crook of
his elbow. "You have to take it easy. Luckily it's not far
to my car."

She hid a smile moments later as he manoeuvred his
tall frame into her tiny Renault Five. She tossed her purse
and his briefcase into the back seat and turned the key in
the ignition, slowly feeding gas. After a slow, hoarse
crank, the engine caught, a little rough but smoothing out
as it warmed up.

"D'you drive this in winter, too?" Theo asked
dubiously.

"Of course." She turned on the headlights, engaged
the gear and drove toward the exit. "It's never let me
down. I could use a new battery but there are still a few
miles left in this one."

Waving at the lot attendant, she pulled into the street.
"Where to?" she asked, pretending she hadn't been listening avidly to every detail he'd given the policeman.

"If you don't know which way, why did you offer?"
he asked.

"Surrey, wasn't it?"

"Yes, but Surrey's a big place."

"You can give me directions after we cross the
bridge."

SHE DROVE WELL, clutching, shifting and braking with
smooth efficiency. But then what would he expect from a
woman who had barely met him, but who rescued him
and took over, displaying solicitude for his injuries and
concern for his state of mind? She hadn't even laughed
at his unmanly horror of snakes. On the other hand, nei-

ther had the burly cop who hadn't shown any keen urge to pick up the snake, either.

His brow ached a little where, despite the seat belt, he'd clipped the door frame of his car, but the pounding in his temples had mercifully subsided. Probably the principle of hitting your toe with a hammer to make a headache go away.

Dusk had fallen but enough light remained for him to study her from under his lashes. Her hands looked small and capable, with unpainted nails cut short. She wore no jewelry except a man's watch. The wide brown leather strap around her delicate wrist subtly emphasized her femininity. That jolt of awareness he'd felt when their hands had touched—what did it mean? If only he hadn't felt faint all of a sudden and been forced to hold himself upright against a lamppost.

She braked abruptly as another car cut into her lane. Her sunglasses slid off the dash and into her lap. She muttered something and handed them to him. "Could you put these in the glove box, please?"

He reached forward and opened it, nearly letting loose an avalanche of maps, tapes and several years insurance papers in slippery plastic envelopes. He pushed the sunglasses inside, and snapped the cover closed. "Gorgeous day today, wasn't it?" she said, her voice a little breathless. "Especially for March. We should be grateful for every sunny day. We can still have plenty of rain. Have you always lived in Vancouver, Mr. Zacharias?"

He hid a smile at her nervous chatter. "Call me Theo. No, I lived in Montreal until four years ago."

"Oh? What made you leave?"

He shrugged, surprised that the innocent question from a virtual stranger could still dredge up old pain. "Business. Wanting to make a new start."

"Mmm." The single syllable seemed weighted. The light from street lamps flashed through the car but it had grown too dark for him to read her expression. "How do you like it here?"

"Fine." Why did he have the feeling there was more behind this than idle conversation?

"Where do I turn?" They were crossing the bridge, streaming across with hundreds of other cars, like a school of fish in a river.

"First exit, then head north. I'm not taking you out of your way, am I?"

"A little but it doesn't matter. Consider it my Good Samaritan act of the week."

The road wound through a forest, emerging into an agricultural area where lights glowed lemon yellow from houses and barns. "Next road to the right," Theo said. "It's the third driveway down." Again a faint unease slithered through him. He knew nothing about this woman. Was it wise to allow her to see where he lived?

Still, there was something about her, some quality of integrity that shone through the evasions and air of secrecy. No matter what she was, his gut feeling told him she wasn't a mad stalker, like that horrible woman in the movie who had tried to kill Michael Douglas.

She steered the car up his driveway. The security light came on, laying a welcome swath of brightness across the front of the house. She gave a low whistle. "Nice. Wish I could afford something like that."

The laugh that escaped his lips sounded rusty. "Maybe you'll be able to, with my financial expertise."

"What?"

"You came for my advice, didn't you?"

He saw her throat ripple as she swallowed, her face averted. He wished he could see her eyes. Duplicity. It practically oozed from every pore of her body.

He hated liars. Setting his jaw, he reached for the door handle as she stopped the car outside the closed double garage. "I can make it from here." He reached between the seats for his briefcase, wincing as pain jabbed through his shoulder. Must have banged that as well. Good thing he'd been wearing his seat belt when the car hit, or he'd be presently languishing in the emergency ward instead of wondering what secrets lay behind the guileless blue eyes of this maddening woman.

"I'll be in my office at nine, no, better make it ten, tomorrow morning," he said. "Be there. And thanks."

He was three strides away from the car before he heard her voice. "You're welcome. Take care of that cut. Oh, do you have a way into town in the morning?"

He had to give her an A for effort. She never gave up. "Yeah. I can get a lift with my neighbor to the Skytrain." He lifted his hand in farewell. "Thanks, again."

"We've got a problem?"

"Yes, the courier lady."

The first speaker remained silent for a long moment. Then, "We'll have to eliminate her as well." The voice was laced with sincere regret, which firmed into resolve. "But give it a little time. We can use this to make him suffer. Give him a chance to start caring about her, then hit her."

The accomplice snickered smugly. "Just leave it to me. He'll go down knowing it was his fault that she got it."

"Why don't you level with me, Miss Gray?" Theo said to Jenny the next morning. "Did you just want an introduction and chose this unique way to engineer it, or is there a real reason you want to see me?"

"Financial advice," she said, picking at a loose thread on the side seam of the jeans she wore today. Along with them, she had on a deep blue sweater that matched her eyes. The white collar of an oxford cloth shirt surrounded the ribbed neck, subtly enhancing the creamy texture of her skin. Her hair was loose today, a dark brown mass of glossy curls.

Exasperated, Theo sighed. "Nice try, but I know you haven't any money unless you've got a source of income I don't know about."

That got her attention. She sat up, looking straight at him, color rushing into her cheeks. "How could you know anything about my finances?"

"I asked around about your company. Swift Couriers is barely solvent."

"We pay the rent," she said indignantly.

He put up his hand. "Yes, but how? Twice in the past year you've asked for an extra couple of days to get the money together. You employ girls who used to live on the streets, former runaways and such. And you pay them a very generous wage in addition to a commission on each delivery. What are you running, Miss Gray? A charity or a business?"

"No one can live on minimum wage," she said, her fingers again worrying the loose thread.

"I agree. No one should have to." He got up and walked around his desk, planting his hips against the edge of it as he faced her. "So what is it you want from me? A loan, perhaps? I understand your line of credit with the bank is already stretched to the limit."

She looked up, her eyes flashing angrily. "Aren't there laws about privacy anymore? How did you find that out?"

"We have our ways, Miss Gray. About your rent, I simply asked your landlord, early this morning."

"You made a quick recovery."

He lightly probed the bruise on his forehead. "A couple of aspirin and I was okay." He flexed his shoulders carefully. "Except for feeling that I've been run over by a truck."

"Will your car be repaired?"

"They'll have it back in a couple of days. It won't take

long once the insurance company gives the okay. A little
straightening, a new lens, some touch-up paint and it'll be
as good as new.''

He left the desk and sat down on the arm of the chair
in which she slumped. He inhaled the faint floral scent of
soap or shampoo. He liked the way she smelled, no heavy
perfume, just natural woman. "Look, Jenny," he said,
dragging his mind back to business, "I think it's great
what you're doing, giving those girls a job, but you have
to know it can't go on forever. You have to get more
business lined up, or cut the number of employees you
have."

"They need their jobs, or they'll be out on the street
again, selling their bodies." Her blue eyes bored into his,
pleading, passionate. For a wild instant, he found himself
wishing some of the passion was for him.

This was crazy. She was lying to him and he was letting
her. And he couldn't make himself move away from her
even when she shrank back against the soft leather cushions to put a distance between them. "Jenny, please, if
you're in trouble and came to me for help, tell me. I will
help, if I can."

She stared up at him while time stretched. Phones rang
in the other offices around them but they hung suspended
in an oasis of silence. Her eyes were as clear as a saint's,
the color of a Madonna's robe he remembered from a
church icon. And as remote.

She could hurt him, he realized with a jolt. If it turned
out that she was involving him in some kind of scam, he
didn't know if he could bear it.

Nervously she licked her lips. He watched in helpless
fascination. The lush pink curves grew wet and glossy as
her tongue crossed them. He wanted to run his thumb over
her bottom lip to see if it felt as soft as it looked. He
wanted to discover how she tasted.

His door opened after a perfunctory knock. Ms. Herrington's perfectly made-up face appeared around the corner. Her smile disappeared when she saw Jenny. "Oh, are you still here?"

"Was there something you wanted, Janice?" Theo asked, part of him glad of the interruption.

"Just bringing in your mail, Theo." She dropped it on the desk, and withdrew, hips swaying under a white linen skirt.

"Sorry about that," Theo said to Jenny. "Now where were we?"

"Did they find out any more about how a snake got into your car?" she said.

He jumped up from his chair and paced restlessly around the room, his fists jammed into his pants pockets. "No, but the cop called me last night and confirmed that the snake was harmless, as you said. He promised to release it in some park."

"Was the car in the garage all the time you were gone or only after four yesterday?"

He paused, midstride. "How did you—? Yeah, come to think of it, how did you know exactly when I'd be back?"

"I asked Ms. Herrington."

"Hmm," he said, irritated. "I'll have to speak to her about discussing company business with strangers."

"I'm not a stranger. I—well, usually one of the girls— we've been making your deliveries for the past year. Ms. Herrington and I may not be bosom buddies but we do know each other. Besides, your return time was available to anyone who wanted to make an appointment."

"Then why didn't you?"

"I was in a hurry." She seemed to find the pattern in the tweed carpet of absorbing interest.

He rolled his eyes toward the ceiling. "And you still haven't told me what it is you want."

"Just some simple financial advice." Her chin lifted. Stubborn as they came, he noted.

"Okay." He sat down again and pulled forms out of a drawer. "I'll need some basic information, your tax forms from the past couple of years, and a list of your assets."

She delved into her purse, a large shoulder bag today, and brought out a tattered envelope. "It's all here."

Theo's eyes widened involuntarily and he swallowed a laugh. This must be the smallest, most pathetic business he'd ever tried to save from the evil clutches of Revenue Canada and bankruptcy.

He sifted through the papers, noting that she had done her own tax returns. "Too expensive to get someone to do them," she explained. "And it's fairly simple if you follow the instructions."

But how many deductions had she missed because she didn't know tax laws? he wondered, inwardly groaning. Scanning the handwritten forms, he spotted several right away.

He opened his briefcase to take out a tax manual. His hand fell on the office mail he'd shoved in there yesterday. He'd been so wiped last night, he'd fallen into bed and forgotten all about it. He glanced through the envelopes, casting more of them aside. A couple he opened and checked the contents. Nothing that couldn't wait.

He came upon a square envelope, stamped but without a return address. He slit it with the letter opener and drew out the card inside. "Welcome Back" trumpeted the black letters on the front. He opened it. On the blank page inside, the words "To Hell" were printed crudely by hand in lurid purple.

"What?" He stared at the message until it blurred before his eyes. He blinked, bringing it back into focus. Picking up the envelope, he looked closely at it. No postmark or date cancelling the stamp. His name and office address were correct, the uniformity of the type telling him it had probably been produced by a laser printer.

"What is it?" Jenny asked.

He started, having forgotten she was still there.

"A message, I think." He forced a laugh. "Most likely somebody's idea of humor. The guys around here are always pulling practical jokes."

"Really?" He could have sworn she paled. "Let me see it."

He handed her the card and the envelope. "This didn't go through the post office," she said, turning the envelope over in her hands.

"How do you know?"

She poked a finger at the bottom of the envelope. "You see, there aren't any lines indicating it passed through the sorting machine. Even if the stamp isn't cancelled, those lines always show."

"There you have it. It's someone in the office, pulling my leg." He tossed the card and envelope to one side of the desk and continued sorting through the mail.

"Or it was delivered by a courier service," Jenny said somberly.

He laid the rest of the mail aside and tapped the letter opener on the desk. "Then why bother with a stamp?"

She shrugged. "Maybe they meant to mail it and changed their mind. Who knows?"

He set the letter opener down with a sharp click. "Never mind. Shall we get on with this? I'm sure you want to get back to your own work."

THE MESSAGE DOGGED Jenny's footsteps as she walked to her office an hour later. Welcome Back—To Hell. Was it connected with the snake in the car? And were both part of the "make him sweat" campaign?

She had to assume they were. But what could she have told him? She knew he recognized her flimsy reason for contacting him as the pretext it was. If she tried to warn him, he might just conclude she had developed some sort of obsession with him, and was behind the incidents. He'd call the police, and then where would she be? Either locked up or under a restraining order to stay far away from him. He would truly be at the mercy of whoever was planning to kill him.

She checked the basement storage area before going up to the office. All the bikes were out, a sign that business was brisk enough to employ a full staff.

Upstairs she found Cindi busy making up the payroll, a job they normally shared. The young woman looked up, biting the end of her pen. "How'd it go with the great financial wizard?"

Jenny's mouth turned down. "He's working on it. I don't know why you aren't in favor of getting an expert to assess our business. He might find a way to save us a lot of money, or to increase our profits."

"As I said yesterday, I don't like to see you throwing good money after bad. Did you discuss his fee with him?"

"Not yet, but he strikes me as an honest man. He wouldn't be in his line of business long if he cheated people. Clients have to be able to trust their financial advisor, don't they?"

Cindi chewed her pen. "Yeah, I guess. But I've always found it hard to trust those dark brooding men. You never can tell what they're thinking." Her eyes narrowed. "You're not falling for him, are you?"

"Of course not," Jenny said, but even to her own ears the denial sounded a little too vehement.

Cindi pursed her lips, her expression sceptical. "Just be careful, is all I can say."

Tell me something I don't know, Jenny thought dismally as she went into her office. She didn't need Cindi to tell her that any relationship between her and Theo was doomed from the outset. She had to stay close to him for the time being, to protect him and try to figure out who was after him, but once this was over, she would never see him again.

The In basket was empty at the moment. Cindi had obviously taken care of the morning's business. Jenny opened the door again. "Do you want me to finish the payroll? If you like, take an early lunch."

Cindi smiled. "Sure. I wanted to get a haircut anyway." She lifted her purse out of the bottom drawer of the desk and gestured at the computer monitor. "It's all yours."

Jenny settled down, typing in the hours from the time cards, the deliveries completed, commissions earned. Occasionally the phone rang, businesses requiring pickups, or the girls checking in for further instructions. She answered it, entering the data on another program in the computer. Her couriers came and went, smartly dressed in the uniforms she supplied, black tights and sweat shirts, with hooded, waterproof jackets for rain and cold weather.

At ten to five Jenny ran downstairs to check in the bikes and make sure they were secured. Sandra, a skinny waif whom she hadn't seen after the theft of her bike, wheeled in a rented bike. "Oh, Jenny, I'm so sorry about the bike. I didn't know that barrier I locked it to could be lifted. And I was delayed—you know how they can be in the bus depot. When I came out, it was gone."

"It's all right, Sandra." Jenny patted the girl's shoulder. Her bones felt as fragile as a bird's. "Are you eating enough?"

Sandra grinned, revealing small teeth with a gap between the two middle ones. "These days I am. And I found a nice place to live with Katie."

Katie was one of Jenny's oldest employees, off the street and clean for two years now. She would provide a stabilizing influence on Sandra who had run away from alcoholic parents and, though the cynicism in her eyes made her look older, was only eighteen. "Good," Jenny said. "So you like the work?"

"Yes, and I'll be more careful with my bike from now on."

"Don't worry about it. If it doesn't turn up, the insurance will cover it." Of course the rates would go up again, but she couldn't worry Sandra about that.

The other girls trickled in while they were talking. "Pay day tomorrow," one of them said.

"If I get it done," Jenny joked. "Okay, shoo, all of you up to the office to clock out. I want to lock up."

Upstairs she found Cindi about to leave. "Do you want the computer on?"

Jenny nodded. "Yes, I'll just print out the checks so they'll be ready."

"Good night, then."

Later, the checks printed, she signed them and locked them in the small floor safe. Turning off the computer, she covered the keyboard and went into her own office to get her purse.

The outer door slammed open. She jumped. Damn, she'd forgotten to lock it after the girls left.

She let out her pent-up breath as Theo Zacharias strode into the room, hair bristling and color high. A white smudge marred the sleeve of his charcoal suit. Jenny gaped at him, her mouth suddenly as dry as chaff. "What? Another accident?"

"Suppose you tell me," he said furiously. "Before I met you, my life was boring and predictable. Now I've wrecked my car, nearly had a heart attack because of a snake, received a threatening note, and to top it off, one of your bicycle couriers ran me down and nearly knocked me in front of a moving bus."

Chapter Three

Jenny shook her head in immediate denial. "Not one of my couriers. First of all, I don't allow them to use those kamikaze tactics that have given the bicycle messenger business a bad name. And secondly, they were all back—" she looked at the clock on the wall "—I checked them in half an hour ago."

"Well, it was forty-five minutes ago that this happened. I wouldn't have bothered with the police but one of the bike squad happened by just after the accident and he insisted on writing up a report. A very thorough report. Then I rushed over here. I was afraid you'd be gone."

"Another minute and I would have been. Why don't you sit down?" She sank onto the chair behind the desk.

"I'd rather stand, thanks." He leaned across the desk, resting his knuckles on the wooden top. "You can say what you want but it was one of your couriers. Black clothes, pink bike."

"Did you see the face?"

"Actually, no. She was wearing dark glasses and a helmet and I was scrambling out of the path of the bus at the time. But there was no mistaking that pink bike."

Frowning thoughtfully, Jenny picked up a pencil and passed it from one hand to the other. "One of my bikes was stolen yesterday. That must have been it."

"Convenient." His voice dripped sarcasm.

Jenny jumped up, pencil bouncing across the desk and onto the floor. "I can prove it." She snatched the time cards from their holders next to the door, stooping to retrieve the pencil as she returned to her chair. "Look at these." She thrust them into his hands. "You'll see all my girls were in by five. They couldn't have been running you down at the same time and had time to get back here. Where did this happen, anyway?"

"On Granville."

"How far up?"

"Near Georgia."

"See," she said triumphantly. "It couldn't have been my girls."

"But it was your bike," he insisted. He dropped the time cards on her desk and shoved his hands into his pants pockets.

"I'll check with the police and see if they've picked it up anywhere." She flipped through the box of business cards sitting on the desk, found the right one and dialed the number. She gave the dispatcher the file number and was transferred to Stolen Property.

Theo watched as she asked about the bike, listened, made monosyllabic responses. She asked about Theo's latest accident, tapping the pencil on the desk as she waited to be transferred. After a moment, she hung up, scowling. "They haven't seen any trace of it, but several bystanders agree with you that the bike was pink. But they say it bumped you accidentally. That a child ran in front of the bike and it swerved to miss the child and hit you."

"If that's true, why didn't the courier wait and explain?" He came over and hitched his hip onto the corner of the desk. Jenny rolled her chair back, uncomfortable with his large frame looming over her. "The courier was already swerving, toward me, when the child ran out. It wasn't an accident."

Jenny believed him, no matter how easily the police dismissed it. She pinched the bridge of her nose, her mind working. There had to be some way to put him on his guard without being too obvious about it. "Neither was the snake an accident, I'll venture," she said at last. "An underground garage is pretty cold. Snakes are cold-blooded. That means they take on the ambient temperature. It wouldn't have been very active until your car warmed up, as it did, sitting in the traffic. Are you sure your car was locked?"

"Yes, but that may not mean much. We've all seen news broadcasts on how easy it is for a car thief to get into a car. They could have stuck that skinny metal strip they use down the window frame, opened the door, put the snake inside and relocked the car door afterward."

"Do your car doors lock without the key?" she asked. "Mine don't. Neither do a lot of European cars."

"The front doors don't," Theo said. "But you could leave the rear door open, press the inside lock down on the closed front door, then do the same on the rear one and slam it shut. It will lock that way."

Jenny nodded. "Yes, that would work and no one would be the wiser. What about the note? D'you think there's a connection between it and the snake?"

Theo kneaded his arm below the shoulder, on the smudge of dust. It was the same one he'd banged up yesterday, Jenny noted sympathetically. "Pretty sore, is it? Can I get you an aspirin?"

"Don't bother." He got off the desk and went over to stand by the window. Jenny swivelled her chair around, her eyes on his back. His suit jacket had another pale smudge of dust on the right shoulder blade.

He was silent for a long moment, leaving Jenny wondering what he found so fascinating about the brick wall outside, which was her only view. That and the untidy collection of poles supporting phone and electric wires, strung down the alley, eerily sinister in the gathering dusk.

Finally he turned, the light in the room hitting his face. A peculiar emotion fluttered in her chest. He looked even more tired than yesterday. The circles beneath his eyes were as dark as bruises.

"Yes, I think there's a connection," he said wearily, clawing his fingers through his hair. "I showed the card around the office and watched everyone's faces but they looked truly baffled. Not a snigger or a smirk among them."

"So that's a dead end." A thought—memory, actually—flitted through her brain. She frowned, but it was gone before she could grasp it. Her stomach growled. She gave an embarrassed laugh. "I missed lunch. Forgot, to tell the truth. And I bet you haven't had dinner. Why don't I treat you?"

"You can't afford it." But he smiled as he said it, the gray eyes turning as silver as rain.

She picked up her purse. "I wasn't planning a four-course dinner at the Pan Pacific. What I have in mind is noodles. I know a great place just down the street."

The smile broadened into a grin. "So do I. It's where all the druggies and winos hang out."

"Mostly outside, especially at this time of day. And it's perfectly safe. I eat there whenever I'm too lazy to cook."

They walked out into the mellow spring evening. The pinkish-orange glow of the streetlights softened the hard edges of buildings and created an almost romantic aura, reminding Jenny of Paris where she'd once spent a spring vacation. Daffodils and tulips made patches of gold and mauve in planters along the sidewalk. The first tender green leaves, as delicate as lace, decorated trees that flourished despite automobile fumes and the other hazards of city life.

"Okay," Jenny said when they were seated at a chipped Formica table and had given their order to the harried Chinese waiter who doubled as bus boy and dishwasher. "We have to figure that someone is deliberately harassing you."

"That's absurd."

"Absurd, it may be, but if it's true, you're going to have to be on your guard." There, she'd said it.

"I'll go to the police."

Jenny made a rude noise in her throat. "The police. Go ahead but you already know what they'll do. Same as they've done about you nearly falling in front of a bus. An accident. Somebody too embarrassed to face you afterward. And the way they perceive bike couriers, they'll just shrug and say typical behavior, what did you expect? You say it was deliberate." She reached across the table and covered his hand with hers, the first time she'd touched him other than accidentally. "I believe you. I don't think you'd make it up, or misread a situation."

He said nothing, staring down at their two hands, as if surprised to see them joined. Jenny's gaze followed his. Her hand looked small and pale against his. His fingers were long, with clipped nails. The back of his hand, tanned skin sprinkled with black hair, tensed into corded tendons. The hairs softly tickled her palm, and she stiffened, starting to pull back.

"No, don't." He turned his hand over and clasped hers. "Jenny, I don't know what to think. Maybe I'm going crazy."

Her fingers tightened around his. "You're not. I assure you, you're not."

His gray eyes sharpened. "What do you know about this?"

"Nothing." Her gaze skittered beyond him, and she gulped in gratitude when the waiter stopped by their table to set bowls of noodles in front of them. The scent of chicken and ginger and garlic swept up her nose, made her mouth water. "Mmm, doesn't it smell delicious?"

She dragged her hand free of his and picked up the chopsticks, twirling noodles around them and slurping them into her mouth. She could feel Theo watching her but she pretended this was an ordinary dinner with an ordinary man.

She knew she was fooling herself. How did he do that? Just the look on his face, cynical and disbelieving as it had been most of the time they'd been together, was enough to make her stomach feel as if she'd gone up too fast in an elevator. A buoyant lightness that was uncomfortable and exciting at the same time.

Was she falling for him? Cindi's question haunted her. Yes, she was, she told herself with brutal honesty. But if she let it go on, it would be the biggest mistake of her life.

"Do you have any enemies?" she asked to drown out her disquieting thoughts.

He laid down his chopsticks and picked up the little ceramic spoon. "Enemies? I'm in a very conservative field. Hardly the place to make enemies."

"Well, maybe somebody's miffed because the stock market is going down and their mutual funds are losing value. Or you gave bad advice."

"I assure you, I have no enemies."

"No jealous women? Wife or ex-wife?"

"No women." His mouth turned down and he stopped eating, pushing the bowl away. "My wife is dead, has been for five years. And her ghost isn't after me. In fact, quite the contrary."

The cutting edge in his voice lashed at her. "I'm sorry." Her breath hitched in her throat.

She found herself looking at the top of Theo's head as he stared down at the battered table. His shoulders slumped. His hand lay palm up, the fingers loosely curled.

They suddenly clenched into a fist, as if he were using them to hold some profound emotion inside.

The sheer dejection in his pose got to her. Was he still in mourning for his dead wife? Or was she right in interpreting his tone as a profound disillusionment? Her throat burned with ridiculous tears that she valiantly held back. She was doing it again, identifying with the victim, or what she saw as the victim, just as she had too many times as a social worker. She'd hoped she'd learned her lesson after countless letdowns, developed a thicker skin.

After all, for all she knew, Theo might be simply playing on her emotions. The warning of some of her friends rang through her head: Watch out for men who show their vulnerability in the early stages of a relationship. You can't trust them.

She blew her nose with a napkin. "Must be catching cold," she mumbled, to explain the thickness in her voice. "You must miss her."

He looked up. "Hell, no, I don't miss her at all. If she hadn't died, she would have been my ex-wife by now."

This time there was no mistaking the bitterness. She could think of nothing to say. Picking up her own spoon, she finished her noodles.

She wished she could tell him the truth, but it was too early. She had to make him trust her first, at least a little. She feared it would be an uphill battle. The way he sounded about his wife, he wasn't going to trust anyone easily.

She had to keep trying. "You mentioned people in your office doing practical jokes. Would anyone carry it further than a joke? Somebody jealous of your accounts, income, or whatever?"

"Not likely. I already had my own clients and brought them with me when I started working for Pacific Rim Investments two years ago."

"Where did you work before that?"

"For a bank, but I did investment counselling on my own time. That's how I built up a roster of clients. PRI approached me to work for them. I accepted. They're an established, conservative firm with an impeccable reputation."

"Did you work in the same field in Montreal?"

"Yes, but the company I was with didn't have any branches here."

"Then why did you pick Vancouver?"

He crumpled the napkin he'd been holding and tossed it aside. "I wanted a complete change of scenery. And I could afford not to work for a while if I needed to. Why are you asking all these questions?"

She looked up at him, her gaze meeting his squarely. "Because I want to help you. You burst into my office practically accusing me of being responsible for your 'accidents.'"

"You're not." He interrupted her. "What I said was in the heat of the moment."

"Nevertheless," she went on doggedly, "I feel responsible. And maybe I can help."

"How?"

That stymied her. She forced a smile. "I don't know yet. We'll think of something."

"DO YOU NEED your briefcase?" Jenny asked later as they walked back up Hastings Street.

"No, I won't bother now," Theo said. "It's locked in my desk. Safe enough. Do you have your car?"

"In the same parking lot as yesterday. Can I give you a lift home?"

"I wouldn't want to trouble you. I can get the Skytrain."

"No, really," she said. "It's no trouble at all."

He smiled at her. "In that case, I accept."

A panhandler dressed in a ragged ski jacket stepped out in front of them. "Spare change, sir?"

Theo dropped a couple of loonies into the outstretched palm. They passed her office building, locked up tight with steel grids over storefront windows. "You should get an office in a better part of town," Theo said. "It's dangerous here at night."

Her mouth turned down. "Easy for you to say. You know I can't afford a better office. And it's not dangerous if you're careful."

"Bad enough."

"If you knew what I did before I started my business, you wouldn't give this a thought."

"Oh? What were you before? A cop? Or maybe a paramedic?"

"Close," she said. "I was a social worker."

His brows shot up. "What made you quit?"

"Frustration. Counselling someone, getting their head straight, and then a month later finding them making the same mistakes. And likely as not, blaming anyone but themselves. I couldn't take it anymore."

Theo nodded, then smiled knowingly. "But aren't you doing the same thing now? Aren't your girls from the same social strata as your previous clients?"

"They are. But at least this way I know I'm doing something to help them. I don't have to get everything rubber-stamped by some government agency."

They turned into the next street, winding their way through well-dressed couples headed for a night out at music clubs and theaters. The wail of a saxophone shivered on the night air, soaring over the dull roar of traffic. Jenny remembered nights during her student days when she and her friends would go out and dance until one or two, dragging themselves heavy-eyed to class in the morning.

All of them respectable now. Mostly married, having

children, working at real jobs to pay off a mortgage in the suburbs. All except her.

"Do you go out much?" Theo said.

Jenny shook her head. "Not anymore." She jogged a couple of steps ahead of him as they entered the parking lot. "Here's the car."

"Why not?" he persisted, obviously seeing through her attempt at changing the subject. "You're young, attractive, single." His eyes sharpened as he fastened his seat belt. "You are single, aren't you?"

"Yes."

"Ever been married?"

"Not even close. No one I dated had the patience to put up with calls at all hours, hanging around women's shelters, trying to find a foster home for abandoned kids at three in the morning." The car lurched as she braked for a traffic light. She raked her hand through her hair. "Theo, I don't want to talk about it. It's too depressing."

"Sorry. I'm just trying to figure you out."

"Are you sure it's worth the bother?"

"You've given me a lift twice now. It wouldn't do for me to accept rides with a stranger, would it?"

Relieved at the bantering note that had come back into his voice, she silently let out a long breath. "I'm not a stranger. You know more about my finances than any one else in town."

"Yeah, there is that."

The subject of her finances occupied them until she turned in at his driveway. She stopped in front of the garage, as she had last night.

"Thanks for the lift," Theo said, in no hurry to get out. He turned toward her, laying his arm along the back of her seat. "And the supper. I enjoyed it and you can always call it a business expense."

Jenny laughed. "Hardly worth the paperwork." She felt his fingers touch her hair. Her breath stalled in her throat.

The car, always small, felt as if it had shrunk to the size of a Matchbox toy. The spicy-citrus scent of his shaving lotion filled the space between them. Somewhere, not far away, frogs sang their night chorus.

"A little ahead of themselves, aren't they?" Jenny said with another nervous laugh.

"What?"

"The frogs. It's only March."

"Oh. Well, it's been warm the last few days. They think it's spring."

"It is, started yesterday."

The security light blinked out, isolating them in darkness.

"Would you like to come in for coffee or something?" Theo asked huskily.

Or something? What did he mean by that? Her heartbeat sped up as he bent closer. His breath brushed her face, warm and minty from the hard candy the café had given them along with the check. He couldn't kiss her. The panicky thought skittered through her.

The darkness prevented her from seeing his face but she felt him hesitate, his body momentarily still.

"Oh, hell, why not?" The softly muttered words washed over her.

She could think of dozens of reasons why not. Her lies. His danger.

She had to get away but her head touched the window. No escape. And did she really want to?

His mouth came down upon hers, cool and gentle, as if he were testing her reaction. He pulled away, staring down at her. His eyes picked up a reflection from the dim light at the far corner of the house, shining silver. Cat's eyes in the darkness. She saw them change, thought she saw a question.

Then all thought fled as he pushed his fingers into her hair, molding the back of her head to bring her to him.

He covered her mouth with his own, his kiss becoming hot and fervent. With a mixture of dismay and satisfaction, she responded, parting her lips to the exploring heat of his tongue.

Shards of light exploded through her body, melting any resistance she might have summoned. She moaned softly, and tilted her head up to his, tasting heat and need and desire, feeling his body hard against hers and welcoming it. "Theo," she whispered when he lifted his mouth to draw a tortured breath.

He looked down at her, his eyes soft and bemused. With one finger he brushed back a curl from her hot cheek.

In the distance, a dog barked sharply. As if some spell had broken, Theo dropped his hands to her shoulders. He briefly rested his face against her hair. "Jenny, you're so sweet but..." His voice trailed off, rough with a need he didn't try to hide. "It's too soon. I don't even know you."

The reminder that he knew even less about her than he realized acted like a dash of cold water. "Good night, Theo," she said as evenly as she could. "Let me know when you've finished the financial report." She curved her tingling lips into a shaky smile. "And don't stand near moving buses."

He pushed open the door. "Good night, Jenny. I'll call you."

"STUPID. Stupid. Theo berated himself as he strode toward the door. He unlocked it before he remembered he hadn't picked up his mail from the box at the road. He spun around and headed down the driveway. Jenny's brake lights flashed briefly as she paused before turning onto the road. He jogged down the driveway, reaching the mailbox just in time to see her taillights vanishing around the corner.

Safe. He grimaced wryly. Why did he feel as if he'd had a narrow escape? Dumb move, kissing her. Hadn't he had enough of deceitful women without adding another to the list?

Hell, he must be lonelier than he thought.

That vulnerability of hers kept tugging at him. Too many times he'd surprised a look in those blue eyes that hinted of pain. And he would have had to be blind not to notice the dichotomy between what she was now and what she must have been in the not too distant past. The suit she'd worn yesterday—his wife, the inveterate shopper, had made him very knowledgeable about clothes—had designer lines. Unmistakably expensive. She hadn't bought that on her nonexistent profits from Swift Couriers.

She was an enigma, and she'd gotten under his skin to the extent that he had to see it through. Find out what she wanted from him.

He could have given her his report on her finances tonight, if he'd wanted to. Instead he'd locked it and her records in his desk to save as an excuse to see her again. It had been a simple job. There was nothing wrong with her business that a major infusion of cash and a few dozen contract clients wouldn't cure.

Mail in hand—mostly junk—he retraced his steps. Halfway up the driveway, a huge yellow cat strolled out of the shrubbery. He sat down in Theo's path, demanding attention. Theo grinned at him. "Missed me, did you, Tiger?"

The cat tilted his head to one side. One of his ears was missing and the other tattered from a hundred battles, giving him a comical, lopsided appearance. He stood up on his hind legs, looking more like a miniature bear than a cat. Theo scooped him up and tucked him under his arm. "Let's get you fed."

At the mention of food, Tiger went into an ecstasy of purring. Theo laughed. Tiger was perfectly capable of hunting down his own food, and had for sometime before he'd adopted Theo to judge by his condition then. But Theo had spoiled him, and didn't regret it for one moment.

He put down the cat to open the door. Once he was inside the house, the memory of the ill-advised kiss came back. Her hair had flowed over his hands, as cool as silk. She'd tasted of ginger and mint, even sweeter than he'd imagined. As he walked to the kitchen, that thought haunted him.

JENNY DROVE HOME, her mind in turmoil. At a traffic light near the mall, she stopped on the green signal, earning herself a rude honk from the driver behind her. She let up the clutch too quickly and ground the gears, compounding her embarrassment.

This couldn't be happening. She'd wanted to go on kissing him, even to risk going in for coffee. Good thing she hadn't, although she'd no reason to congratulate herself on her common sense. He had stopped, not she.

But why had he kissed her? It was clear he didn't trust her, and he didn't strike her as the predatory kind of male who had to make a move on every female he met. That left one possibility. He was attracted to her despite his own misgivings. She groaned. She didn't need that kind of complication.

Don't you? a little voice in her head asked craftily. Her mind backtracked abruptly. Maybe she could use his apparent interest in her as a woman, as long as she curbed her own attraction to him. She'd already decided she needed to check out the people he knew. What better way than to see him outside of work as well? She would be close enough to protect him.

On that comforting, if still uneasy, thought she parked her car and let herself into her apartment.

In her bedroom, she changed into tights and a long sweatshirt, staunchly relegating the kiss and her uninhibited response to the back of her mind. Sitting down at the desk in the corner of her room, she turned on her computer.

While it booted in, she got an apple and a glass of milk from the kitchen. She set the milk beside the computer and took a bite of the apple. Tart-sweet juices burst over her tongue, reminding her of Theo's kiss.

The heat came flooding back. Dangerous, foolish fantasies. Much more of this and she would drive herself crazy. What did she know about him anyway? She should be concentrating on finding a reason why anyone would want to kill him rather than waste her time going all soft and mushy inside every time she thought of him.

She clicked to open a new document, which she titled Observation. Someone wants to kill Theo Zacharias, she typed. Who? Good question. One she didn't know how to answer unless she had some means of learning more about him. The irony was that he had access to nearly all of her financial affairs, yet she had no way of accessing any information about him.

Okay, start with the simple. She typed: someone close to him. The transient thought that had flitted through her mind in the café earlier—she suddenly knew what it had been. The voice she'd overheard yesterday. The caller saying he or she was watching Theo all the time. She added to the words on the screen: It has to be someone in his office. Which meant he had an enemy there.

But he denied it. He'd said, quite adamantly, that he had no enemies, including his wife's ghost.

She paused, staring at the blinking cursor. Why was he so bitter about his wife's death? Or was it her death? Hadn't he said they would have divorced if she hadn't died? What was the story behind it?

She leaned back, tossing the apple core into the trash can with an expert hook shot. Staring sightlessly at the screen, she finished the milk and let her thoughts roam.

Why had he left Montreal? Had he been in trouble?

She'd seen plenty of newspaper stories about brokers arrested for things like insider trading, going to jail. She couldn't imagine Theo being a crook, cheating little old ladies out of their life's savings, but what did she know about him? What did crooks look like? From the news reports, most white collar criminals were ordinary people you would pass on the street.

That didn't fit Theo. Any woman with red blood in her veins would notice Theo. Any woman's heart would beat faster at the sight of that tall, lean body, that dark, hawk-like face, the pale eyes like jewels. He gave off an aura of danger, and the promise of delicious, reckless sex.

She'd be a liar if she considered herself immune. Even now her body warmed and softened at the thought of him.

She rebuked the feeling. Mooning over him wasn't solving her dilemma.

If he had left Montreal under a cloud, how had he gotten his jobs in Vancouver? In his line of work, references were not only followed up, but they were also thoroughly scrutinized.

The motive for the harassment could not be in the past. She typed the words, then added a question mark. Not *likely* in the past. Start with the present.

She had to find out more about his co-workers, and his clients, if possible. But how? She didn't know. The only thing she could do for now was to keep her eye on him, even if it meant leaving early and maybe staking out the parking garage once he got his car back.

She clutched her head in despair. She couldn't follow him every time he went out to meet a client. She just didn't have the time. And if he caught her hanging around where she had no business to be, he would more than jokingly accuse her of an unhealthy obsession.

No, there had to be another way.

She let her hands fall on the keyboard and the computer

let out a startled bleat. Lifting her fingers, she stared in dismay at the last line she'd typed.

I can't let myself fall in love with him.

Jerking the mouse along the incriminating line, she highlighted it and pressed delete, wishing she could annihilate the thought as easily as she did the words.

THE STRIDENT RING of the phone woke her. She groped across the night table. The receiver clattered on the hard wooden surface as she knocked it over. She dragged it by the cord to her ear. "'Lo. Sorry 'bout that," she mumbled.

A high-pitched squeal shot into her ear. Pain ripped through her eardrum. She jerked the receiver away and held it at arm's length, suddenly wide-awake. What was this? Was her home phone malfunctioning as well? That was all she needed. She was about to drop it when she heard a voice.

A weird, disembodied voice that sounded as if it came through a tunnel. The caller spoke, in a singsong tone that sent shivers up her spine. "Leave Theo Zacharias alone and you might live to see your thirty-third birthday. Otherwise, you're next. You'll be seeing each other in hell."

Chapter Four

Jenny dropped the phone. It thudded to the floor, the steady drone of the dial tone mocking her. Clammy sweat broke out on her palms but her mouth felt as dry as sand. She stared at the clock radio. The red numbers told her it was 3:35. Outside, rain fell, pattering against the window. A car swished wetly by on the street.

Normal. Her stomach heaved, and she swallowed to moisten her throat. Would her life ever be normal again? She'd dropped into a nightmare.

Her birthday. On April 10 she would be thirty-three. The caller knew more about her than most of her current friends.

Logic. Think. Her mind cleared, although her heart still hammered inside her chest like a ponderous drumbeat. Who had access to her birth date besides any traffic cop who looked at her driver's license? Cindi, obviously, from the personnel records to which she had access. Even though Jenny was the boss, her statistics were in the computer. Theo, also, must know. The information appeared on her tax records, of which he had copies.

It wasn't possible for either of them to be the caller. Cindi was her friend, and depended on her for her living. Theo didn't know about the money she'd dropped off, and in any case, why would he threaten her? It had to be someone else. And that could be anyone. Perhaps one of her couriers had seen the date on the computer when she'd come in to get a delivery schedule from Cindi. From there the information could have gone anywhere.

Theo might have had his secretary or an assistant do part of the work on her finances. People in his business kept the confidences of all their clients. No one thought about it; it was ingrained in their code of ethics. But the person who had received the thousand dollars she'd delivered wouldn't be worried about a little thing like client confidentiality. Not when he or she planned murder.

Yes, her caller had to be one of the two people she'd overheard on the phone on Monday. Although he or she would have no way of ascertaining that Jenny knew about the money and the contract, Jenny's immediate efforts to contact Theo must have aroused suspicions. And the killer was taking no chances.

No chances. It hit her suddenly. He'd taken one. He'd called her. Grabbing hold of the cord, she dragged the now silent phone toward her. She pressed the Disconnect button and then, hearing the dial tone, she pressed *69, last number recall. A recorded voice droned out the number. She quickly scribbled it down.

Local. The voice repeated the number. She cut it off, and punched out the number. "The number you have dialed cannot be completed."

Her mouth twisting in frustration, she tried again, dialing the long distance access number and the area code. "The number—"

On impulse she dialed zero for operator. To her relief, she didn't get a recording. "I can't get through on this number," Jenny said.

"The number?"

Jenny recited it, her heartbeat speeding up, then plummeting as the operator told her, "I'm sorry. That number connects to a pay phone. Your call cannot be completed."

Swallowing her disappointment, Jenny thanked her and hung up.

"ANOTHER ROUGH NIGHT?" Cindi greeted her the next morning.

Jenny smothered a yawn. "Insomnia. Worry about the business and how we'll pay the taxes and the rent."

Cindi arched a perfectly plucked brow. "I thought your new friend was supposed to wave a magic wand and all our problems would just disappear."

Jenny forced a smile. "Even Theo can't work miracles."

"And here I was counting on it." Cindi shrugged. "Sorry, Jenny. I didn't mean to give you a hard time. We need a miracle. Our overdraft is going into shock." She rifled through the papers on her desk. "On the other hand, there is some good news. We've got a contract with one of the biggest car dealers in town to pick up and deliver their parts. I put Tracy on it. Good thing we kept that little Civic."

Swift Couriers boasted one car as well as the bicycles, an almost antique Honda whose body was about to expire from terminal rust. The engine, however, ran like a clock, and would probably last through another couple of hundred thousand kilometers.

Jenny nodded. Unless the car did fail, they would be able to make ends meet for the next few months. If the Civic died, she could use her own car for the deliveries.

And if Theo managed to work a miracle—

No, she couldn't let herself hope.

She had barely sat down at her desk when the phone rang. Cindi answered it, then called out, "Jenny, it's for you."

"How's it going?" Theo's deep voice caressed her ear.

"Fine, I guess," she said, dismayed at the way her

pulse sped up. She had to stop this; she was worse than a teenager in love with the football hero.

"I've got a problem."

Alarm skittered along her nerve endings. Had someone attacked him again? At least he was alive, and it didn't sound as if he were calling from a hospital. "What's wrong?"

"Some of your tax stuff is missing. And so is the report I did on your finances."

"What?" Her voice rose before she could control it. "How could that happen? Did you have a break-in at your office? I thought businesses like yours were safer than a bank."

"Usually they are." He stopped, then cleared his throat, clearly embarrassed. "I'm really sorry about this but my desk wasn't locked and some other stuff was taken as well. It could have been the cleaning crew, although the same company has been doing the janitorial work for years without any problems. But Doug just told me they hired a new kid last week. I called them and they say they checked him out, but he did clean my office."

"But what would he do with the documents?"

"Good question," Theo said, sounding as baffled as she felt. "Maybe he thought the papers he took would give him a lead on a hot investment. I don't know."

Jenny's intuition, fine-tuned during her years in social work, jumped into high gear. "Was anyone else's desk touched?"

"Apparently not. At least not obviously."

She let out a long breath. Just what she would have figured. Another instance of harassment against Theo. "Have you tried to get hold of the kid who works for the janitorial service?"

"You sound like a detective," he said sharply.

"I sound like a person whose personal papers are missing," she said, exasperated. "How am I supposed to react? *Have* you talked to the kid?"

Theo sighed, and she could imagine him raking a restless hand through his hair. "We've tried. There's no answer at his place."

Jenny gripped the phone tighter. "You mean you haven't gone there? What about the police?"

"We'd rather handle this ourselves. The fact is, we have no evidence that this kid is even responsible, so we can't go around making charges without foundation."

"Then let me try."

"You? Why should you get involved?"

"It's my stuff, isn't it? Maybe he still has it. Not that it's irreplaceable—lucky you gave me photocopies, but I'd rather not have somebody find the papers in a Dumpster or something."

Theo was silent for a long moment. His voice, when he spoke, betrayed his reluctance but also his frustration. "You know, maybe that would work after all. I'd go myself but I have appointments all morning. By the way, you'll get the report. It's in my computer and all I have to do is print out another copy."

"Okay. Give me the kid's address. I'll see if I can get the papers back. If he took them."

THE STREET SHE DROVE to was in one of the poorest sections of the city, lined with old houses, most of which had been converted to housekeeping rooms. She frowned as she noted the signs of poverty and lost dreams. The residents of some of the houses probably all shared one bathroom and one kitchen.

Under a leaden sky that was beginning to break up, she drove slowly along the potholed pavement. She found the house, which had a British flag draped inside the front window in lieu of a curtain. Parking the car behind a rusty relic from the sixties, she got out and walked through a gate that hung on one hinge. Scattered toys and a battered tricycle lay on the lawn that was more weeds than grass. Dandelions sprouted gaily between cracks in the cement walk.

She climbed the sagging wooden steps and pressed the doorbell. The old-fashioned two-tone ring echoed inside the house. She could see the front hall through the screen door, faded linoleum and painted walls scarred by years of use.

Theo's words echoed through her head as she waited. Be careful. Don't go inside the house. Let him come out.

If he only knew some of the places she'd been in when she'd worked for Social Services—seedy bars looking for an errant father, crack houses, unsanitary hotel rooms, houses in which the only furniture was a bed. She'd seen it all. Interviewing one twenty-year-old kid was elementary.

An old man sucking on the foul-smelling stub of a cigar lumbered down the hall. He didn't open the screen door. "Yeah? Help you?"

"I'm looking for Eddie Dixon."

"Ain't here. Said he'd be back by ten. Said he's expecting a call." He rolled the cigar to the other side of his mouth. "Only one phone in the house."

Which might explain why Theo had gotten no answer when he'd called. Everyone who'd heard the phone might have expected someone else to pick it up. She glanced at her watch. Ten to ten. "Thanks. I'll be back."

He grinned, showing large yellowed teeth. "Wouldn't want to come inside, would you? Pretty lady like yourself isn't safe on these streets."

She stepped back, her skin crawling. Safer out here than inside with him, she was willing to bet. "No, that's all right. Thank you."

She almost ran to her car, got inside and locked the door. She checked the passenger door, making sure it was locked as well and that the windows were rolled up tight. She wasn't used to this anymore. In the past, she would have brazenly stood outside, leaning on the fence, ignoring passersby.

The adrenaline rush died, leaving her tired and dispirited. The sun peeked out from a break in the clouds, warming the inside of the car. Jenny's eyelids drooped, her restless night catching up to her.

She started awake when a set of rough knuckles rapped on the car window. She blinked at the sight of the old man peering through the glass. "Eddie's back."

She got out of the car, feeling dozy and rumpled and at a distinct disadvantage. How could she have slept? "Can you call him out here?"

He hitched up his baggy trousers, snapping the suspenders against the grimy T-shirt that stretched over a large belly. "You're not a cop, are you? I wouldn't turn anyone over to a cop."

"I'm not a cop," she assured him. "I just want to talk to Eddie."

The old man nodded. His work boots clumped up the steps and he vanished into the house. Jenny waited, leaning against her car fender, her keys in her hand.

The screen door opened and a tall skinny lad stepped out. A faded plaid shirt, several sizes too large, hung on his bony frame, over jeans that would have fit the old man. His sallow skin showed remnants of acne and he slumped as if he were constantly ducking under low doorways. "Yeah?"

"You're Eddie Dixon?"

"Yeah." He pulled a cigarette package out of his shirt pocket, stuck one between his lips and lit it with a lighter clipped to the pack. He inhaled deeply and blew out the smoke.

"You work for Miranda's Cleaning Service."

"Yeah. What about it?"

Surly kid, she thought, squelching an urge to punch him. Excellent communications skills. "Did you clean Pacific Rim Investments' offices last night?"

"Sh—" He broke off. "You're a cop." He dropped the cigarette, spun away through the gate and took off toward the back of the house, long legs churning. Jenny sprinted after him.

Luckily for her the backyard was enclosed by a high fence. He made an abortive leap to scale it, but fell back, breathing heavily. "Stop smoking," she advised. "Your lungs will thank you for it."

She planted her fists on her hips, rocking slightly on her heels. "Now, tell me about it. Nobody's been able to call you this morning so why did you run? And just in case you're wondering, I'm really not a cop."

"Yeah? Well, you sound like one." Defiantly he lit another cigarette, deliberately exhaling the smoke into her face.

She glared at him, refusing to move. "Look, wise guy, I can call the police. Or you can talk to me and no one will find out about it."

He let his body sag against the warped boards of the fence, the bravado draining out of his face. "You mean you won't make me lose my job?"

She pretended to consider. "Why? Should you?"

His lower lip trembled and she realized that he was only a boy, playing at being a man. "I need that job."

"Fine. Then do it properly. Who got to you?"

"I dunno. Somebody phoned me. Real weird voice, metallic, you know. Said I'd get fifty bucks if I took some papers out of a guy's desk and shoved them behind the filing cabinet in his office. It wasn't stealing. Sooner or later somebody'd find them. Please, lady, that's all it was. Just a joke."

"You've inconvenienced several people," she said severely. "That goes beyond a joke. How was the payment made? Did you see the person?"

"Uh-uh. I got it in the mail, express post, you know, those red-and-white envelopes that only take a day. In cash."

Dead end. She tapped her foot, thumb and forefinger tugging at her bottom lip.

"Lady, I won't do it again." His voice shook and she sensed that he was on the verge of tears. "Just let me keep my job."

"Okay," Jenny said. "But this sort of thing can't happen again. I'll be keeping track of you." She turned and walked away from him. At the corner of the house, she looked back. "And quit smoking. Put the money into an RRSP and you'll not only have something for your old age but you'll live long enough to enjoy it."

Theo would have been proud of her, she thought as she drove back downtown. Oh, maybe not for her foolhardiness in chasing the kid around the house, but for being a quick learner where finances were concerned. He didn't need to know the kid had tried to run.

"I TALKED TO THE TEENAGER," she told Theo half an hour later, cradling the receiver between her neck and shoulder as she initialled the invoices Cindi handed her. "I promised I wouldn't report him. He needs the job."

Warmth spread through her as he laughed. "Another poor lamb you have to save from the slaughter, I suppose."

"So what?" Elated with her success, she couldn't take offense. "You'll find the missing papers behind the file cabinet."

"Just a second." A light thump indicated he'd put down the phone.

Jenny gave the invoices back to Cindi, nodding at her.

"Thanks, Cindi." Phone against her ear, she waited until the rustle of papers told her Theo had returned to his desk.

"Yes, they're all here. Stupid kid."

"My feelings, exactly. But I think he won't pull a stunt like that again."

"But why'd he do it in the first place?"

Here was the tricky part. Should she tell him? She'd debated the question all the way back from the kid's place. Yes, she had to. The decision made, she felt as if part of the weight of her secrets from Theo had shifted off her shoulders. "He says somebody paid him fifty dollars." She attempted a laugh but it stuck in her throat. "Must be one of your practical jokers."

Theo said nothing, the silence filled only with the faint sound of his breathing. "Yeah, must have been," he said at last but he didn't sound any more convinced than she felt.

After perfunctory farewells, they broke the connection.

Jenny sorted through the messages on her desk, making calls to acquaint potential clients with her rates and terms. Her major coup of the morning was another contract, with a computer company that needed disks carried at various times to and from their branch stores. If she planned routes efficiently these deliveries could be combined with those of the car parts, making the Honda and one driver do double duty.

A renewed sense of well-being filled her as she heard the noon horn playing the opening notes of "O Canada."

SHE KNEW IT WAS TOO GOOD to last. At five after the hour, Tracy staggered into the office, her face a delicate shade of green. She held her stomach, collapsing into a chair. "I'm sick but I have six more deliveries to make." She swallowed hard, her eyes rolling. "Must be something I ate, or flu."

Cindi pushed her chair back, wheels clacking across the

tiled floor. "Don't come near me. I don't want to catch it."

"If it's something she ate, it's not contagious." Jenny, who had been going over accounts on the computer with Cindi, stepped around the desk and rested her hand against Tracy's forehead. Hot. Definitely hot. "Can you get home okay, Tracy? Never mind, I'll give you a lift and after that I'll do the deliveries."

AT THREE Jenny called the office from a pay phone. "You have to pick up a box of parts in North Van and deliver it to the auto mall in Richmond," Cindi said.

Jenny groaned. She'd be lucky to complete the route by five. And she'd hit rush hour traffic on the way back. "Anything else?" she asked.

"Yeah. Theo Zacharias called. Says he needs you to get in touch with him."

Now what? Jenny thanked Cindi and hung up. Immediately dropping another quarter into the phone and dialing Theo's office number. "Mr. Zacharias is in a meeting and cannot be disturbed," Ms. Herrington said haughtily. "May I take a message and have him call you?"

"No, I'll try later. Thanks." She slammed down the phone. Even if she gave her pager number, she'd have to find a phone to call him back if he contacted her. Not for the first time, she cursed the inconvenience of not being able to afford a cellular phone.

An accident on the Oak Street bridge delayed her return. Traffic crept by the two smashed cars and their disgruntled drivers, two lanes merging into single file. And to make matters worse, it began to rain, a slight drizzle that made the roads slippery and slowed traffic further. By the time Jenny parked the little Honda in the lone parking space she rented next to the Dumpster behind the building, it was well after six and rapidly growing dark.

She found a note on Cindi's desk that Theo had phoned twice since three-thirty. Knowing it was futile, she dialed his office number. Sure enough, she got a recording that listed the hours they were open and a suggestion that she call in the morning. She had her finger poised on the number pad when she realized she didn't know his home number.

Pulling the phone book out of the desk drawer, she ran her finger down the Z section. This time she could match him with the name of his street. He was the only T. Zacharias without a middle initial. The phone rang three times before his voice came on. "I am unable to speak to you at the moment. Please leave a message."

She smiled. Brisk and straightforward, as she would have expected. She waited through several beeps indicating other messages, then spoke. "This is Jenny. It's six-thirty." She calculated rapidly, swivelling to glance out the window. Had the rain stopped? She compromised with, "I'll try you later."

She spent several minutes checking through tomorrow's schedule, which included a gratifying number of parts deliveries. However, unless Tracy had recovered, Jenny would have to deliver them herself, which would take her away from the office again for much of the day.

As far as she knew, none of the other girls had a driver's license. Perhaps Cindi would spell her, but that wasn't likely. Cindi hated battling the traffic. Better let her do what she was best at, calling up potential clients and convincing them to use their services.

The building creaked around her as she sat at the desk and made up the delivery schedules. By the time she was through, it was close to seven. Hurriedly putting the sheets into the desk, she left the office, carefully locking the door.

The elevator took forever to come. She was about to use the stairs, poorly lit as they were, when it wheezed to

a stop. It took her down one floor. The number two lit up
and the car stopped, the inner door opening. Jenny peered
through the grill. No one was there.

They'd probably gotten tired of waiting. Jenny jabbed
the Close Door button. It rolled shut but try as she might,
she couldn't get the infernal machine to move, either up
or down. Finally she pushed the Open Door button and
to her relief, it opened once again. Pushing aside the steel
grill, she got out and headed toward the dim red Exit sign
marking the fire door and emergency stairs.

Unoiled hinges groaned as she entered the stairwell.
The bare concrete stairs disappeared into the darkness below her. Only the bulb on the landing was lit; the others
farther down must have burned out.

Cold air wafted up the stairs. For a moment Jenny
wouldn't have been surprised to see the shadowy outline
of a ghost, arriving to escort her to the ground floor. She
shivered, almost giving in to an insane urge to laugh.

The lobby was actually two floors below her since the
building was numbered in the European style, with the
floor above the ground designated as the first. Somewhere
she heard a door slam, up or down, she couldn't tell. She
peered down the space between the flights. A light glowed
below her, like a red eye, most likely on the main floor.
Overhead, she could see the red Exit sign on the floor
above but nothing beyond that. Not even spooky shadows
or stealthy footsteps on the stairs.

Holding onto the cold steel rail, she crept downward,
placing her feet carefully on each tread once she was out
of range of the light. Good thing she wore sneakers and
not the high heels she'd had on the day before yesterday.

By the second flight, she couldn't see the stair treads.
She slowed her pace even further, feeling for each step.
Eerie noises filtered upward from the basement. Unable
to see in the dense darkness, she used the faint red beacon
of the Exit sign below her as a guide.

Suddenly it winked out. Jenny froze, her heart thundering in her ears. Was that a rustle of feet or clothing she heard, or only the rush of air currents from the basement? She strained to hear, then cautiously placed her foot on the step below her. By her calculations, there were only three steps left before she reached the main floor landing. She stepped down from the last one, pushing her foot ahead to make sure she hadn't miscounted. No, the reassuring feel of solid ground transmitted itself to her brain.

She put down the other foot and groped for the door handle. She clamped her fingers around the smooth metal and braced herself to pull it open.

An arm snaked out of the darkness to wrap itself around her throat. The scream rising from her chest emerged as a thin squeak. Multicolored dots danced before her eyes, and a dull roar filled her head, blocking rational thought. She jabbed her elbow back and had the satisfaction of hearing a grunt of pain, but the arm around her neck tightened.

She couldn't breathe. Her throat burned as if a blow torch seared it. She felt the world go black, which was odd because it had been black before, without the lights. All strength drained out of her and her body went limp.

The pressure eased marginally. Desperately grabbing the last vestiges of consciousness, she dragged in a shallow breath, trying to get her vocal cords to process the scream stuck in her brain.

He was strong, too strong. She flayed her arms as he tried to grab them, to pin them behind her. Her fingers clawed at his neck, encountering crisp hair and a smooth collar, beneath a rougher one. He grunted again as her other elbow hit some vital spot, but she couldn't get the right angle to do much damage. He only tightened his hold again.

She stamped her foot, trying to kick her assailant in the shins or ankles, but the soft sneakers made little impact.

For the first time in her life she wished she were wearing the torturous high heels. At least they would have been useful as a weapon. The sneakers proved their further weakness when he placed a hard foot on one of hers, painfully grinding the bones together.

Her attacker suddenly stiffened, as if a noise had startled him. The pressure on her throat eased again, and Jenny gasped in air. She smelled the sweet odor of shaving lotion or cologne, heavy and musky. Suddenly he let her go. She slumped to the floor, her legs as limp as overcooked noodles.

She lay there shivering as she dragged in a lungful of blessed air. It didn't matter that it smelled strongly of old cement, mold and mildew. She was alive. He'd let her go.

Below her, a door slammed and she knew her attacker must have run into the basement. From there he could get out into the alley behind the building through the fire exit.

Cold seeped through her clothes and she struggled to her feet, shaking her head as dizziness made the darkness spin around her. Steadying herself on the stair rail, she groped for the door. It wasn't there. Fighting the panic that threatened to choke her, she forced herself to think.

Somehow she'd gotten turned around. She leaned forward, reaching out again. Her palm scraped on the rough cement block wall. She took a step, and touched the warmer wood of the door. Strange, her muddled mind said, that the fire doors in this building were made of wood; wouldn't steel be safer?

She found the handle, and pulled on it. It opened so suddenly she almost fell. She lurched into the lobby, which was also dark except for the pallid orange light from the street outside.

Behind her a sharp thud made her spin around. No one. She laughed shakily. Merely the fire door closing, its worn hydraulics failing to ease it slowly shut.

Hands trembling so badly she could barely stick her

key into the outside lock, she finally managed to wrench
the door open and let herself out into the street.

"Jenny, what are you doing here at this time of night?"

Chapter Five

Jenny groaned. Theo. Just what she needed, for him to come on all male and protective.

"I work here, remember?"

The wobble in her voice betrayed her. Weak, stupid tears filled her eyes and overflowed. Her humiliation complete, she let herself slide down the door until her bottom hit the dirty cement step.

Theo, with a fine disregard for his suit, sat down beside her and pulled her into his arms. "Jenny, Jenny," he murmured. "I knew something like this would happen."

There it was, a repeat of his earlier warning about the neighborhood. As if she could do anything about it. Not to mention she was sure the attack had nothing to do with the perceived danger of the neighborhood. And everything to do with the early-morning phone call.

The tears dried up abruptly. Jenny pulled her head back. She groped in her pockets for a tissue, sniffing dismally as she came up empty. Theo passed her a clean white handkerchief, waiting while she mopped up. "I'll wash it and get it back to you," she said shakily.

The cement felt hard and cold beneath her. She went to stand up but her legs wobbled alarmingly. Maybe it would be prudent to stay where she was a moment longer. Next to her, Theo showed no sign of impatience, sitting on the grimy concrete in his navy, pin-striped suit.

"Somebody grabbed me from behind," she said at last.

Theo nodded. "That's what I mean. It's not safe here, especially after dark. Where did it happen, in that dungeon of a basement where you keep the bikes?"

She shook her head. "No. The elevator stopped so I took the stairs. He jumped me on the landing outside the entrance lobby. And he took off through the basement. I don't know why he let me go. I think he heard a noise."

"Was he after your purse?"

"I'm not carrying a purse. I've got my wallet in my pocket but he didn't seem to be interested in it. He could have grabbed it anytime." She dragged in a long, shuddering breath. "No, I don't think this was an ordinary mugger. He smelled too good."

"He smelled too good?" Theo echoed incredulously. "What do you mean?"

"Yes, he smelled like after-shave or something. Most of the people on the street smell of sweat and unwashed clothes, or of hamburger grease and beer because they spend so much time in bars and fast-food restaurants."

"Okay, so we have a clean mugger. Any idea what he wanted? Did he say anything?"

"Only a grunt when I buried my elbow in his belly." She almost smiled as she realized she had at least scored one point.

"Soft or hard?"

"Hard, of course. As hard as I could. I'm not a wimp."

Theo laughed, the sound so normal after her fright that it did much to restore her equilibrium. "Not how you hit him. I meant his belly. Was it soft or hard?"

She closed her eyes, thinking. A shiver ran through her once again as she recalled the feel of her assailant against her back. "Neither. Just a regular belly, I guess. But he wasn't fat or flabby. I could feel his chest but it wasn't particularly hard, either. He was strong, though. I couldn't break free.''

More sensory details rushed into her mind, things she hadn't registered at the time. "He was taller than I am. And probably not too old. Oh, yeah, he wore gloves, leather gloves. I could smell them. I think they were new. And he had on a dress shirt. I felt the collar. And probably a tweed jacket. I think his shoes were also dressy. I could hear them scraping on the floor when he was trying to hold me. And he stepped on my foot, hard.''

She flexed the wounded foot, wincing. All the bones seemed intact but it hurt to move it. No wonder she was having trouble standing.

Theo nodded. "You're good at details, aren't you?"

"Yes, I've always been," she said absently, her mind still on her assailant.

"So we're looking for a man about my height and age, who's not some scruffy person living on the street."

"With scratches on his neck," Jenny said, holding up her hand. Little bloody bits of skin were imbedded under her fingernails. She shuddered as she examined them. "Can they do DNA tests on them to identify him?"

"I doubt it. Who would they match it up with?" Theo smiled faintly as she scrubbed them clean with his handkerchief. "Dress clothes? Clean? He's either the best-dressed mugger in town or he had some other purpose in mind." His eyes bored into hers. "What would that be, Jenny?"

She looked back at him, keeping her gaze open and candid. "I have no idea. Unless it was somebody come back to avenge the way I bullied Eddie Dixon this morning."

Theo rubbed his chin, beard stubble rasping beneath his fingers. "Could it have been Eddie?"

"No. He's skinny and smells of cigarette smoke. And he's really bony. No, it definitely wasn't Eddie. I don't know what this guy wanted but whatever it was, he didn't want me to see him. He managed to turn off all the lights in the stairwell.''

"Unless a fuse blew," Theo suggested, his mouth turning down. "The wiring can't be too reliable in a building like this."

"Maybe not, but if that's what happened, it was an awfully convenient fuse."

"Would you recognize him if you saw him again?"

Jenny pondered that one. "Maybe, if he grabbed me from behind, but not likely if I came face-to-face with him. The after-shave was familiar so it's probably a common brand. I've smelled it before." She leaned toward him and sniffed. "No, it wasn't you."

Theo jerked back, a scowl knitting his black brows. "Yeah, sure. As if I'd wait in a dark corner to mug you. What for? To steal your purse?"

"Well, I don't know much about you, do I?" she said seriously.

Theo stood up, pulling her to her feet. "You know that I don't have to make my living as a mugger."

"That's true." Jenny grimaced as she brushed dust from the seat of her jeans. "What I need is a bath. Or at least a place to wash my hands." She shook her fingers, her skin crawling. "I think I can still feel that guy's blood under my nails."

"Come along." Taking her arm, Theo walked her briskly along the street. "There's a washroom in the mall below my office building. After that, I'll take you to your car. You did bring your car, didn't you?"

She nodded numbly. Just as she'd feared, he was bound and determined to portray the knight in shining armor, but she found to her surprise, at the moment she didn't care.

In the washroom she stared aghast at her reflection. She'd used makeup to disguise the dark circles that a lack of sleep had left beneath her eyes but during the day it had worn off. Her eyes looked like black holes in her pale face. Her dark brown hair sprang in uncontrolled waves on her head, emphasizing the pallor of her skin.

She squirted liquid soap onto her hands, and scrubbed them, paying particular attention to the undersides of her nails. She rinsed with the hottest water she could stand, and then soaped some more. Finally, for good measure, she washed her face, grimacing as she dried off with the rough paper towels.

Since she had only a lipstick with her, there wasn't much she could do to make herself look more presentable. She dotted spots of lipstick on her cheeks and rubbed her fingers over them to create a little color. It didn't help much.

Her hands still felt dirty. She was debating whether to scrub them again when she heard a knock on the door and Theo's voice calling, "Jenny, are you okay in there?"

Tucking the lipstick into her pocket, she went out, forcing a bright smile. "I hate days like this, don't you, when everything seems to go wrong."

He gave her an odd look but didn't say anything.

SHE GOT ANOTHER ATTACK of the jitters when they stepped out of the elevator into the parking garage. Although brightly lit, the low ceilings, thick concrete pillars, the scent of oil and exhaust, and the echoing roars of unseen engines made her think of movies in which the hero got run down by a car in just such a place. In fact, she kept expecting her attacker to step from behind a post and jump them.

Theo, feeling her shiver, laced his fingers through hers. "Don't worry. My car is just up ahead."

She dragged her mind out of the shadows, glad of something else to focus on. "You mean they finished repairing it? That was quick."

"Yeah." He let go of her hand as he paused next to

the dark gray Saab. Pulling the keys from his pocket, he unlocked the passenger door. He ran his hand over the repaired fender. "The damage wasn't as bad as it looked. I would have had it back yesterday but they had to wait for the paint to dry. Dark colors seem to take forever. And it's pretty dusty down here. I didn't want to take any chances of messing it up."

"That's good," Jenny said. "So you won't need me anymore." There went her excuse to spend time with him.

He'd moved around to the driver's side. He looked at her over the top of the car, his eyes gleaming in the shadows. "Oh, I'll still need you, Jenny. How about if I follow you home?" He tapped his briefcase. "I've got your financial report in here. I'd like to go over it with you. Unless you've got plans for the evening."

Yeah, she thought, vacuuming her apartment. She hated vacuuming. "No, I have time."

"What about dinner? Would you like to stop somewhere?"

"I can eat later, when I get home."

Theo grinned. "Nothing doing. I'll order a pizza with my car phone and pick it up on the way. After all, you bought last time."

"Yeah, like you owe me." Her laughter bounced off the damp cement wall beside her. "You don't know where I live."

He tossed the briefcase into the back seat. "Sure, I do. Your address was on your tax forms."

"Oh, that's right." So was her birth date, for anyone to see.

They drove out of the garage, along streets teeming with late-night shoppers. Over Theo's objections, Jenny got out at the entrance to the parking lot. Now that she had her wits back, she wasn't going to let a random, or not so random, mugging interfere with her life. "My car is in the first row. You can see it from here."

"Well, check the back seat before you get inside," Theo said, his scowl back.

"I always do," she said calmly. "Even though in a car that size, anybody hiding there would have to be a midget."

"Okay. I'll see you at your place. Set the table." The window started to close, then stopped halfway up. Theo leaned across the car. "Oh, Jenny, there's something else I want to ask you. Later."

If his intention had been to make her think of him all the way home, he succeeded. And she finally admitted that the feeling of being pampered and cared for, unfamiliar as it was, wasn't as hard to take as she'd expected.

"HOW WOULD YOU LIKE to go to a party with me?" Theo, slice of pizza suspended midway to his mouth, kept his eyes on Jenny as he waited for her answer.

She took her time, he had to say that for her. In fact, she took so long, sitting there staring at the pattern of pepperoni on the pizza, that he began to question why he'd asked her. His throat closed as he realized how much he wanted her to say yes. "Forget it," he said, putting an offhand tone in his voice that didn't quite come off. "If you don't want to go—"

To his surprise, she offered him a sunny smile. "I'd love to go to a party with you. When?"

The breath he let out must have been audible to her. Why did it matter so much? No other woman had been able to get under his skin this quickly and with this little provocation. "Tomorrow night." He frowned. "I hope that's enough notice. I'll pick you up at seven. The party's just drinks and snacks. We can go out somewhere to eat afterward."

A line appeared between her straight brows. "Formal dress?"

It struck him that, despite the suit she'd worn the day

they met, her wardrobe might be limited. She probably thought she had nothing to wear. In contrast to her normal, rather frightening self-sufficiency, that little, oh so female element of her personality struck him as endearing. His nervousness fled. "It's not formal. Most of the people there will be coming straight from the office."

She lifted her head from her study of the cooling pizza. Her gaze sharpened. "People from your office?"

"Yeah, some of them. I'll introduce you, if you're worried about not knowing anyone. And don't worry, some of our clients will be there." He lifted another slice of pizza, grinning disarmingly. "They're just regular folks."

"Not as poor as me, I'll bet."

"It won't matter, will it?"

"I guess not."

They finished the pizza and a second glass of the wine Theo had brought along with it. He helped her carry their dishes to the sink. "No dishwasher?" he asked in mock horror.

"Sorry." She shrugged, at ease, he was pleased to see. "Leave them. I'll do them tomorrow. You wanted to show me the financial report you've done."

"Yeah." He wouldn't have minded doing the dishes, standing close to her while one of them washed and the other dried. Inhaling that fresh, delicate scent that was uniquely hers. Ordinary, mundane, but somehow he wanted that with her. Maybe if he saw her doing the tasks of everyday life, he could figure her out, break through that enigmatic reserve she'd erected like a wall between them.

Not that her personality was reserved. Quite the contrary. He'd already seen her to be impulsive, optimistic and courageous, with a healthy dose of common sense and self-esteem. No, it was the things she hid, the little barriers she put up to keep him at an emotional distance. He was still convinced she was hiding something. But even though he'd grown to like her—far too much, perhaps, he kept warning himself—he hadn't made any progress as far as knowing her better.

Maybe the party would change that. He'd see her interaction with others. It was a risk, bringing her to a gathering where so many of his co-workers would be present. Monday morning's gossip would no doubt feature Theo and his date, a novelty since he'd never brought a woman to an office party before.

He'd steered clear of women since Lisa's death, except for the most casual dates. Not that he was mourning her. But he had to admit she'd destroyed his trust, his faith in his own judgment. He'd thought himself in love with her, only to discover within a year that it was an illusion.

Now, he wondered if he'd recognize love if it walked up and smacked him in the face.

Still, he knew that meeting Jenny had shaken him out of the rut that had seemed comfortable and safe. What he did about it, however, remained to be seen.

"Where will you pick me up?" Jenny asked. "If the party's downtown, I can wait at my office. There's always something to do."

"Nobody works late on Friday night," Theo said forcefully. "No, I'll pick you up here. The party's in the Sheraton on 104th."

They sat back down at the table and he opened his briefcase, withdrawing the sheaf of papers she'd given him. They were somewhat wrinkled from their night behind the file cabinet, except for the final report that was printed on PRI letterhead.

He silently handed it to her. Jenny nodded as she scanned the figures. "Depressing, isn't it?" she said. "Looks like the only cure is if I win the lottery."

Theo rolled his eyes. "Don't bother wasting your money. By the way, I didn't make a complaint against Eddie Dixon. I talked to his boss, saying the papers had been misplaced. Eddie's been transferred to a different floor, anyway, so we shouldn't have any further trouble, especially since he seems serious about keeping this job.''

Her smile warmed him right down to his toes. "I'm glad,'' she said. "It's hard for kids to get jobs, especially when they're unskilled. If he lost it now, I expect we'd be supporting him in prison soon.''

Amused, he squeezed her hand. "You're still a social worker at heart, aren't you, Jenny?''

She shrugged. "Too soft, by far. That's why I couldn't stand it to beat my head against the system any longer.''

"Bet they're sorry they lost you, though.''

Her mouth turned down. Disillusionment. He'd felt it so often he had no trouble recognizing it. Still holding her hand, he used his other hand to turn her face toward him. "Jenny, don't sweat it. You're probably doing more good now. You're dealing directly with the problem, not using the issues to distance yourself.''

His heart lurched as he saw tears swimming in her eyes, turning them the color of rain-washed pansies. "Jenny, don't,'' he whispered. "I can't stand it if you cry.''

"I'm not crying.'' She gulped, her voice cracking.

Unable to stop himself, he leaned closer. He kissed her, drinking in the single tear she let fall. She tasted salty and sweet at the same time. Delectable. He inhaled the faint flower scent of her hair and thrust his fingers into the glossy curls to draw her nearer.

Why did she have the power to tug on his emotions, to make him forget all his questions and misgivings about her? Then all thought evaporated as he covered her mouth with his own. Slick wet heat molded them together. Her nails dug into his shoulder, pricking through his shirt. Her other hand stroked his hair, soft and gentle, then gripping hard as the kiss deepened.

It couldn't go on. They had to breathe, although he thought he would rather drown in the sweetness of her.

"Jenny," he murmured, resting his forehead against hers. "This is supposed to be business."

"Is it?" She sounded dazed. Her eyes remained closed. He could see the tracery of blue veins under the pale skin. She wore little makeup; her creamy skin didn't need it. He liked her naturalness, better than he'd liked the businesswoman she'd been the day they met.

Tuesday. Only Tuesday. The reminder that he didn't know much more about her now than he had then brought him back to complete sanity. He cleared his throat, straightening on the hard kitchen chair. "Shall we finish this? You look like you could use some sleep."

Her eyes opened, the deep blue almost black. She blinked and the dazed look vanished. She picked up her pen. "Yes, business."

They spent an hour discussing various ways she could enhance efficiency and increase her profits. She told him about the car parts contract. "That's great," he said. "I'll keep my eye out for more business for you as well. You know, it might just work out after all."

"I certainly hope so," Jenny said fervently.

At the door, he paused, fighting himself. He wanted to kiss her again, sink his hands into the soft hair that curled around her face. He wanted to carry her off to the bed he glimpsed through the open bedroom door.

He contented himself with touching a fingertip to the bruised looking skin under her eyes. "You need sleep. Good night, Jenny."

"Good night, Theo." Her voice was husky, as if she were already half asleep. "Send the bill to the office."

"No rush."

He was halfway down the hall when he looked back. She still stood in the doorway, weariness in the angle of her body against the frame. He reached her in three strides, pulled her into the curve of his body and let his tongue slide over her lips and into her mouth. She gasped, then responded, opening her mouth and welcoming him.

She wrapped her arms around his neck, her fingers combing through his hair. Her breasts pressed against his chest. He felt the nipples harden and knew he wasn't the only one feeling the passion. He lifted his mouth from hers and kissed her cheek, then her closed eyelids. She ducked her head and laid her mouth on his chest. He'd long ago discarded his tie and loosened half the buttons on his shirt. He suddenly wished he could tear it off, lay her down and let her explore all of him.

He jerked himself out of the daydream he couldn't afford to indulge. "Jenny," he said. "I have to go. But not before one more."

He covered her mouth with his, drinking in her sweetness, not caring if she felt his longing. For one moment he would have this, then he would find the strength to go.

When he pulled away, her cheeks were flushed, her eyes languorous. "Good night, Jenny. I'll pick you up tomorrow night at seven."

This time he didn't allow himself to look back.

AT THREE O'CLOCK Friday afternoon Jenny had a brain wave. She'd lost sleep overnight mulling over Theo's situation, even when her thoughts kept trying to dwell on the kisses they'd shared. False pretences. He would hate her when he found out. Yet, shivers of pleasure ran through her, almost keeping the guilt at bay.

All morning she'd been so absentminded that Cindi had finally suggested she get her brain in gear. Now she sat in the Honda after making the last parts delivery, breathing fumes and listening to car horns futilely trying to speed up the stalled traffic. She profoundly hoped that Tracy would be back on Monday.

At the intersection ahead of her a billboard advertised the urgency to get income tax forms filed, touting the wisdom of using a tax preparation company. Safe, reliable, member of the Better Business Bureau.

A light flashed in Jenny's brain. How did you know if your financial planner was safe and reliable? The Securities Commission. She could check Theo's credentials by calling them.

As soon as the traffic light turned red, she gunned the little car past a truck and sped all the way to the office, raising a cloud of dust as she braked beside the Dumpster.

Cindi grinned at her as she charged into the office. "Traffic must have moved faster today."

"Gotta make a phone call before they close," Jenny said, panting from her run up the stairs.

At her own desk, she looked up the number and punched it out on the phone. Quickly, before guilt at spying on him took over. It was for his own good, she reminded herself. The more she learned about him, the better her chances of finding out who was after him.

The woman who answered took her time replying to the request. Impatiently Jenny tapped a pen on the desk. "Theo Zacharias has had one alleged complaint filed by a client in Montreal."

Jenny's pulse jumped. "When was this?"

"Four and a half years ago. The complaint was dropped a week after it was made."

"What was the nature of the complaint?" Jenny asked.

"Mismanagement of funds but it was never substantiated."

"What about now? Is he considered reliable and capable?"

"Yes, very much so. You must realize that often complaints are made out of spite, someone disgruntled with the market, which is, of course, out of the broker's control. Since it was withdrawn so quickly, we feel this was of that nature. I hope I've been of help."

"Yes, thank you."

Jenny's mind churned with confusion as she put down the phone. A complaint but it had never been followed up. Did that mean he was innocent? It would seem so. She knew brokers had to comply with certain regulations, although almost anyone could set himself up as a financial planner. Theo was licensed, which meant he was honest.

Didn't it? She twisted her fingers together, suddenly cold. Did that complaint have anything to do with what was happening now? Logic told her it didn't. Again, like whatever reason he'd left Montreal, it was too long ago. Presumably long forgotten.

She swivelled her chair around and stared at the brick wall outside her window. Was the complaint the reason he'd left Montreal? Theo hadn't been very forthcoming when they'd talked about his past.

The bigger question was, could she confront him with this information, ask him to elaborate on it? Would he be angry that she'd belatedly checked up on him, after allowing him to analyze her finances?

Maybe it would be better to keep her mouth shut. More dishonesty. Not to mention she wouldn't find out if someone in the past might be after him now.

Unable to reach a conclusion, she turned to the invoices on her desk. She'd see him tonight, and play it by ear.

THE CROWD eddied around her as she balanced a glass of wine and a small plate of hors d'oeuvres. She'd somehow got separated from Theo. She stood on her tiptoes, trying to spot his dark head.

Failing to do so, she looked around for a chair. Since the point was to circulate, to make and enhance business contacts, there weren't nearly enough to go around. She edged between groups of people talking too loudly and cheerfully, reminding her again why she didn't like this kind of party. Everyone trying to impress everyone else. In the past, she'd gone to enough charity fund-raising events to recognize the sometimes pathetic need to see and be seen.

She'd had time to change her clothes before Theo had picked her up, and was glad she'd taken his advice. Dressed in a tailored skirt, silk shirt and blazer, she fit the dress code. Most of the other people had come straight from work, she guessed, since power suits appeared to be the dress of choice for either sex.

Miraculously she found a chair, behind a potted palm in a corner. She sat down, wiggling her toes out of her shoes. She just stuffed a crab-covered cracker into her mouth when she heard her name. "Jenny, there you are."

To her disappointment it wasn't Theo who came around the palm, dragging his own chair. The man who'd stopped by Theo's office on Tuesday afternoon sat down beside her, so close his knee bumped hers. She swung her legs to one side, trying to think of his name.

He came to her rescue, grinning. "Doug Stevens. We met. Well, maybe not met, but I saw you in Theo's office." He nodded at his burden of plate and two wine-glasses. "Sorry, I'd offer to shake hands but they're kind of busy."

He handed her one of the glasses. "I saw you coming over here and I thought you might like a refill."

"Thank you, but I still have mine." She frowned. "How did you know my name?"

He shrugged. "I don't remember. Either Theo mentioned it or maybe I got it from Janice." At her puzzled look, he added, "Ms. Herrington, our receptionist?"

"Oh, yes." Jenny hid her amusement, amazed that Ms. Herrington actually knew the name of a lowly delivery person. Still, she probably processed the billing.

"Theo seems to have abandoned you," Doug said. "Good luck for me. How about dinner tomorrow night?"

Jenny bit her lip, a smile tugging at her mouth. "You don't know me."

"That's why I want to have dinner with you. I want to know you."

Should she say yes? He was a stranger—Theo hadn't talked about him—but her need to get to know the people at PRI drove her to recklessness. She opened her mouth to accept but before she could say the words, Theo appeared around the tall palm.

"Oh, there you are, Jenny." He scowled at Doug. "Jenny's having dinner with me tomorrow night," he said pointedly. "Get your own woman."

Doug stared at him for a moment, his smile as stiff as if he'd set it in cement. "Okay, Theo." He gathered up the two glasses and his plate and stood up. "Better circulate. Nice meeting you, Jenny."

"Thank you," she murmured gently, biting down on her temper.

As soon as the noisy crowd swallowed Doug she turned on Theo. "That was rude. You don't own me."

He muttered something that sounded like, "No, but I'd like to."

She gaped at him, sure that under the chatter of voices around them, she'd misunderstood. She knew she had when his expression hardened and he shrugged. "Of course, you're free to do what you want. Our dinner date is for tonight, not tomorrow. Would you like to go look for him?"

"No, but how about introducing me to some of the other people from your office?"

"Fine," he said shortly.

She abandoned the plate and glass, knowing it was easier to navigate with her hands unencumbered. To her surprise, she knew several of the people Theo introduced her to, including a couple of her former co-workers from Social Services. "There's someone there I need to talk to," Theo said. "Will you be all right for a moment?"

"Sure, go ahead." She found it interesting to catch up

on the latest news from the government agency, the frustrations that still existed in the system.

"You should come back," one of the women urged her. "You were so good at your job, and you can't be setting the world on fire with a courier service."

"Sorry, I'd rather be my own boss," Jenny said firmly, although she couldn't deny she sometimes missed the camaraderie of the office she'd worked in.

She moved back to the side of the room, taking a glass of orange juice from the drinks table and cradling it in her hands. She idly watched the people milling around. She paid little attention to the sifting conversations until she heard Theo's name. She couldn't see the speakers, a man and a woman, to judge by the voices. They stood on the other side of the potted tree next to her.

"Nice-looking lady Theo brought tonight," the man said.

"She's a new client," the woman said. Suddenly Jenny recognized the purring voice. Ms. Herrington—Janice, hadn't Theo called her? "Although I wonder about her solvency. She runs the courier service that PRI uses."

"Well, you know how Theo is. Always encouraging marginal businesses. Must be the Greek in him. There, virtually every business is a small one. Still, there must be more to it with this woman. Theo usually doesn't date clients."

Janice laughed. "Theo rarely dates at all. I've been trying for months. He doesn't seem to notice. But there was that awful business with his wife's death and the estate. I wonder if his new lady knows about that."

"Theo, being Theo—" To Jenny's disappointment, they moved farther away, and she couldn't hear what he would typically do.

All her senses went on full alert, however. Was there some scandal attached to his wife's death? She wondered if the complaint that had been made against him before he left Montreal had anything to do with that. Did she dare ask him?

That was the trouble with lying. Start with a little lie and soon you found yourself mired deeper and deeper in the quicksand of deception. She shoved the pervasive guilt away. She'd worry about it later.

The crowd had started to thin when she saw Doug Stevens again. He stood across the room. Amusement sifted through her. He hadn't wasted any time. He'd already latched onto another woman, a curvy blonde whose red leather skirt clung to her bottom like fresh paint. She had her arms around Doug's neck, whispering into his ear. He laughed and, catching Jenny's eye, winked conspiratorially.

He said something to the blonde and she turned. A frisson of unease ran up Jenny's spine as she recognized the woman.

Chapter Six

Pasting a smile on her face, Jenny hurried across the room. "Hi, Blossom. It's been a long time. How are you doing?"

Blossom threw her arms around Jenny in an exuberant hug. "Just great. I'm doing great, Jenny. I've got a job in the office of a trucking company."

Doug's gaze bounced from one to the other. "You two know each other?"

Blossom playfully tugged at Doug's ear. Jenny saw that her fingernails were painted the exact crimson shade of her skirt. "Jenny and I go way back. I was her first receptionist. I was good, too, wasn't I, Jenny?"

"You were. A lot better than the girl I got after you left to go back to school, the one I had to fire before I hired Cindi."

"Well, I made it. Told you I would."

Jenny grinned at her, her initial uneasiness evaporating. She couldn't think of a logical reason why Blossom's appearance bothered her except that it seemed too much of a coincidence that one of her former employees knew Theo's co-worker. What if all of this, her delivery of the money, her overhearing the conversation on the phone, the harassment of Theo were all part of an elaborate plan? She shook away the thought, telling herself it was too crazy. "I'm so glad you did make it, Blossom. How about calling me sometime? I'll buy you lunch."

Blossom laughed. "No, I'll buy. It's the least I can do after you gave me a chance. How about one day next week?"

"Sure. Call me at the office." Jenny scanned the room. "You haven't seen Theo, have you?"

Doug shook his head. "Not lately. But a while ago I saw him talking to Janice."

Janice who would like a date with Theo. Intrigued by the thought, Jenny wondered how he had responded.

At that moment Theo walked up to them. Alone. "Hello, Blossom. I didn't realize you were here with Doug."

"I wasn't. I had to work late so I came on my own. I just got here." She tucked her hand into the crook of Doug's elbow. "We're going out for dinner."

"Why don't you join us?" Doug said. "Two pretty women are always better than one."

Blossom poked him in the shoulder. "Doug, don't be greedy."

Doug winked at Jenny. "Why not, if I can get away with it?"

Holding her breath, Jenny waited for Theo to agree to join the other couple. She let it out in relief when he shook his head. Not that she would have been averse to spending time with Blossom, but Doug made her uncomfortable. He'd barely met her but he acted far too familiar. She hated predatory men. "Sorry, Doug," Theo said. "Maybe some other time. Jenny and I have business to discuss."

Doug's leering grin broadened. "Business, huh?"

Jenny's temper flashed but before she could say something that would deflate him, Theo glared at Doug. "Yes, business," he said so coldly she shivered.

Doug appeared oblivious, taking a long swallow from the glass he held. Judging by the slight tremor of his hand, it wasn't his first drink, or his second. Jenny found herself hoping that Blossom was planning to drive. "I wouldn't mind doing business with Jenny myself," Doug said. "How about it, Jenny? My connections are at least as good as Theo's. Maybe better. I've been here longer."

Blossom gripped Doug's arm, her mouth set firmly although her tone remained teasing. "Come on, Dougie, give me the keys. You promised I could drive."

"Let's go," Theo said. "Good to see you again, Blossom," he added as he led Jenny toward the door.

THEO TOOK HER to a restaurant in the country. The building was a converted farmhouse, the cuisine Italian. On the drive there she tried to sort the events of the evening into some kind of order. Blossom knew Doug, but the relationship was apparently casual. Blossom must have seen Doug trying to come on to Jenny but she had shown no particular reaction. Of course, Blossom wasn't inclined to settle for any one man. When and if she did, it wouldn't be a confirmed flirt like Doug.

She recalled the overheard conversation. What about Theo's leaving Montreal? Was there something he should have told her about that?

"You were surprised to see Doug's friend Blossom weren't you?" Theo said, breaking into her thoughts.

"What makes you say that?"

"The look on your face when she turned around."

Jenny smiled sheepishly. "My mother always told me never to try to bluff anyone. My face always gives me away. It drives me crazy."

"I think it's charming."

"Inconvenient," she declared.

"Only if you've something to hide."

But I have, she thought, the smile slipping. If you only knew. "I hadn't seen Blossom since she stopped working for me," she said, making conversation to keep herself from thinking about her deception. To top it off, she wasn't any closer to resolving it than before.

None of Theo's co-workers appeared to be anything but what they were—friendly and kind, and admittedly curious about her. A couple of them had told her how nice it was to see Theo at an office party. Apparently he rarely attended them. Jenny was credited with getting him out of his shell.

"How did you meet her?"

Jenny almost blurted out, "Meet who?" when she realized he was still talking about Blossom. "She came to me for help when I was with Social Services. She'd been a dancer at a club but she was on probation at the time. She would have gone to jail if she'd been older."

"How old was she? And what did she do?"

"She was barely sixteen then. She must be twenty-one or two now. She was blackmailing a number of men, alleging they'd had sex with her when she was under age."

"Had they?"

Jenny shrugged. "Probably, but it wasn't my job to judge her. I couldn't send her home because she had a worse life there than on the street. I had her declared an emancipated minor and got her back into high school. When I opened my business, she worked for me the first year, then went on to take a word processing course. She seems to be doing fine now."

"Looks that way," Theo said. "I've seen her a few times. The manager of the company where she works is a client of Doug's. She's been to the office a couple of times on business for him."

"I'm relieved she's doing well," Jenny said. "She used to phone me now and then, and keep me up-to-date but I hadn't heard from her in the past year." She bit her lip. Should she ask him? She started to speak but the words stuck behind her teeth. Clearing her throat, she tried again. "I got the impression you don't like Doug much."

He glanced at her sharply as he steered the car into the parking lot of the restaurant. "Funny, I got that impression from you, too." He wheeled into a vacant space and set the hand brake. "He's okay, just young, a little too brash."

"He doesn't look much younger than you."

"I'm thirty-four. He's thirty but it's more that he hasn't learned to moderate his impulses."

"And you have?" she asked, amused.

Theo made a sound of frustration. "A bad marriage will do that to a man. It teaches you to test the water first, before you jump in."

Against her will, disappointment stabbed her. Was that what their shared kisses had been, testing the water?

She got out of the car before he could walk around to her side, breathing in the astringent scent of sprouting leaves on the willows that grew around the parking lot. The murmur of a stream beyond them nearly drowned out the sound of traffic on the road. Jenny lifted her arms and inhaled deeply. Stars, usually invisible under city lights, twinkled in the sky. Lulled by the peaceful rural ambience, her feeling of unease melted away. "This is great. Just like being in the country."

"I thought you'd like it," Theo said. He took her arm and led her up the steps and onto the wide veranda where tables sat in secluded niches separated by trellises covered in bare branches. "Too bad it's too chilly to sit out here. Oh, well, we'll do it in summer."

So he saw a future for them, at least to the summer. The warmth that invaded Jenny's heart was quickly doused by guilt. By summer, if she managed to keep him alive, he would have forgotten her.

He'd obviously made a reservation because as soon as he gave his name the hostess led them to a booth next to the crackling fireplace. After they ordered, Jenny sat staring at the flames, trying to think of a way to bring the topic back to Doug Stevens.

Theo saved her by asking, "Why the interest in Stevens? I wouldn't have thought he'd be your type."

"Oh?" She raised her brows, her eyes sparkling. "What do you see as my type?"

"Someone less superficial." He grinned suddenly. "Someone like me, if you want to know."

She laughed, taking a sip from the water glass the waiter set before her. He showed Theo the bottle of wine he'd ordered, and opened it, pouring a little into a glass. Theo sampled it and nodded. The waiter filled the glasses and left the bottle on the table. "Try it," Theo said.

She drank, savoring the fruity flavor of the wine. It settled warmly in her stomach. "Is Doug good at his job?"

"Good enough, I guess," Theo said offhandedly. "He bought a BMW last year. He does tend to skate a little too close to the edge of ethics once in a while but there've been no major complaints. He's sharp at guessing the right stocks to invest in. He's into the party and night club scene but that's where he meets many of his clients. Why? Thinking of dumping me and letting him handle your money?"

"No, I wouldn't do that. I've got confidence in you."

In the dim light, she saw his eyes darken. The lowered lashes lent a brooding intensity to his expression as he fixed his gaze on his wineglass. "Maybe you shouldn't. You don't know that much about me, either."

"Why, have you had complaints?" There, she'd said it. She held her breath, dreading his reply, bracing herself for evasions.

Relief filled her as he shrugged. "Once. By one of my wife's lawyers, after her death. He accused me of giving her bad financial advice. It turned out he was robbing her blind."

"Would he hold a grudge against you?" she asked without thinking.

He looked at her sharply. "I doubt it. He'd made enough to retire, and no charges were ever laid against him. He's living in a cottage in the Laurentians and spends his days fishing. I think it gave him a great deal of satisfaction to know she didn't leave me anything."

"Your wife was wealthy, was she?"

"You might say that. Gossip had it I married her for her money. Maybe killed her for it, too. But by that time, there wasn't much left, so the gossip died down pretty quickly." He said it all in an expressionless voice but Jenny could see pain in his eyes. Then it vanished, to be replaced by hard cynicism. "Forget it. It was over a long time ago."

He smiled but his eyes remained remote and bleak, as if the memories festered inside him. "Let's talk about you. Tell me all about yourself."

"That would take about five minutes and put you right to sleep," Jenny said, her light tone belying the confusion and dread that churned within her.

THEO WALKED her to her door. It was close to midnight and the only sound in the building was distant music from one of the suites upstairs. "Can I make you coffee?" Jenny asked.

He hesitated. The attraction he felt for her pulled at him, but at the same time, he knew he needed a breathing space. "Thanks but I think I'll head home. Don't forget our dinner tomorrow night."

"Tomorrow night?" she echoed, a blush climbing up her cheeks. "I thought, uh, I mean…"

"You figured I only said it to get at Doug." Placing a finger beneath her chin, he tilted her face up so that their eyes met. "I never say things I don't mean. I want to have dinner with you." As he uttered the words, he knew he was sinking deeper into an involvement with her, instead of listening to the sober part of his mind that urged him to step back and assess where this was heading.

"Well, then let me cook it," she said. "Come about seven."

"Okay," he said before he could question the wisdom of indulging the implied intimacy of eating at her apartment.

Still, he settled for bestowing a chaste kiss on her forehead instead of pulling her against him and sating himself on that pink mouth.

Congratulating himself on his restraint, he drove toward his house, which suddenly seemed too large and too lonely. Watch it, he told himself, remember Lisa. You thought you were in love with her and that it would last forever. The so-called love didn't last a year.

Of course he'd been much younger then. All the more reason to be careful. The lesson was only valid if he used it to control future situations.

Tiger didn't appear when he parked the car in the garage. Not that it worried him. The cat did his prowling at night, although he usually didn't go far and came running when he heard the car. Theo hoped he was having a good time, not going to a lonely bed like his master.

He walked across the lawn, dew dampening his shoes, to the shrubbery at the edge of the woods. "Tiger, where are you?"

No answering meow. At the side of the house, he called again. The frogs in the pond suspended their serenade. New leaves rustled in the forest, a light wind combing the trees. The cat didn't come.

Giving up, Theo headed back to the house. The security light flicked off as he approached the front door, plunging him into darkness. He fumbled with his key, swearing when it fell from his hand. An unfamiliar, musky odor hung in the still air. He sniffed, trying to find the source.

Perhaps disturbed soil in the flower bed, some animal digging the loose dirt.

He groped along the brick step for the keys. Instead of cool metal, his hand encountered soft fur and a sticky substance. His blood ran cold, his breath suspended painfully between chest and throat.

The cat? Savaged by a coyote? He'd seen them but, bold though they were, they'd never come this close to the house.

Without taking his eyes off the dark shape that lay on the step, he moved back and waved one arm. In response to the motion, the light came on, flooding the front of the house.

A rhododendron bush cast the step in shadow but when he moved back to the door, he saw his keys glinting in the light. He grabbed them, stepped carefully around the furry body and unlocked the door. He flipped the switch inside, grimacing as he felt his fingers slip on the smooth plastic.

Light spilled out and illuminated the furry creature that lay on the ground. Dark blood still trickled from beneath the body, slowly seeping into the paler red bricks. The breath Theo had been unaware of holding gusted out. Not Tiger. The fur was too dark, too long. The striped, bushy tail didn't belong to a cat, and neither did the black mask around the glazed eyes.

A raccoon, considered a pest around here because they upset garbage cans and sometimes killed pets. Cats like Tiger. No, Tiger wouldn't let a raccoon overpower him, Theo thought, staring at the spread-eagled, bloody corpse in horror. Tiger was big enough and fierce enough to put up a fight, perhaps even kill a raccoon the size of this one. The unfortunate creature looked to be young, perhaps half grown.

Where was the cat?

Theo ran into the house, slamming the door after him.

He turned on lights as he went, finally reaching the kitchen. The door leading outside was closed and locked, undisturbed as far as he could tell. He opened it and scanned the back patio. Nothing.

Relief rushed through him. He always left an old lawn chair out there, sheltered by the roof overhang. Padded with a blanket, it was Tiger's favorite place to sleep outdoors. Tiger also used it as a recuperation spot whenever he got into a fight with neighborhood cats or dogs. Lately, though, he'd been good; he hadn't come home wounded in months. Nor had he brought Theo little gifts of dead birds or disemboweled shrews for some time.

He wasn't on the chair. The blanket was folded neatly, as Theo had left it that morning.

Which must mean he wasn't responsible for the dead raccoon.

Unease crawled up Theo's spine. Who had left the grisly corpse like a gift on his doorstep? A dog, maybe. Not likely another cat; cats only offered to share their kills with those they loved, and they were extremely territorial.

A human, then. His stomach clenched at the thought of someone sick enough to kill a defenceless raccoon, much less leave it on a doorstep.

He relocked the back door and moved to the sink. He closed his eyes briefly as he saw the blood on his fingers. Squirting liquid soap into his palms, he held them under running water as hot as he could stand, scrubbing his knuckles and nails until the skin was red and tender. For good measure, he soaped his hands again, and rubbed them together. Shades of Lady Macbeth? The wry thought crept into his mind, shutting out some of the horror.

He sobered immediately. If a demented human had left the raccoon, maybe he'd tried to break into the house as well. Theo dried his hands and took a marble rolling pin out of the kitchen drawer as a makeshift weapon. Walking through the house, he checked in closets and behind doors, telling himself he was probably a paranoid fool. But, he figured, better a live fool than a dead hero.

The house appeared undisturbed. No sign of an intruder.

He began to breathe easier, chiding his overactive imagination. Back in his bedroom, he changed into jeans and a sweatshirt, laying his suit on a chair to take to a dry cleaner in the morning. He stopped in the kitchen to pick up a flashlight and yesterday's newspaper. Under the sink, he found a pair of rubber gloves he'd last used to repot a plant. Pulling them on, he went to the front door.

The raccoon lay there, exposed under the porch light. The puddle of blood no longer glistened but had faded to a dull rust stain on the bricks. He crouched down and played the flashlight beam over the body. The skin gaped open from its throat to its abdomen. He frowned, pulling gingerly at the edge of the incision. He shuddered, stomach flip-flopping, threatening to back up. Swallowing hard, he settled back on his heels, turning off the flashlight.

He didn't need to see any more. This was no animal kill.

The cut was clean, not ragged as the tearing of fangs would have left it. A knife had done this. Which meant...

He turned on the flashlight again and shone its light behind the bushes next to the door, then farther out, into the flower beds. The soil lay flat, undisturbed, under its blanket of mulch. Daffodils nodded their yellow bells, and here and there little shoots of green that would become tulips nosed out of the ground.

He found no sign of a knife.

He sat on the shallow step for a moment, debating whether he should call the police. Would they bother to come, just on his saying he thought the raccoon had been deliberately killed? Maybe they would, if it was a slow night. But on a Friday night, especially at this hour—he saw it was nearly one—they would probably tell him to wait until morning.

He snapped his fingers. Morning. He'd call them and make a report if they considered it important enough to open a file.

Carefully, he rolled the raccoon into a layer of newspaper and carried it into the garage. There he pushed the bundle into a clean garbage bag, tied the top securely and put it into his half-empty freezer. At least if they wanted to examine the corpse, it would be preserved.

Back outside, he ran the hose to rinse the bricks, spraying the water until no trace of blood remained except for a darker stain on the more porous grout. It looked as if he was doomed to live with the reminder of the kill.

Sick and dispirited, he went back into the house, double-checking to see that the door was locked. He put away the flashlight and washed his hands again, drinking a glass of water when he was done.

The phone rang, slicing through the silence and making him jump. Before he could stop himself, and let the machine take it since it was probably a drunk with the wrong number, he snatched down the kitchen extension.

"Yes?"

Crackling noises filled his ear. Then a metallic voice, devoid of expression, spoke. "Did you like my gift?"

Stunned, Theo couldn't say a word. His lack of response didn't seem to bother the caller who waited in equal silence. The static in the phone had faded to a low hum. Some sort of electronic equipment, he thought with the single rational part of his mind.

"Cat got your tongue?" The caller laughed ominously. "By the way, where is your cat?"

Theo felt the blood drain from his head into his midsection. He gripped the counter to keep himself from collapsing under the sudden wave of nausea. "What have you done to him?" His voice cracked. "If you've hurt my cat, I'll—"

"What will you do, Theo Zacharias? You'll have to find me first." The voice rose, becoming an eerie singsong. "Can't catch me, can't catch me."

The caller broke into cackling laughter, which had an oddly mechanical ring to it. "You'd better watch out for the other little cat, too. This is only the beginning."

The phone clicked loudly. A moment later the dial tone told him he'd been disconnected.

He smashed it down on the wall hook. The other little cat? What other little cat?

The implication of the term slammed into him. Did the caller mean Jenny?

He grabbed the phone and punched out her number, which he hadn't been conscious of memorizing. After four rings, she answered. "This better be good, if you're calling me this late."

The husky sleepiness of her voice did things to his libido that he'd almost forgotten. Sexy didn't begin to describe how she sounded. He'd had only a glimpse of her bedroom but memory of the double bed covered with a yellow-and-white afghan leaped into his mind. She would be lying there, propped up on her pillows, dark hair flowing over flowered cotton. He'd only seen the afghan but she probably used flowered bed linen to go with the floral scent, which so tantalized him.

Did she wear a T-shirt to bed? A silk nightgown? Or did she sleep naked?

"Hello? Say something, damn you." Her voice didn't sound languorous as she snapped out the words.

"It's me, Jenny. Are you all right?"

"Why wouldn't I be?" she asked, sounding wide awake and puzzled.

He suddenly felt foolish, wondering if paranoia over the dead raccoon had made him jump to the wrong conclusion. Still, he had to make sure. "Your doors are locked, aren't they?"

"One door, and the balcony. Yes, Theo, they're locked. I'm not stupid."

"Nobody said you were." His knees felt rubbery as the adrenaline high receded. He raked his fingers through his hair and let himself slide down the wall until he sat on the floor.

His involuntary sigh must have penetrated the phone lines. "Theo, are you all right?" Jenny asked, concern in her voice.

"I don't know," he said honestly.

Her chuckle caressed his ear, soothing him, making the whole traumatic night fade as if it were a half-forgotten nightmare. "That sounds reassuring."

He closed his eyes, wishing he could drown in the sound of her voice. Wishing she were here, holding him tightly. "I had this phone call," he said at last. "A crank call."

She was silent for so long that he wondered if she'd fallen asleep. When she finally spoke, her voice sounded strained. "What did he say?"

"He, she, or it. I couldn't tell. It seems someone left a dead raccoon on my doorstep and then called to brag about it. He or she threatened my cat."

"Is your cat missing?"

"He's not here but then he's often out at night. The caller also said something I thought referred to you but I could have been mistaken."

Again, silence. Then she said, "Did you try to get the number by using call return?"

Call return? "Damn! No, I didn't think of it, and it won't work now that I've called you."

"No, it won't. Are you going to phone the police?"

"What will they do? It wasn't an overt threat. I was going to report the dead raccoon in the morning."

"You're sure an animal didn't kill it?"

"Positive. Well, maybe it was an animal, but it was the two-legged kind and he used a knife."

"Are *your* doors locked?"

He laughed humorlessly. "Yes, all of them. I checked twice."

Silence stretched between them. The fridge clicked on, a gentle, homey growl. In the living room, a clock chimed once for the half hour. Peaceful, ordinary sounds. Sitting there, he could almost let himself believe that this was a regular occurrence, two friends catching up on the day's news before going to bed.

He heard claws scratching on the door next to him, the door he'd locked only moments ago. "Hang on, Jenny. I think the cat's here."

"Or someone else," she said at once. "Theo, don't open the door."

"I have to go see. I can reach it from here."

"Theo—"

"Don't worry, Jenny." He leaned over, reaching up to disengage the dead bolt. Turning the knob, he opened the door an inch.

He found himself face-to-face with a triangular nose framed by long white whiskers. Green eyes glittered like pale emeralds. He pulled the door wider. Tiger stalked in, ears flat, hair standing out in a ruff around his neck. His tail was as big as a bottle brush, hanging low.

He walked past Theo, growling softly in his throat.

"Theo." Jenny's peremptory voice came over the phone.

"I'm here," he said. "The cat just came in. He looks as if something spooked him."

"Is he hurt?"

Tiger had completed his circuit of the room, sniffing at all the corners and finally sitting down in the middle of the floor. He lifted a paw, licked it and began to groom his fur. Theo extended his hand, rubbing his fingers together.

Tiger pricked up his good ear but he eyed Theo suspiciously for a long moment. He rose, his tail lifting, a signal that he was no longer in the hunter-defense mode. He came and sat by Theo, licking Theo's hand before resuming his own washing.

Theo probed the cat's fur with gentle fingers. Tiger began to purr, rolling over to have his belly rubbed. "No, he seems okay," he said into the phone. "Look, Jenny, I'm sorry I bothered you. Good night."

"No bother." She paused, then said softly, "Good night, Theo. Be careful."

"I will," he said but the line had gone dead.

He opened a can of tuna for Tiger, who looked at him wide-eyed as if he couldn't believe his luck, before gulping it down. Best to leave him inside for the night, if there was an animal-killing stalker out there somewhere. Tiger might not like it but at least he'd be alive in the morning.

In the bathroom, Theo stripped off his clothes and stepped under the shower. Bracing his arms against the tiled wall, he let the hot water pummel him. Slowly the tension seeped out of his muscles. When the water began to cool, he soaped himself vigorously, rinsed off, closed the tap and grabbed a towel. He rubbed his skin dry, brushed his teeth and walked naked to the adjoining bedroom.

His nostrils flared as he noticed a faint, coppery odor. Tiger sat beside the bed, his tail again bristling. Now what was the matter with the cat? "You're sure spooky tonight, aren't you?"

Tiger looked at him, the green eyes inscrutable. "If only you could talk," Theo added.

He took hold of the quilt to turn it down. Before he could move it, Tiger jumped onto the bed, growling.

Theo's patience began to fray. "Come on, cat, it's a little late for games."

He picked him up and set him on the floor. With a flick of his wrist, he turned down the bed.

Bitter bile flooded up into his throat. Right in the center of the white sheet lay a bloodstained knife.

Chapter Seven

Theo sat at the kitchen table, his hands wrapped around a coffee mug in a desperate attempt to warm them. At intervals, shudders he couldn't control racked his body.

The policeman—what was his name? Baldwin, he thought—tossed him his sweatshirt. "Here, you're in shock. Put this on. You'll feel better."

Theo shoved his head and arms through neck and sleeves, pulling the soft fleece down over the waist of the jeans he'd yanked on before calling 911. He nodded gratefully as Baldwin, a thirtyish man whose matter-of-fact attitude instilled confidence, topped up his coffee mug.

Baldwin filled another mug from the pot. "We know how your intruder got into the house."

Theo looked up, alarm cutting through his exhaustion. "How? I checked the whole house."

"What about the basement?"

"There, too."

"Did you check the windows closely?"

"Not that closely," Theo admitted. "They're pretty small and they looked closed and locked." He returned to his listless contemplation of his coffee.

"One of the windows at the back had the glass removed, and then carefully propped back in place. It looked undisturbed until we touched it. The glass is still there. You can have it reinstalled. In the meantime, one of my men nailed a board across the opening to hold it for tonight."

Baldwin scratched his head. "It takes a little time to pry away the rubber seal from the window. On the other hand, your burglar could have done it before tonight and taped it closed again so you wouldn't notice."

"Things only started happening to me since Tuesday."

"Oh? Can you tell me about it?" Baldwin took a notebook from his pocket and turned to a clean page.

"I got back from Japan, banged up my car when I found a snake inside it, and then a bicycle courier nearly pushed me in front of a bus. You can get the complete report from the Vancouver police."

"I will," Baldwin said. "You wouldn't happen to know the file number."

"Not offhand. I can look up the card in my briefcase, if you want."

"Never mind. I'll call you tomorrow." Baldwin frowned. "Since Tuesday. Hmm."

I met Jenny that day, Theo thought, her image as vague as mist. He couldn't think, and he didn't dare let himself feel. The body's defense against overload.

"You know," Baldwin said, chewing on the end of his pen, "the intruder could have prepared the window while you were away."

Theo shook himself out of his lethargy, summoning up outrage. "But why?"

"Good question, Mr. Zacharias. One I was hoping you could answer." He broke off as one of the other policemen spoke to him. Turning back to Theo, Baldwin asked, "Mind if we have a look at the dead raccoon?"

"No. Hell, take it away. It'll save me burying it."

"It's in the freezer in the garage, did you say?" At Theo's nod, Baldwin set his mug on the table, and walked into the hall. Theo could hear his low voice as he gave instructions to the other man.

Baldwin came back and sat down on the opposite side of the table. He took a sip of his coffee and opened the notebook again. "Okay, tell me everything that's happened tonight."

"I came home and found a dead raccoon." Theo heard his voice relating the events of the evening but his mind and emotions remained detached, as if the horror had happened to someone else. At one point, Tiger nudged his leg and he picked him up, sinking his fingers into the lush fur. Tiger, serene now that he'd unearthed and routed all enemies, purred rhythmically.

"Does anyone have reason to hate you, Mr. Zacharias?" Baldwin asked when Theo fell silent.

Theo gave a rusty laugh, remembering that Jenny had asked the same question several days ago. "I would have said no, but it appears there's at least one person around who must dislike me."

"Any idea who it might be?"

"None." Theo shook his head.

Baldwin closed the notebook and tucked it into his jacket pocket. "That's that, then," he said. "I'll call you tomorrow about the file number. It'll likely be Monday before I can tell you anything about the raccoon and whether there are fingerprints on the knife."

Theo set the cat on the floor and got up, grimacing at the stiffness in his joints. Baldwin nodded sympathetically. "Shock will do that. You feel like you've aged in one hour."

He put out his hand and shook Theo's. "I'd suggest that you have an alarm system installed. They're not foolproof, especially out here. On second thought, just get stickers for your windows that say the house has an alarm. Works as well as anything to deter most burglars." He smiled thinly. "Or move to a less isolated house."

Theo's mouth twisted wryly. "I'll look into it. Thanks."

Locking the door after the police cruisers pulled out of the driveway, he leaned back against the cool painted metal and closed his eyes. Around him, the house made the usual creaking sounds as it settled but for the first time they seemed menacing rather than friendly. Was that faint series of thumps footsteps coming up the basement stairs?

Heart racing, he ran to the basement door and threw it open, raking his fingers over the light switch in the same motion. The steps yawned below him. No one was there.

He choked on a laugh, and shook his head, punchy with the need for sleep. Closing the basement door, he turned to let out the cat who was meowing at the back door. "Don't talk to strangers," Theo warned him.

Tiger flicked his tail and Theo watched him saunter off. The forest behind the house looked hazy and mysterious in the gray light of dawn. A light mist pearled the grass. The cat's paws left dark blots in the dew as he paced across the lawn. A robin sang ecstatically, half hidden among the tender, newly fledged leaves of the lilac bush.

Normal. Theo dragged in a deep breath and made himself push the horror to the back of his mind, pretending it had been a nightmare that would fade in the daylight.

Reality struck him in the face when he entered his bedroom. They'd taken the knife, photographed the entire scene, but the sheets, stained with rusty dried blood, still lay on the bed. He bundled them up, along with the quilt and the mattress pad, and carried them out to the garage. He stuffed them into a garbage bag and tied it.

Then he went back inside and spent the rest of the night in his guest room.

He didn't expect to sleep but he must have, because he dreamed. In an odd, surreal way he knew he was dreaming but at the same time he was powerless to control the images that played across his overtired mind.

He saw Lisa, his dead wife, laughing at him as she prepared to go out for the evening. "Come with me, Theo. Don't be so stuffy. You can do those reports some other time."

"They have to be done by tomorrow," he said, knowing she was only asking for appearance sake. She didn't want him; she was much happier by herself. She'd go to some club and meet her friends, perhaps go off to someone's apartment later. Or to a hotel. She'd come home at dawn, smelling of stale perfume and cigarette smoke, her makeup and hair askew, her eyes as innocent as a child's no matter what debauchery she'd engaged in that night.

He would eye her dispassionately as he went out for his morning run, too inured to her infidelities to care anymore.

The dream shifted. Lisa was driving her car, and somehow he knew it was the night she had died. In his dream he was with her. He warned her to slow down. He tried to take the wheel, to steer to the side of the road, but she only threw back her head and laughed. Her foot punched down on the gas pedal and the car leaped forward, engine howling at redline.

Rain darkened the streets, and lightning fractured the night sky. "Are you crazy?" Theo yelled. "You'll kill us both."

She lifted a bottle to her lips. Vodka. She said she liked it because it went down so smoothly before burning in the stomach. She liked both the smoothness and the burning. Theo, in a split second of coherent thought, wondered why she felt the need to constantly punish herself.

She hurled the bottle out of the open window of the car. He heard it smash on the wet asphalt. "Would you care, Theo, if I died?" she asked, her voice almost sober.

"Look out," he shouted. The car careened into the curve, lost traction and skidded wildly. Lisa laughed, expertly easing up on the gas pedal and controlling the spin. The car righted itself, hurtling on through the night.

Another curve appeared ahead, the twin headlight beams glistening on a large puddle. Lisa whipped the heavy vehicle to the left to avoid it. The right wheels caught the water. As if in slow motion, Theo felt the car spin around and head for the embankment next to the road. For an instant, it was airborne, then it slowly tumbled over and splashed into the river, on its roof.

Water poured through the open windows. Theo groped for the seat belt buckle, unlatching it. Bunching his muscles, he flung himself upright, and reached for Lisa's seat belt. Too late he remembered she hadn't fastened it. He searched in the wet darkness, hands flailing. Under the water, he found her soft hair. Tangling his fingers in it, he dragged her above the surface.

The car had almost filled with water. They had to get out of there before it sank. He heard voices shouting, a bright light probing the darkness. The beam did not reach into the car. No help there.

Lisa lay against him, half afloat. He called her name but she was either unconscious or— His mind refused to form the thought.

Her satin dress was soaked, slippery. He couldn't get a grip on it. He pulled her head toward him, dragging her by her hair.

His fingers felt sticky and a thick coppery scent filled his nostrils. He shook his head, fighting the sickness in his stomach. He probed gently. Hot blood seeped over his hand, sluggishly melting into the water.

The light finally found the inside of the car. Theo looked down. Two glazed eyes, surrounded by a black mask in a furry face, stared at him. Sharp, pointed teeth sank into his hand. He screamed.

And bolted upright in bed.

He hauled the sheet around him, goose bumps rising

on his sweat-drenched body. What a nightmare; he couldn't even begin to analyze the psychological significance of it.

He'd never dreamed about Lisa's death in the five years since it happened.

He'd been at home when she had her accident, waking out of a sound sleep when the police had knocked on his door with the news. At their request, he was present when they winched the car out of the river at daybreak. He hadn't even flinched when they'd used the jaws of life to remove her body from the car, not even when he'd seen her temple crushed, blood matting her hair, from the impact with the window frame.

Only after the ambulance left, ominously silent since there was no hurry to get to the morgue, did reaction set in. He'd watched the tow truck haul away the car, with the seat belt dragging on the road through the damaged door. And he'd been dismayed to realize tears were running down his face.

For her life or her violent death—he just didn't know. But in that moment, he'd vowed never to love again. Never again would he expose himself to this laceration of his soul. And later events, the damage to his reputation, the allegations that he might have somehow caused Lisa's death, the sordid mess about the estate, had cemented that vow deep in his heart and mind.

The shivers subsided. He heard the furnace come on. Getting up, he walked over to the window, standing naked above the heat register, letting the warmth seep into his body.

The sunshine of the past few days had gone. Leaden clouds crawled across the sky, pregnant with rain. Perfect for the mood he was in.

The morning Lisa had been pulled from the car it had also been spitting rain, carried on the biting wind that pushed a storm over the city.

He banished the memory. Only the guilt remained. Although why he should feel guilt he didn't know. But he blamed himself because he hadn't perceived the depth of her despair, hadn't understood her self-hatred.

He still didn't.

Poor Lisa, hunting desperately for an elusive happiness she'd never found. Well, maybe a merciful God had given her peace after her death.

The image of Jenny's dark blue eyes swam into his consciousness. Eyes which were troubled. And troubling. With one look, she'd cut through the icy shell encasing his soul.

Jenny and Lisa couldn't be more different. Lisa, constantly laughing and rushing around to fill her emptiness, oblivious to the feelings of those around her.

Jenny, sure of herself, but caring too much. He suspected her life also wasn't particularly happy, but she didn't bother to fake anything she didn't feel. She carried on, bucking the odds against her, no matter what the obstacles. She just pushed them aside or climbed over them. Theo had no doubt that despite her money problems, she would eventually win.

He still didn't know why she'd come to him. But he'd decided she would tell him in her own time. While he didn't exactly trust her, he no longer distrusted her.

Last night, he should have accepted her invitation. Who knew where it might have gone, after the coffee? But he'd seen the uncertainty in her eyes. Despite her often brash, outgoing demeanor, like him she'd learned to keep her emotions in check. She just didn't let anyone see that control.

He did. With him, she slipped, let her worry show.

Did he see it because he was the object of her worry? He couldn't figure it out.

He would see her tonight. The thought of spending the evening with her sent a rush of pleasure through him. For the first time he questioned the vow he'd made on the stormy morning beside the river. He'd never anticipated meeting Jenny. Why should she have to pay for his heartache, his hurt pride, and what might have been temporary insanity?

Tonight they would talk. Maybe she would finally decide she trusted him enough to tell him what had brought her into his life.

After that…anything could happen. Heat curled inside him, pooling in his abdomen. Anticipation driving out the dark memories, he strode to the kitchen to let the cat in.

"DO YOU WANT ME to get rid of her?"

"No, not yet. Just scare her enough that it brings them closer together."

"Okay, but it seems to me they're pretty tight now. He's going to take her to dinner. Second night in a row. You know, I've been thinking. I'm not convinced she knows that the envelope she delivered is connected to what's happening to Zacharias."

"Oh, come on. Don't be a fool. She came in and picked up the phone. I heard the click on the line. She heard enough to make her suspicious. Good thing the call was masked and I got away before she caught me."

"She doesn't suspect you?"

"How could she? There's no reason to. Just take care of it, will you? Something that gets them together and makes him protective. Can you get into her place?"

"I'll find a way. And I don't think you need to worry about them being close. I saw the way he looked on Friday night. He's totally besotted. I never would have expected it. Theo Zacharias and a bike courier."

"Good. Then he'll feel responsible and suffer when she dies. But not yet. I'll be in touch when it's time."

"YOU'RE EARLY," Jenny said when she opened the door. "I haven't started to cook."

Theo handed her the flowers he'd brought, tiny purple violets. Simple flowers but their intense fragrance reminded him of her. The way he felt when he was near her, excited, almost giddy, uncertain.

Jenny buried her nose in the violets, inhaling the perfume as her eyes sparkled with pleasure. She smiled, a secretive, womanly smile, which stabbed straight at his heart.

Last night he'd been more objective, but tonight he felt as uncertain as a teenager, and as excited, in an uncomfortable state of semiarousal. That sort of thing hadn't happened in years. Sure, he enjoyed sex but he'd learned to control his appetite, had become extremely discriminating in choosing the women he dated, or took to bed. It had been a long time since he'd indulged, now that he thought of it. A very long time.

He frowned. Maybe that was all it was, chemistry, her proximity combined with months of celibacy on his part. Yes, that must be why she turned him on so easily. A simple explanation.

But when he met her eyes, saw the flush that heated her skin, he knew it wasn't simple at all. In fact, to call it simple diminished and belittled his awakening emotions.

He'd fallen for her, crashing without a parachute.

WAS SHE READY FOR THIS?" Jenny asked herself as she filled a brandy snifter with water and arranged the violets in it. If he'd brought her a dozen roses, she would have been flattered but not touched. The violets, humble little flowers from his own garden, costing nothing when he could afford the best, moved her as nothing else would have. He'd put thought into it. It wasn't a casual gesture; she wasn't a casual date. He'd seen deep inside her, where few people had ventured or been admitted.

The knowledge that after less than a week he understood her better than anyone on earth scared her spitless.

"Remember the snow we had the second week of March?" Theo said. "Well, the violets were blooming then, sticking out above the snow as if defying it to crush them." His voice dropped to a whisper. "I didn't know you then but now that I do, I realized you're a lot like these flowers, fragile but resilient."

For a moment emotion thickened her throat and she couldn't speak. The accumulation of lies made a knot in her chest. She swallowed, forcing a light laugh. "I never guessed you for a poet, Theo."

His eyes widened momentarily, then he smiled. "Even us number crunchers have our moments."

Jenny gestured toward the kitchen, such as it was. "Come and sit down. I'll pour you some wine and get the dinner cooked." She pushed aside the plastic bags printed with a red supermarket logo. "Actually I just got home. I got stuck at the store in an endless lineup."

She found the paper bag that held the wine and rummaged in a drawer for the seldom used corkscrew. "Maybe I should chill it a little?"

Theo's hand came around and covered hers, prying her fingers loose from their grip on the corkscrew. "Jenny, don't be so nervous. I'm not going to jump on you."

She couldn't believe the heat that surged through her at the image her treacherous mind displayed. She could only pray that it didn't show in her face. Handing him the bottle and the opener, she clutched the edge of the counter so he wouldn't see her hands shaking.

"Not that I haven't thought about it, mind you," he added conversationally as he twisted the metal point into the cork.

Her fingers tightened, cramping. "But you left last

night." She clapped both hands over her mouth, trying to stuff the words back inside. "Oh, no, why did I say that?" she wailed.

Theo stared at her, a slow smile spreading over his face. "Probably because you were thinking the same thing I was, but also knowing it's better to wait. Because you're honest."

But I'm not, she almost blurted out. She moved to the table and busied herself emptying the grocery bags and putting the food away. "Can I do anything?" Theo asked.

Covering her unease, she thrust a cello-wrapped head of butter lettuce into his hands. "You can wash this. The salad spinner is in the cupboard under the sink."

She heard the click of his wineglass on the counter as he set it down, then the water running. She folded the bags and stuffed them into the blue recycling box. Taking a pot from the cupboard, she measured rice into it. "Could you please fill this with water?" She handed him a large measuring cup.

"Full?" he asked.

"Yes, please."

She took the water from him, and poured it into the rice, adding salt and herbs. She set it on the stove and turned on the gas under the pot. The flame ignited with a loud pop. Jenny jumped back, shaking her singed fingers.

"Does it always do that?" Theo asked.

She laughed a little shakily. "Sometimes. It's an old stove, inclined to be temperamental."

He frowned. "Maybe you should have someone look at it. The gas company won't charge you for an inspection and they'll adjust the orifice if necessary."

"I'll tell the landlord. He'll take care of it. It's his stove, after all."

Theo nodded, smiling faintly. "Yeah, I guess it would be. It's been so long since I've rented that I'd forgotten what it's like."

"I could have moved into my mother's house when she died," Jenny said. "But I sold it to get the money to start my business."

"I hope you kept enough for emergencies."

Always the financial planner, she thought, amused. "I did, but I can't touch it until I retire. But at least then I won't be living on the street."

Theo's smile broadened. "Do you really think there's any danger of that?"

"Maybe," she said, deadpan. "Are you aware what a high percentage of single, elderly women live in poverty?"

"Yes, but I doubt if you'd be one of them. You'd figure out something." He took the bowl she gave him and began to tear the washed and dried lettuce into pieces. She couldn't take her eyes off his hands, dark tanned fingers lightly sprinkled with soft black hair, working with a competence that showed he was used to preparing food for himself. She remembered how his fingers had felt sliding warmly over her face last night just before he'd walked away, and shivered.

Get a grip, she told herself. Quit mooning over a man you can't have.

The sizzle of water hitting a hot stove spun her around. "The rice!" She turned down the burner and the foaming water subsided at once. Only a couple of drips had escaped the pot. She grabbed a paper towel, leaning past Theo and briefly inhaling the tangy, citrus scent of him. "You smell like a lemon tree," she muttered.

"What?"

"Oh, nothing." Heat blazed in her cheeks. She bent over the stove and mopped up the spill, nearly setting the towel on fire. If she kept on like this, she was going to burn the place down.

She unwrapped the lamb chops and rinsed them in the sink, patting them dry with paper towels. They would only take a few minutes to broil. She could wait until the rice was nearly done.

"Did you speak to the police about the dead raccoon?"

"Yeah, last night." He paused, taking great care to align the knives and forks precisely next to the plates on the table.

"Last night?" Jenny felt the blood drain from her face. It had been another attack on him. She hoped it was only some kid playing a gruesome prank. If this accelerated, she would have to tell him. And deal with the consequences.

"I called them when I found the knife that had been used to kill it," Theo said.

Jenny pressed her hand against her stomach. The sight of the raw lamb chops sent a sickening nausea through her. She kept her back to Theo to hide her reaction. He would know at once it was out of proportion to simply hearing the story. "Where was the knife?" she asked, her voice hoarse and barely audible.

"In my bed," he said bluntly. "Look, Jenny, if it bothers you, we won't talk about it."

She hadn't fooled him, she realized. Turning, she raised her stricken eyes to his. "I want to know. And what was that threatening phone call you mentioned? Could you tell who was calling?"

"No. They used some kind of masking device."

Just like the call she'd overheard, and the one she'd received. "And you found the knife afterward," she said, concealing her agitation with difficulty.

She felt the warmth of Theo's body against her back. Reaching around her, he took the shredded paper towel from her hand. "Don't you think you've dried the meat enough?"

"I guess so." She spurred herself into action. "I'd better light the broiler."

"Doesn't it have a pilot light?" Theo crouched down beside her as she opened the oven.

"Not this stove, not in the oven. It's too old."

The pungent smell of gas curled out into the room. Jenny wrinkled her nose. Was it stronger than usual? When she turned on the oven she'd noticed a smell before but this seemed more pronounced.

She reached for the knob on the front of the stove, twisting it as she flicked the lighter on.

"Jenny, no!"

She turned her head at his sharp explanation. Before she had time to think, the weight of Theo's body flung her to the side.

A deafening roar filled her head as the oven exploded.

Chapter Eight

The oven door clanged to the floor, five feet from the stove. Theo's body lay over her, heavy and warm. Was he okay? She gulped to restart her breathing, reassured by the up and down motion of his chest against her back. Alive, yes, but conscious?

His breath feathered her ear. "Are you all right?"

Still shaking, she laughed. "I thought that would be my line. You're on top of me."

He heaved himself to one side. "Oh, sorry. I must be crushing you."

"Did you hear me complaining?" Fresh laughter bubbled up into her throat. She swallowed it. If she dared let it loose, she'd dissolve in hysterics. "What happened?" She flipped over and pushed herself up by holding the counter. Her ears rang and she shook her head to clear them. "As if I didn't know. The oven exploded."

She leaned forward and peered into the dark cavity. A yellow flame licked with deceptive sloth toward the paper towel, which the explosion had dropped from the stovetop onto the floor.

Jumping to her feet, Jenny grabbed the small extinguisher she kept above the stove and pulled the lever to activate it. White foam shot out, burying the infant fire.

She let the device drop with a clang. In the distance, sirens wailed, becoming closer.

Theo reached past her and turned off the gas knob, as well as the one operating the burner under the rice. Hands on hips, Jenny surveyed the disaster area. The rice pot lay upside down on the floor, rice grains scattered everywhere. Less of a mess, she thought dispassionately, than if the mixture had been more liquid. Soot blackened the walls and cabinets, and a pall of smoke hung in the air.

The sirens grew louder, then died. Bloodred light washed into the room through the window.

"Oh, no, somebody called the fire department. There's nothing left for them to do."

"They'll make a report for the insurance," Theo said as a loud pounding threatened to break down the door. He strode across the apartment to let in two firemen armed with axes and big red extinguishers. In the hall outside, several people craned their necks to peer into the open door. The explosion must have reverberated through the whole building.

"Anybody hurt here?" The fireman's voice boomed over the buzzing in Jenny's ears.

She looked across at Theo. Black soot streaked his blue sweater and faded jeans. Damn it, if she were paying his laundry bills, for which she'd lately been responsible, she'd soon be broker than she already was.

Not that her own clothes were in better condition. Her shirt was also peppered with bits of carbon, and she had a brown-edged hole in one sleeve. She picked at the edge of it, finding the skin underneath red but not particularly painful. Lucky, again.

Lucky? It hit her that they could have been killed. She pressed her hand against her chest, trying to slow her suddenly racing heart. She must have made a sound because Theo stepped up to her, his eyes dark with concern. She sighed as she rested her head against his chest, welcoming the strength of his arms around her.

The burly fireman pulled the stove away from the wall and shut off the gas connection. "Get your landlord to call the gas company to inspect the lines. The stove is probably a write-off and I wouldn't advise using it again in any case."

"What could have caused the explosion?" Theo asked. "We smelled gas but it wasn't that strong."

"Doesn't take much in a confined area," the fireman said. "You must have had a leak in the line where it feeds the burner. It's not uncommon in these old stoves. But lucky it happened now. If it had built up in the closed oven for several days, you would have blown up this whole apartment."

The fireman left. Without letting go of Jenny, Theo closed the door. He led her into the living room and sank onto the sofa, his arms around her. His hands, as he smoothed back her hair, shook. Jenny looked up, noticing how pale he looked, almost as green as Tracy had been the day she went home with flu.

She laughed shakily. "Here I was beginning to think you were the original Mr. Cool."

"Oh, yeah?" He managed a wobbly grin. "You should have seen me last night. I nearly threw up all over the bloody bed."

They sat holding each other, drawing reassurance from the simple act of touching. Jenny was aware of the sexual tension simmering beneath the comfort but it was safely banked. Theo's hands stroked up and down her back and she breathed in the scent of him, citrus cologne and the sweat of fear, a combination more heady than the finest perfume.

Heat coiled in her midsection. He must have sensed the moment the embrace changed to something more potent, the moment passion reasserted itself. His arms tightened, and he murmured something she didn't understand, his breath stirring the hair at her temples.

For a moment she was tempted. She turned her face toward his and opened her eyes. The hazy room, clouded with smoke, swam into her field of vision. Smiling gently, she laid her finger across Theo's lips. "Later. I have to report this or the landlord will have a fit."

Theo reluctantly let her go, and walked into the kitchen to survey the damage.

Jenny picked up the phone and dialled the building manager who lived on the top floor. The phone rang and rang, and finally an answering machine cut in. She covered the receiver while it played its message and glanced across at Theo. "I wondered why he didn't show up when the firemen came. He must be out."

She briefly spoke into the phone, asking the man to call her when he returned, adding that the damage would be covered by her insurance.

She and Theo had just finished mopping the floor when a knock sounded on the door. She opened it to find Mr. Smith, the building manager, standing there with a worried frown on his wrinkled face. "I got your message," he said without preamble. "What happened?"

"The oven exploded. The firemen said it was a small gas leak. The stove is done for."

Mr. Smith walked in and peered at the ruined stove. "I'll have to report it on Monday." He glanced around the room. Although they'd washed the walls down, scorch marks remained on the cupboards adjacent to the stove. The vinyl flooring would have to be replaced. The section in front of the oven had curled up, brown and wrinkled from the heat of the blast.

The man's nose twitched. Jenny sneezed. The place still reeked of smoke and fire extinguisher chemicals. "You can't stay here, obviously, until it's been repaired and cleaned," he said. "Do you have someplace to go?"

"She can stay with me," Theo said.

Mr. Smith pursed his lips. Jenny stifled a chuckle. Did he now feel he had to be the guardian of her morals? "It's a large house," Theo added, "with three bedrooms."

"I'll be all right, Mr. Smith," Jenny said. "I'm sure the insurance will cover a hotel for a few days, if necessary."

"Might take a week," Smith said morosely. "Smoke damage takes time to get rid of."

Theo handed Smith one of his cards. "My home and office numbers are both there. Call me when the flat is ready."

He walked him to the door. The old man shuffled down the hall toward the stairs, muttering to himself.

"Okay, Jenny," Theo said briskly. "Pack what you'll need. Looks like the only salvageable parts of our dinner are the lamb chops and the salad. We'll take them along and cook them at my place."

Guilt ate at her. She wanted to stick close to him, but staying at his house, especially with the burden of lies she carried, was a little too close. She dragged in a breath, feeling claustrophobic. "You don't have to do this, Theo," she said. "I can stay in a hotel."

He walked over and gave her a little push in the direction of the bedroom. "I don't want to hear it. I've got a perfectly good guest bedroom. In fact, two of them."

Suddenly too weary and dispirited to argue, she packed clothes for the rest of the weekend and Monday's work. After that, she could always stop here and pick up more things. Thanks to the closed closet door the clothes hardly smelled smoky.

They were on their way to the door when the phone rang. Jenny picked it up. "Boom," said a flat, metallic voice. "Just a little boom, though. Wait till next time. I'll be in touch."

The connection clicked and Jenny was left holding a

dead phone. Her horror must have shown in her face because Theo took a step toward her. "Who was that?"

She hitched her tote bag more securely on her shoulder and dodged around him. If he touched her, she would break down into hysterical tears. Her eyes blurred and her throat closed, warning her how close she was to losing control.

Her escape attempt was thwarted by the need to lock the door, which meant she had to let him pass her.

"Who was it?" he repeated. He was too close, big and warm and tempting. She couldn't go on with this.

"A robot," she said in a strangled tone as she locked the door and walked out to her car.

THEY DROVE in separate cars to Theo's house. In the apartment parking lot he had suggested that she leave hers, since they could ride together into town on Monday. "No use driving two cars for two people going to the same place," he said.

But she had insisted on taking her car with her. She didn't want to depend on him for transportation, although she did concede that commuting together was a good idea.

The drive gave her a welcome respite, a chance to reinforce her fortitude, and consider her next move.

It was obvious that she had become a target of Theo's tormentor as well. Even if she dismissed the mugging, the two phone calls and the explosion made it impossible to ignore. Was it because he or she knew Jenny had overheard the conversation on Monday? Or was it merely her association with Theo?

He was going to be asking a lot of questions in a few minutes. She'd felt her face turn white and cold. He'd seen it. She could try to convince him it was a random crank call but she'd already said too much. After all, he'd gotten phone calls, too, and would recognize her description of the voice.

She had to tell him the whole story. Her hands clenched on the steering wheel. No, she couldn't. He would go ballistic. He would rage at her for not telling him sooner. He would hate her. She didn't think she could bear that.

And he was bound to call the police who would take a very dim view of her concealing evidence or obstructing justice or something. And they would conveniently ignore the certainty that if she'd called them at the beginning they would have written her off as an overimaginative wing nut.

By the time they reached Theo's house, her head ached, its pounding in counterpoint to the erratic hammering of her heart.

Theo showed her into the guest room. Belatedly he remembered he'd slept there last night. He stripped the sheets off the bed and bundled them in a heap on the floor while he went to get fresh ones from the linen cupboard.

Jenny twisted her hands together to hide their renewed trembling. "What do you do, try out the guest rooms to make sure your visitors will be comfortable?" The attempt at humor sounded flat to her own ears.

She broke off as she saw his expression turn cold and bleak. "Oh," she said, gulping, "I'm sorry. You found the knife in your bed and you didn't want to sleep there. Will you be all right tonight?"

His mouth tightened. "I'll have to be, won't I? I've no intention of letting some maniac put me out of my own room."

She turned and rummaged in her tote bag. "D'you have any aspirin? I forgot to pack mine."

"In the medicine cabinet," he said briefly, pulling the corner of the bottom sheet snug around the mattress.

A yellow cat with emerald green eyes met her in the hall. He sniffed at Jenny's leg, then raised his tail and began to wind himself between her ankles. His purr vibrated against her, and she picked him up. "You're a beauty, aren't you?" she crooned, sinking her fingers into the dense fur.

"No, he's not," Theo said behind her. "He's been in one fight too many. Probably lost that ear to a coyote."

Jenny held the cat away from her and smiled into his lopsided face. "Never mind. You're still gorgeous, and a few scars give you character." She nuzzled his neck and he rewarded her with a gurgly sound between a purr and a meow.

Theo watched her with the cat. For once she looked completely at ease, unguarded. It was the first time he'd seen her like this, he realized. Always, there was a barrier, of her making, he was sure.

"Where did you get him?" she asked, her eyes shining.

He had a sensation of falling into a sea of blue, sinking into an ocean that embraced him and made him feel as buoyant as a cork. What was it about her that drew him in? She must be a sorceress. He thought Lisa had made him immune to another woman's wiles.

It was Jenny, that basic integrity that shone from her eyes, the forthrightness that was the foundation of her personality. Even though something was worrying her and she kept secrets from him, he sensed that despite the dichotomy in the messages he received from her, she didn't have any wiles.

"Where did you find him?" she asked again, giving him an odd look.

He cleared his throat. "I didn't. He found me." Even to his own ears, his voice sounded strange. "He just showed up here a couple of days after I moved in. He hadn't been a stray long, I'd say. He looked well fed and his coat was glossy."

"He must have had an owner somewhere." Jenny nuzzled the cat again. "Did you—what's his name?"

"Tiger. I advertised in the paper and I contacted animal control. No one asked about him. But the SPCA told me that pets are abandoned on country roads all the time. People get tired of them and just dump them out of cars, thinking they can take care of themselves. Most of them can't.''

"Well, this one looks as if he can," Jenny declared.

"He can. He catches mice and shrews and brings me gifts I can do without. Once he ate a whole squirrel and brought me the tail. I wondered at first whether he'd dragged home the raccoon."

The raccoon? Her arms tightened around the cat, and he squirmed out of her arms and jumped to the floor, giving her an affronted glare. He stalked off, tail and head high. A moment later they heard him yowling at the back door.

"I'll have to let him out," Theo said. "He'll keep that up until I do."

By the time he got back, Jenny had finished making the bed. Theo gathered up the sheets he'd dumped on the floor. "Will you be all right here?" he asked politely. He'd gotten himself back under control, and was determined to keep his personal feelings to himself. She was a guest in his house. No kissing—not that he wouldn't like to, no fooling around.

"Come to the kitchen when you've put away your things. Take a shower first, if you want. We'll cook the chops and eat."

"Oh, there you are," Theo said fifteen minutes later when she entered the kitchen. "I was about to call you."

An appetizing smell of broiling meat swirled around the room. Jenny's stomach growled. She realized she was hungry. Not just for the food. Theo looked good enough to eat, his hair damp from his own shower. He'd also changed, into snug jeans and a loose white sweater with the sleeves pushed up on his forearms.

Nerves or lust—she wasn't sure which would get the upper hand as she imagined those hard muscled arms sprinkled with smooth black hair wrapped around her. She made up for her inner turmoil by sitting sedately at the table and spreading her napkin on her lap. She kept up a stream of bright chatter as she ate her salad, the baked potatoes he'd cooked in the microwave and the lamb chops. "These are good," she said, reaching for another one when he passed the platter.

"Thank you."

They were crisp and brown on the outside, tender pink inside, just the way she liked them. He'd sprinkled them lightly with oregano. "Is this how you cook them in Greece?" she asked.

His mouth quirked. "I didn't cook in Greece. I was a kid when we came to Canada. But yes, my mother cooked them like that. And she taught me. Said just because I was a boy that was no reason not to know how to do household chores. My dad scolded her sometimes, but she knew how to get around him."

"Do you see much of them now?" Jenny asked, gazing at him, her fork resting on the side of her plate, forgotten.

A shadow crossed his face. "Not often," he said and she heard pain in his voice.

"Why not?" she asked boldly.

"Why not?" He gripped his knife, cutting into his meat as if he were slaying a dragon. "It's a complicated story."

"Tell me," she coaxed.

"It's boring."

"Not likely. I like to hear about families."

He looked at her, curiosity kindling in his pale eyes. "Why? Didn't you have one?"

"Sure I did but my father left when I was a toddler. My mother worked long hours to support us. I had to grow up pretty much on my own."

"Well, you seem to have come out of it okay."

"Maybe," she conceded. "I'm just sorry my mother

died so young. She should have had an easier time of it. Come on, Theo, what happened with your family?''

He was silent for so long, she wondered if he would pretend she hadn't asked the question. Finally he sighed, laid down his fork and knife and took a sip from his wineglass. Not the wine she'd bought; the blast had knocked the bottle into the sink and the wine had spilled down the drain. ''The violets,'' she said suddenly. ''We left them behind.''

''I'll get you some more. There's plenty in the garden.'' His gaze moved past her to fix upon an invisible object beyond her shoulder. ''My parents didn't even like Lisa, even though she'd been part of the group of kids my sister ran around with.''

''You have a sister?'' Jenny said, surprised. He had such a solitary, self-sufficient air about him, one that she recognized, that she'd been sure he was an only child.

''She's a couple of years younger than I am, married with two children. She's living in Toronto now.''

''What about your parents?''

''Still in Montreal. Still running the deli they've had for years. I haven't seen them since I left Montreal.''

This shocked her. It wasn't that he couldn't afford a plane ticket. ''But you hear from them?''

''At Christmas and Easter. It upset them a lot, the business of Lisa's death and what happened afterward.''

What happened afterward? The question echoed in her head but she didn't dare ask it when he abruptly pushed back his chair and asked her if she was finished eating. ''In a minute.'' She cut a couple of pieces from her meat and quickly ate them. But the flavor was gone, her fault.

Briefly they'd forgotten the tension between them, talking like two ordinary people on a date. But the conversation about his family had brought dissonance into the room, as heavy as the smoke that had filled her apartment. She shouldn't have pushed him. She should have respected his privacy. She could see it hurt him, the estrangement.

The business around Lisa's death had been ugly and traumatic, she surmised. Could the present harassment relate back to that? She had to know more but not now.

Jenny handed him her plate, an apology poised on the tip of her tongue. "Forget it, Jenny," he said, his eyes as cold as a frozen lake. "It doesn't matter anymore. Someday things will be better."

But when? he wondered bleakly. Greeks tended to hug slights to them like well-loved teddy bears. He guessed it was the centuries of persecution and invasion that had made them fatalistic. They didn't trust good times. Instead they embraced tragedy as if it were expected, what they deserved.

Jenny sat at the table, her chin resting in her lifted palm. Dark circles under her eyes reminded him that she must be tired and stressed. Had she found the aspirin?

"How's your headache?" he said, forcing himself to shake off the hurt that talking about his parents, remembering the good times, always brought.

"Fine." She smiled sheepishly. "I never did take the aspirin. I guess all I needed was food."

"Well, I've got some cheesecake for dessert."

Her eyes lit up. "Did you make it yourself?"

"Actually, no. There's a bakery not far from here that does them better than I ever could."

It occurred to him that his parents would like Jenny. She was genuine, enjoying simple pleasures without worrying about political correctness or her waistline. She was refreshingly normal. Perhaps—

If they both lived that long.

He waited until she had polished off the slice of cheesecake with childlike gusto before he asked the question. "Who was on the phone and scared you?"

She looked up, her eyes as wary as those of a deer

coming face-to-face with a mountain cat. "Wrong number."

"Yeah, sure," he said derisively. "A wrong number that sounded like a robot? What did you mean by that anyway?"

"That's what the voice sounded like."

"Yeah? Then it's probably the same person who phoned me last night. That means they're after you as well."

Jenny shook her head. "I don't know," she said in a small voice. "I just don't know."

"So tell me what this robot said."

She twisted her fingers together, then unlaced them to rub at her temple. He guessed her headache was back. "Excuse me a minute," he said, and strode down the hall toward the bathroom.

Coming back, he set the aspirin bottle on the table and poured her a glass of ice water. "Take a couple of those. I just want to get this settled and then you can go to bed. You'll feel better in the morning."

She tapped out two of the tablets, popped them into her mouth and gulped down half the glass of water. "Where did you get your medical degree?" He was gratified to see a glimmer of humor in her eyes.

"Okay," he said, sitting down again, and folding his hands together on the table between them. He thought about taking hold of hers and warming them. He knew her fingers would be icy. "Tell me what this person said to you. You turned as white as a ghost."

A muscle clenched in her jaw. But when she spoke, her voice was cool and unemotional, as if she were reciting a lesson. "He—or she—said there would be a bigger boom next time. You know, it could have been somebody playing a joke, someone who heard the explosion and saw the fire trucks. He didn't say my name." She sounded breathless, the words tumbling over one another. "You know how some people get their jollies from arson or from other people's misfortunes. It could have been any crackpot.''

Theo leaned forward and placed his finger across Jenny's lips to stop the flow of words. "Don't, Jenny. You don't believe that any more than I do. It's too much of a coincidence. First you get mugged, then your oven explodes. Something's going on here and I'd like to know what it is.''

"So would I," she said honestly, again arguing with herself. The cowardly side of her won again, with disconcerting ease. "But more things happened to you that couldn't have been accidents, didn't they? How do we know this wasn't aimed at you and I just got in the way?"

"Then why wasn't it my oven? It's gas, too."

Jenny glanced across at the glossy appliance with its four burners that looked like shiny black spiders. "Yours wouldn't look like an accident. Mine's worn out and nobody would question a leak. I don't think this person wants the police involved, or at least doesn't want them to take it seriously.''

"But why me? That line, if it was damaged, had to have been doctored some time before I got there. Does anyone have a key to your apartment?''

"Only the building manager.''

Theo's mouth turned down. "I doubt if the prim Mr. Smith would want to blow up any part of the building. He doesn't seem the type.''

"I've known him for nearly three years," Jenny said. "He's very protective of the building and all the tenants.''

"Still, locks can be circumvented, and windows can be opened, as I found out. Who knew I would be at your place at that time?''

Jenny kneaded the back of her neck, as if her tension had settled there. "Your friend Doug knew. And so did Blossom. And your Ms. Herrington might have as well. I thought I saw her still around when we were leaving. And anyone else who might have been standing nearby could have heard.''

"That's not conclusive," Theo argued. "I said I was having dinner with you, not where. I could have just come and picked you up, taken you out.''

"But if you'd come inside afterward and the gas had built up to a denser level, just turning on the lights could have triggered an explosion.''

He pinched the bridge of his nose. "Yeah, I suppose that's true. Has it occurred to you that maybe we're both the target?''

She sighed, her eyelids drooping. "Yes, it has, but I can't imagine why since we never laid eyes on each other before Tuesday.''

"And we had nothing in common before that." Theo passed his hand over his eyes, his own fatigue catching up. "Unless you count some people we both knew. Like Blossom.''

"It's not Blossom." Jenny forced her eyes to meet his. Theo saw what an effort it cost her not to let her head crash down on the table. "Just as likely to be Ms. Herrington." The words slurred as she said them. "She's chasing you.''

Theo laughed grimly. "A fatal attraction? I doubt it. She's not energetic or inventive enough to pull these stunts." His voice softened, his eyes as gentle as rain. "Go to bed, Jenny. Maybe something will come to us in the morning.''

She blinked slowly, eyelids drooping as she pushed her chair back from the table. "I'll phone Blossom first thing Monday morning and arrange to have lunch with her. Maybe she has some ideas.''

BLOSSOM MET JENNY on Tuesday for lunch in a quiet pub frequented by Vancouver's downtown elite. Her treat, she insisted, adding that she wasn't expected back at work until three since it was a slow day and she had some overtime to work off.

"I tried calling you on Sunday," the young woman said. "It rang and rang and I didn't even get your answering machine. Is there something the matter with your phone?"

"Not with my phone," Jenny said. "My oven blew up on Saturday night."

Blossom's mouth, perfectly outlined in copper lipstick, formed an O of surprise. "Your oven blew up? How did that happen?"

"A leak in the gas line, it appears. The fire department came."

"You've got insurance, haven't you?" Blossom smiled. "I remember how you counselled us to make sure we had insurance even if we rented."

"Yes, the insurance will cover it. And the landlord is putting in a new stove."

"So where are you staying? You can bunk with me if you want, if you don't mind sharing a bathroom with two other people. I've got an extra bed."

Jenny shook her head. "Thanks, Blossom, but I'm staying at Theo's for a few days until they repair the damage."

Blossom's eyes grew wide and calculating, her mouth twitching around a smile. "Sounds serious. Is he the guy for you? Finally?"

Jenny twirled fettuccine around her fork. "I don't know. I really don't know. He likes me but..."

"What's not to like? And he's a hunk. I'd hang onto him."

"He had a bad marriage. He's very bitter. And there are other complications as well." Were there ever! Jenny stared down at her plate, the creamy sauce congealing in her stomach.

She looked up and saw the questions trembling on Blossom's lips. To forestall them, she asked quickly, "How about you and Doug Stevens? Is that serious?"

A shadow crossed Blossom's face. "Naw, it's just a bit of fun."

"Did he take you somewhere fabulous to eat on Friday night?"

"Him? Not likely. He's always short of money. We went to a fast-food place and then I drove him to his place in his car, since he'd had a few too many drinks at the party. He did give me taxi money to get home, though."

Was Doug the man watching Theo? Jenny's mind turned over the possibility as she ate her lunch and chatted casually about Blossom's job and her own. He needed money—that was an interesting piece of information. Why? Theo had said he was good at his job.

What was his vice? Drugs? Gambling? It had to be something that consumed quantities of cash.

But when it came to motive, she could think of nothing. Unless it was simple jealousy or envy. She'd sensed a certain antipathy between the two men, but it was probably professional rivalry, nothing to be enemies over.

"Blossom," she said, leaning forward, "how did you meet Doug?"

"One of my former clients—" She winked at Jenny who responded with a mock scowl. "One of the guys who used to visit me introduced us just before I met you. So I've known him five or six years."

"He wasn't one of your—" Jenny could hardly force out the words.

To her relief, Blossom shook her head. "No, nothing like that ever went on. He was just a guy the other guy knew. We used to meet at night clubs. That's a big thing in Doug's life."

At two she left Blossom to walk back to work. The young woman had insisted on paying the bill, saying she couldn't repay Jenny if she tried. They hugged as they parted, each promising to be in touch regularly.

Cindi greeted Jenny with a handful of messages. Jenny thanked her absently. "Have you had lunch?"

"Yes, I ate it here, but I could stand a break if you're going to be around."

"Sure," Jenny said. "Take half an hour or so."

She glanced through the pink slips as she went into her own office. Most were routine, but she lifted her brows in surprise when she saw Eddie Dixon's name and a phone number. He'd called only fifteen minutes ago and would be there until two-thirty.

She picked up the phone and dialled the number. A gravelly voice she recognized as belonging to the boy's landlord answered. "May I speak with Eddie, please?"

"Jus'a sec. I'll see if he's here." The phone clanked against the wall, and rebounded several times.

She heard a crackle of static as someone retrieved it. "Hello?"

He sounded different on the phone, more mature. "Eddie? This is Jenny Gray. You called."

"Yeah. I wanted to thank you for saving my job. I get a raise next month."

"That's wonderful," Jenny said with genuine warmth.

"Yeah. Well." He hesitated, seemingly a at a loss for words. "Say, Miss Gray, you know the dude whose office I did?"

"Yes."

"Have you seen him lately?"

"Yes, I have," she said carefully, wondering where this was going.

"Well, this guy I know says the word is someone's after him. And this morning I get this call from someone wanting to buy a gun. You know, a gun that can't be traced."

A chill scurried up Jenny's spine. "Yes?"

"Your name was mentioned, too, and they said you've been riding into town with him. Looks like they're after both of you."

"And what did you tell them." Jenny was amazed at the control in her voice.

"I told him to, uh, flake off. Guns—I never was into guns. I dunno where anyone got the idea I might sell them one. I'm clean, man. I'm not doin' that sort of stuff anymore." He took a deep breath. "What kind of business are you mixed up in anyway? You seem like good people. Who's after you?"

"I wish I knew. Eddie, you don't have any idea who called you, do you?"

"Nope, sounded like Darth Vader. Oh, Ms. Gray, I'm tryin' to quit smoking. See you round."

She laughed and thanked him for the call. But as she put down the phone, her body felt as if she'd fallen into a deep freeze.

Chapter Nine

Numb, Jenny folded her icy hands in front of her on the desk. This couldn't go on. Her nerves were fraying and she felt as if she'd aged ten years in the past ten minutes.

But what could she do? She was no farther ahead than she had been a week ago, stonewalled behind an electronic force field.

The phone rang. She jumped as if she'd been shot. "Good afternoon, Swift Couriers." Switched to professional mode, her voice remained steady.

"Hi, Jenny. How's business?"

Theo. She gulped in relief. "Fine. How are you?" What was he doing calling her in the middle of the day?

They shared his house with surprisingly little friction. He was the perfect host, looking out for her comfort, always polite and solicitous, even taking her in his car to her apartment to meet the insurance agent yesterday evening. He hadn't leaned on her to learn her secrets.

In fact, he hadn't made a single personal overture although she'd surprised a hot blaze in his eyes when he was unaware that she saw him watching her. He wanted her, no question, and if she hadn't been weighted down by her lies, she would have welcomed him. But whatever he wanted, he hadn't acted on it, possibly held back by some archaic Greek code of honor regarding guests in one's house.

It was driving her crazy. In fact, in the dark hours of the night when the room seemed overly hot and her hormones screamed for release, she'd seriously considered walking into his bedroom and jumping his bones.

Fortunately, up until now, sanity had won over her fevered imagination.

"I'm fine." His deep voice drew her out of her speculations. "Look, Jenny, I'm seeing a client after work so I'll be a bit late. How about meeting me someplace for dinner?"

In a hotel with room service? She squelched the image that rose in her mind. She sat silently, listening to his breathing in her ear. As long as he was on the phone both of them were safe.

"Come on, Jenny," Theo said, his voice laced with amusement. "You only have to say yes. Is that so hard?"

"Yes," she said.

His laughter caressed her, brushing along her nerve endings as if his fingers slid up her spine. "Yes, what? Yes, it's hard, or yes, you'll meet me?"

"Both."

"Okay." She heard a sound in the background. "Just a second, Jenny." He put down the phone and paper rattled. "Here are the papers you wanted, Doug. Sorry about that, Jenny. Can you get to Granville Island by six?"

"Sure. I can ride the bus, or use one of the bikes."

"Take a taxi. I'll pay you back." He named a restaurant, one she'd wanted to try. "Is that all right? I'll make a reservation so you can just go to the table if I'm late. See you then."

"Yes." She hesitated. "Theo, please be careful."

"Careful?" He laughed. "This client is eighty and can hardly walk. He's not a threat."

"Yes, but someone is."

He sighed, and she could picture him dragging his fingers through his hair, destroying its ordered layers. "Yeah, I guess I have to remember that. I'll be careful."

AT FIVE-THIRTY, the golden sunshine slanting in the window beckoned her. She had spent the afternoon preparing the payroll, although it was a day early, and signed the last check with a flourish. She bundled them together and locked them in the safe.

In the little washroom, she combed her hair and smoothed the silk shirt she'd worn with faded jeans. She wasn't dressed to go to a proper restaurant and suddenly wished she kept a change of clothes at the office. Oh, well, Theo wouldn't mind, and if he did, they could cancel the reservation and go somewhere else.

Stiff after sitting at her desk the whole afternoon, she stretched her arms over her head, and heard a joint pop. Exercise, that was what she needed. She would ride down on one of the bikes. No problem with traffic since it was only a short run down Granville Mall, which was closed to private cars.

Construction beneath the bridge delayed her. She got off the bike and wheeled it around piles of lumber and mud puddles. A huge dump truck cut in front of her and backed toward the pit in the ground. She waited while the driver adjusted the hydraulic lift to raise the box and send tons of gravel sliding into the hole. He touched his finger to his forehead in greeting as she inched her way around the vehicle.

She got back on the bike and pedalled toward the restaurant. For this late in the day there seemed an inordinate amount of activity in the market area, vehicles coming and going, people milling about. She kept an eye out for Theo's car but the lot was crowded and she didn't see it. Of course, he might not have arrived yet.

Outside the art institute, a sign proclaimed the opening

of an exhibit by a famous wildlife artist who would be present in person. That explained the crowds, she realized. Part of the parking area was roped off and fitted with a stage where a band tuned their instruments. A saxophone wailed plaintively over the rumble of a drumroll, sending a shiver up her back.

The bike rack at the restaurant stood behind a row of shrubs around the corner from the entrance. She locked the bike to the thick pipe, frowning. Too isolated. She hated using bike stands that were invisible from the road or walkway. Too easy for a potential thief to work in privacy although she guessed this stand was well used. Several bikes besides hers were parked there, and one was a sleek Italian racing bike. At least it provided a more tempting target than her well-used, pink mountain bike.

The head waiter glanced down at her jeans but, beyond a faint, disdainful curl of his lip, made no comment. "Right this way, madame."

By six-thirty, the restaurant had filled up, and the waiter had already come by twice to ask if she wished to order. "My dinner companion is late. I'll wait a little longer," she told him, wishing she hadn't drunk the three glasses of ice water he served so far. "Could you direct me to the washroom?"

He pointed to the back of the room, leaving the menus on the table and topping up her glass once more.

When she returned to the table, she saw Theo. He strode across the crowded room, sinking onto the padded seat in the booth. His hair curled over his forehead and the knot of his tie hung halfway down his chest. The narrow end stuck out at an angle and there was a gray smudge on his white shirt collar.

He extended his hands, palms up. "I'm sorry. I got held up."

"Literally, it looks like." She clenched her hands together in her lap, afraid to hear what had happened to him now. Obviously something had. The rumpled state of his grooming and the glitter in his eyes told her he hadn't just come from a routine meeting with an eighty-year-old client.

He laughed, a reckless sound that had diners at adjacent tables turning their heads. "No, it wasn't a mugger, unless you call a crate falling off a truck that."

She felt her face go pale and tight. "A crate? At the construction site?"

His eyes narrowed, and the laughter died. The suspicion on his face chilled her. "Yeah. How did you know? Unless it was you?"

"Me?" Her voice squeaked ignominiously, and she swallowed audibly. "Why would you think it was me?"

"Tell me you took a taxi."

"No, I didn't." Comprehension dawned. "You saw a pink bike again and you think it was me or someone who works for me."

"Yeah, I saw a skinny person on a pink bike, beating it out of there. I would have caught him or her but a busload of students for the art show was unloading and I got caught in the crowd. How long have you been here?"

"Half an hour. A bit more."

He stared at her, his eyes as pale as ice in the dim light. "How do I know you're telling the truth?"

Her temper rose, superseding the sick feeling in her stomach. "You don't, do you?" She grabbed her glass and gulped down more water, nearly choking when a chunk of ice slipped into her mouth. "Listen, Theo, it wasn't me. You can ask the waiter. He's been glaring at me for taking a table and not ordering."

"Okay. I believe you." He spread his hands. They were shaking and he quickly clenched them into fists. "This whole thing is getting to me. Did you ever recover the stolen bike?"

She shook her head. "No, there's no sign of it."

"And I suppose all your couriers clocked out at five."

"Yes. And the bikes were all there. I know, because I checked when I took the one I rode over here."

Theo drummed his fingers on the table. "Then it looks as if someone on a pink bike, either yours or another like it, is following me around."

"What?" Alarm skittered through her. "How many times have you seen it?"

"Four or five times, but every time except that time at the bus stop and tonight were during normal working hours. So it could have been coincidence."

"Do you remember the exact times and days?"

"Sort of." He looked up at the waiter who had opened the menu in front of him. "Yes, we'll order now. Bring me the chicken *Cordon-Bleu*. And a plain salad. Jenny, what'll you have?"

Her mind racing, she hadn't heard a thing. "The same as you," she said, hoping it wasn't liver.

"What about wine?" Theo asked.

"Not for me, thanks." She had to keep a clear head. "I'll have coffee."

Theo turned back to the waiter. "I'll have a glass of the house white, please."

"Very good, sir."

"Why did you make a point of telling me to be careful this afternoon on the phone?" he asked as soon as they were alone again.

Jenny closed her eyes. She had a sensation of standing on the edge of a tall building in a high wind. At any moment she would plunge toward the hard pavement below.

"And don't bother to lie," Theo added with a hard edge to his voice. "I'm sick to death of lies."

Jenny's eyes popped open. "I had a phone call from Eddie."

"Eddie?" His brow furrowed, then cleared. "Oh, yeah,

Eddie, the janitor. How's he doing? Not in any trouble, is he?"

"No, but he could have been. He phoned me instead."

"Wise of him, after all the trouble I went to to save his job. What was the problem?"

"Someone—Darth Vader, he said—called him with a proposition."

"Our Darth Vader, I presume."

Jenny nodded. "Sounds that way. The caller offered to pay Eddie to get him a gun. A gun that couldn't be traced."

"Oh? And what did Eddie say?"

"He told them—" She paused delicately. "Quote, to flake off."

Theo laughed, the sound harsh and humorless. "Yeah, right."

Jenny frowned at the candle flickering on the table between them. "You've been careful with your car since the day you found the snake inside it, haven't you? If they can't readily get a gun, they may try something with the car again."

Theo's expression hardened. "Well, they won't find it easy. Since the day I found the snake in my car, I've parked in a different place every day. Anywhere but in my designated stall. In fact, today I parked at the Sandman Inn."

"Where's your car now?"

"On the other side of the construction site. Under a streetlight. Unless someone saw me park, they'd have to search far and wide to locate it."

"That's why you were walking past the site. What happened?"

The waiter set their salads before them. Theo dribbled dressing on his and set aside the little cup. "I went past a truck unloading crates of rivets or something. The driver wheeled the dolly away. The back of his truck was open.

A crate fell out and nearly hit me. Luckily his helper was just coming around the truck and pushed me out of the way. He said he thought he saw somebody jump from the back of the truck afterward but couldn't be sure."

"You weren't hurt."

"Only my pride. But this is getting annoying."

"When did you see the pink bike?"

"After I dusted myself off. The driver and his helper were arguing about who'd left the crate so close to the edge in the truck."

"Could it have been an accident?"

"Could have. There was a machine compacting gravel in the pit and the ground was shaking."

"The gravel I saw dumped," Jenny muttered.

"The crate could have fallen from the vibrations if it was precariously balanced."

Their food came. Chicken, Jenny noted in relief, not liver. Despite her worries about Theo and the tugging of guilt inside her, her mouth watered in anticipation. She picked up her knife to cut into the succulent meat. "Maybe you should get an alarm for your car."

"I'll put a sticker on it, same as I did for the house. Alarms are a nuisance more often than not, and they don't deter professional thieves. Anybody who'd be willing to damage the car would have been stealing hubcaps when he was eight. Tampering with a car would be child's play."

"At least Eddie warned me about the gun."

"He did, but what about the next person our caller asks?"

The dismal thought hung between them during the rest of the meal despite Theo's efforts to banish it with casual conversation. Maybe the falling crate was an accident. Jenny tried to convince herself it had been but her uneasiness remained. She only managed to shake it off when he tempted her into sharing a slice of chocolate cheesecake with raspberry sauce.

AFTER DINNER they walked along the sea wall. The city lights stained the water red and orange and green, and the waves slapped against the stone wall, a soothing murmur. Overhead, stars glittered the dark sky.

Tension tightened Theo's muscles as he watched and listened for anyone following them. He'd never been nervous walking in the city at night but during the past week the shadows had become threatening, hiding places for potential danger.

He hid his tension from Jenny, lacing her fingers through his. Her floral aroma drifted around him, along with the green scent of freshly cut grass.

They came to the park. A jogger passed them, his feet thudding rhythmically. Crickets sang in the shrubbery along the path. A couple stood locked in each other's arms beneath a tree. Soft words and kissing sounds carried on the night air. Absorbed in each other, oblivious to the world. Theo envied them.

"Shall we go back?" he said softly. They would go home and he would somehow find the strength to let Jenny go alone to the guest room while he lay awake in his own room, denying himself. And her.

"Sure," she whispered, her fingers tightening around his.

Footsteps sounded behind them. The couple who had been embracing beside the path caught up to them, laughing as they broke into a run. They got into a car and drove off, tires squealing.

Theo wondered what Jenny would do if he threw her over his shoulder and drove her home and made love to her until neither of them could think straight.

Headlights briefly touched them as a car circled the parking lot. Stepping into denser shadows, Theo pulled her into his arms. He pulled her close, feeling her momentary resistance, but almost at once she buried her face against his chest. Her hands gripped his shirt, as if clutching a lifeline. He inhaled her perfume, light, innocent, and all his suspicions of her seemed ugly and petty, receding under the reality of holding her, protecting her, loving—

He threaded his hands through her hair, the soft glossy waves cool against his fingers. Tilting up her chin, he lowered his mouth to hers. She tasted of chocolate and raspberries, and he increased the pressure of his mouth, using his tongue to gently request deeper intimacy.

Giving a little cry, she turned her head aside although she didn't let go of his shirt. He stared down at the top of her head, wishing he knew why she always managed to keep that little distance between them. She wanted him, but something held her back. What was it?

"Jenny," he said, swallowing his frustration. "Let's go."

They unlocked her bike from the rack, and Theo wheeled it across the lot and past the construction site. Several spotlights illuminated the pit and the surrounding chain-link fence. The gate was closed and locked.

"It must have been an accident," Jenny muttered.

Theo, one hand supporting the bike, groped for her hand with the other and squeezed reassuringly.

"Here's the car," he said. He set the bike on its kick stand and walked around the car, checking for any sign of tampering. Feeling foolish, he even crouched down beside it, checking underneath as he'd seen beleaguered spies do in the movies. He wasn't sure he'd recognize a bomb if he saw one.

The car, spotlighted by a street lamp, appeared undisturbed. He loaded the bike into the trunk, where it fit neatly, to Jenny's surprise.

They dropped the bike off at her office building. Theo shook his head at the decay of the neighborhood, the drunk staggering along the street, singing something about spring. "At least he's got the season right," he said wryly. "Jenny, it isn't safe here."

"You've told me that before, Theo," she said. "Don't nag."

He clamped his mouth shut, determined that if things did work out with them, he would find her a better location, even if he had to subsidize it himself.

JENNY'S UNEASINESS increased as Theo drove the Saab into his driveway. She stared out the open window at her side, frowning. Something wasn't right. The hair at her nape prickled. The cat hadn't come out to meet them as he usually did.

Was that what felt wrong? No, it was more than that. Theo braked in front of the garage, reaching for the remote control. Jenny laid her hand over his, stopping him. "The crickets," she said suddenly.

"What?"

"They're not singing. And neither are the frogs."

The car idled, a gentle growl that wouldn't normally drown out the animal and insect sounds of the spring night.

"Damn." Theo dug his cell phone out of the storage pocket in the car door. One-handed, he punched in 911. "Maybe it's nothing but after the other night, I'd rather be safe."

He spoke into the phone, tersely explaining his suspicion about a prowler, mentioning Constable Baldwin. Disconnecting the phone, he laid it on the dash. He pressed the remote control. The garage door slid slowly up.

He had his hand on the gearshift when a sharp crack shattered the uncanny silence. His foot jerked on the clutch and the engine died. He threw himself across Jenny and bore her down on the seats. Their heavy breathing filled the car.

The gear lever dug into his ribs but he ignored it as he lifted his head slightly to peer out. "What was that?" she gasped.

"Dunno yet," he said, keeping his head low. The woods were thickest on Jenny's side of the car, and the sound seemed to have come from that direction.

The security light blinked out. Good, he thought. They were safer in the dark. He cautiously unlatched the door at his side, and pushed it open. The light came back on. "Just what we need," he muttered. He pulled the car door until it clicked closed again. To Jenny he said, "Keep down. I'm going to drive into the garage."

He reached down between the seats and twisted the ignition key. The engine cranked to life. Easing the gear into first, he let it roll slowly forward. The car seemed to hesitate as it began to move. With his foot at an awkward angle, he fed it more gas. The car moved but through the open window he heard a scraping sound. "Flat tire. Bloody hell!"

He gave a little more fuel, sliding his foot over the brake when the bumper thumped against the plastic garbage can. Killing the engine, he hit the remote control, holding his breath until the door hit the pavement.

He edged out of the driver's door and crept around the car, checking out the garage. Jenny's little Renault appeared undisturbed. Hunched over, he moved to the back of the Saab. No one between the two cars or hiding beneath the work bench. He moved to the other side of the car. No one there, either.

"Is any one here? It's the police." The voice was quiet but authoritative. Theo stood up. Headlights shone through the narrow windows at the top of the garage door.

Theo pressed the door control on the wall beside him. The door creaked upward. Baldwin stood outside, a dark figure outlined by the lights of his cruiser. "You're not hurt?" he said. "What about Miss Gray?"

Jenny emerged from the Saab. "I'm okay."

"Good. I came in without lights. I've already had a look around but I didn't see anyone."

"They're probably long gone," Theo said, disgustedly. "There's a road over there on the other side of the woods. They could have parked a car there."

Baldwin's eyes sharpened. "You saw a prowler?"

"No, but someone shot at us. Got the tire." Theo gestured to the car, which listed noticeably on the passenger side.

Baldwin knelt down next to the wheel. "Looks like small caliber, probably a twenty-two. Why don't you give me the jack and I'll take the wheel off. You've got a spare, haven't you?"

Nodding, Theo opened the trunk and heaved out the spare. He let the tire iron clank to the floor and carried the jack around the car. "Loosen the lug nuts while I jack it up." He turned to Jenny who was standing shivering, her arms wrapped around her chest. "Why don't you go inside?"

"Unless Captain Baldwin wants me?"

Baldwin gestured with one hand. "I'll come inside if I think of something. But at the moment, it looks like a random shooting."

"Directed at us."

"Not necessarily." Baldwin grunted as he put pressure on the wrench. "There've been other incidents. A house about a kilometer from here had its windows shot out. Not that I think it has anything to do with this, though. The residents were known to the police."

Yes, thought Theo, that ominous phrase you didn't want applied to anyone you knew. Jenny had retrieved her purse from the car and headed out to the front door. He heard her calling the cat and realized that was why she hadn't used the inside door.

"Tiger, here, Tiger."

He straightened from adjusting the jack and walked to the entrance of the garage. "Jenny, don't go—"

She screamed.

"Jenny!" Fear choked him, his heart slamming against his ribs. Baldwin leaped to his feet, his hand on his holster.

Both of them reached her at the same time. She stood in front of the steps, her face gray in the dim light. A funeral wreath complete with a wilted purple bow leaned against the front door.

Theo ran forward. "Don't touch it," Baldwin said sharply.

Clenching his jaw to contain the rage that ripped through him, Theo pulled Jenny close. He could feel the shudders that ran over her, hear the thud of her heart. "Jenny, it's all right. It can't hurt you."

A rustle in the bushes next to the door spun them around. Tiger stalked out, his fur ruffled. As soon as he saw Theo and Jenny, he gave a plaintive meow and rubbed his nose against Jenny's leg. Jenny's laugh sounded as if it were filled with tears. She pulled away from Theo and picked up the cat. "You're safe."

"He's never friendly to strangers," Theo said. "I don't think we need to worry about him even if there are prowlers about."

Baldwin came toward them, holding a square envelope with his handkerchief wrapped around it. He used a corner of the cloth to extract the card inside. "Next time it may be for real, Theo Zacharias. Better order flowers," Baldwin read aloud. He looked across at Theo. "Any idea what this is about?"

"Same as everything else that's been happening," Theo said furiously, balling his fists and shoving them into his pockets.

"Not much use trying to trace it," Baldwin said. "Looks like it came from a cemetery. You see how the flowers are starting to dry at the edges."

He walked to the car and placed the card in a plastic bag. "Not that there's likely to be any fingerprints." Coming back, he used his handkerchief to pick up the wreath

by its wire stand. "We'll check it out. Your tire, as well."
He stowed both items in the trunk of the cruiser and
slammed it shut. "I'll check out the house, if you like,
just in case."

"I'd appreciate it," Theo said, his arm tight around
Jenny's shoulders.

They waited in the front hall while he walked through
the house but Theo could tell from Tiger's demeanor that
Baldwin would find no intruders. The cat purred and
paced toward the kitchen and food, casting back questioning looks when Theo didn't follow. "In a minute,
cat," he murmured. He gave Jenny a little squeeze. "Are
you all right?"

She smiled tremulously. "I think so."

Baldwin came back. "All clear. Lock your doors. I'll
be in touch."

Theo locked the door after him, and went into the
kitchen. He opened a can of food for Tiger, wrinkling his
nose as he dumped the odorous mess into the cat dish and
set it on the floor. Tiger nearly bit his hand in his eager-
ness to gobble it down.

Theo grinned at Jenny who sat slumped at the table.
"His favorite brand, the cheap stuff that smells like...
Never mind."

He threw himself down on a chair, then jumped up to
put on the kettle. "Want some coffee?"

She stirred herself. "At this hour." She glanced at the
stove clock. He followed her gaze, saw her eyes widen.
"Is it only that time? Barely ten? I thought it would be
at least two in the morning."

He held up the jar of instant coffee. "So, d'you want
some?"

"Make it tea, if that's no trouble."

"Okay, tea it is."

The kettle whistled. He poured the hot water over tea
bags and returned to the table, setting down the mugs.

Jenny wrapped her fingers around hers and raised tortured eyes to his.

"Theo, there's something I have to tell you."

Chapter Ten

Beyond a slight narrowing of his eyes, she couldn't detect any change in Theo's expression. "Yes?" he said.

She'd wrestled with herself the whole time the policeman had been there. It couldn't go on; it was getting too dangerous. Yet, she hadn't been able to speak in front of Baldwin. It was only fair that she tell Theo first, give him the chance to decide what he wanted to do.

"Yes?" he said again.

She gripped her mug as if it were an anchor in a raging sea. "I don't know where to start."

His mouth twisted into a parody of a smile. "At the beginning. That usually works best."

Her stomach bunched into a knot of pain. *I didn't know you at the beginning,* she thought miserably. *And now that I do, I don't want to jeopardize what's happening between us.*

The phone rang. Her breath rushed out of her lungs, along with the tension in her limbs.

Theo swore, debating for the length of two rings whether to let the answering machine pick it up. He scooted his chair back and snagged the receiver off the wall phone. "Yes?"

"Baldwin, here. Any more disturbances?"

"No, nothing," Theo said. Wasn't this carrying the slogan to serve and protect a little far? Baldwin had been gone barely half an hour.

"Good, good. I checked your tire."

"That was fast work," Theo said.

"Yes, well, I was curious. It was a twenty-two that did it. I'd like to come back in the morning and check out the woods where you say the shot seemed to come from. So don't worry if you see me poking around at daybreak."

"Okay. I usually leave by seven-thirty to go to work. Feel free to check anything you want."

"Thank you, Mr. Zacharias. Just be careful." He paused, then added, "Miss Gray is all right? None the worse for the fright she had?"

"Miss Gray is fine." Theo turned to look at her. Her head lay on the table and her mouth was slightly parted as she breathed gently. Miss Gray is asleep.

Curious as he was, he knew he wouldn't find out tonight what she wanted to tell him. It could wait until morning.

He barely heard Baldwin wish him good-night, and answered absently before hanging up the phone.

She lay against him, a sweet, light weight, as he carried her down the hall to her room. Balancing her awkwardly, he turned down the bed and laid her on it. She snuggled into the pillow, mumbling something he couldn't understand. Tiger jumped up on the bed and settled himself next to her, purring.

"Traitor," Theo muttered, feeling stupid for being jealous of a cat.

He started to pull the blanket over her. Wait, she wouldn't be very comfortable with those jeans on all night. And from the look of her, she was unlikely to wake before morning. He'd have to take off her clothes, never mind the strain on his willpower.

JENNY DRIFTED UP from a deep sleep to find Theo's face so close to hers she could see the little black stubs of his growing beard. She opened her eyes wider. Something akin to pain darkened his gray eyes and he closed them, the thick upper and lower lashes meshing.

"Theo," she said softly. She didn't know where they were, or how they'd gotten there, but she felt warm and safe and he was close to her. No one could hurt them.

His eyes popped open. His pupils dilated until only the barest ring of silver surrounded them. The black rims of his irises looked as if they'd been drawn with marker pen. "Gorgeous eyes," she mused. "I thought so from the first time I saw you."

He gave a strangled laugh. "That's why you were staring at me."

"Was I?"

"Not that I was any better. I stared, too."

"Yes, as if you'd found me under your shoe."

The straight brows drew together. "I was tired, jet lagged."

She lifted her arms and clasped his neck, burying her fingers in the soft thickness of his hair, drawing him down to her. Her blood throbbed through her body, hot and as thick as honey. She had to have him. She had to store up the memory because tomorrow whatever relationship they'd developed would shatter. Because tomorrow the lies would be exposed.

She had only tonight.

"Theo, stay with me."

His eyes widened and his mouth dropped open. "Are you sure?"

"Yes, I'm sure."

His breath gusted out noisily and he stood up, scooping the cat off the bed. "I'll be right back."

She lay, heart pounding, listening to him speak softly to the cat as he opened the back door and let him out. She heard the snick of the lock, then his footsteps whispering on the tiled floor as he went into the bathroom.

He came back, tossing several foil packets on the night table. Even as embarrassment at her own recklessness in not considering birth control heated her face, she felt gratitude that he had thought of it.

He took off his shirt and lay beside her, reaching across to dim the lamp. His mouth came down upon hers, soft, coaxing, soothing away her nervousness. The crisp black hair on his chest tickled her palms as she flattened them against him. His heart beat rapidly, echoing the throbbing of her own.

He clasped her closer, molding her against him. Through the fabric of her jeans and his dress pants, she could feel him, hard and aroused against her belly. He wanted her. The wonder of it made tears sting her eyes, and she opened her mouth beneath his, responding with hot desperation.

"Jenny. Sweet Jenny. If you only knew how much I wanted this." His voice was hoarse, rough with a need he couldn't hide.

"No more than I've wanted you," she said.

"Then why the secrecy, the hiding?"

Reality jolted her. She stiffened. Theo clasped her tighter, pressing his face into the curve of her neck. "No, Jenny, don't. It doesn't matter. It can wait."

He kissed her again, his mouth clever and mobile, igniting fires throughout her body. No, it didn't matter. Not now. Plenty of time for regrets and second thoughts later. And they would come, she knew. But instead of pushing him away as she should have done, she took the coward's route and hugged him so tightly he grunted and laughed.

"Yes, hold me, Jenny. There's no past and no tomorrow, only this."

And *this* was the pleasure that surged through her when he traced a path of heat from her mouth down her throat and between the buttons of her silk shirt. Jenny let her head fall back on the pillow and let her spirit submerge in the feeling, the ecstasy.

He undressed her slowly, kissing each new spot he bared. He nipped at her, sweeping his tongue around the little dimple of her navel, his hands shaking as he removed the final garment, her white silk panties.

He knelt beside her, and touched her gently. Heat, as sweet as honey, rushed through Jenny's body. Forcing her eyes to remain open, she watched his face. His eyes closed, his mouth parted in an expression of profound pleasure as he stroked her. The toughness vanished, leaving him open, vulnerable, trusting.

A trust she didn't deserve. Quickly, before it could steal the pleasure, she pushed the thought away. She gave herself up to the rapture his hands ignited within her. So clever, his fingers, touching all the sensitive parts of her body. His mouth kissing her, wet and hot and making her burn.

Making him burn. His breath grew labored, his pulse too fast under her hands. She saw his face, eyes open now, hot and desperate, a man poised on the edge.

The caresses slowed, gentled. She whimpered, desolate, as he moved away. Softly he touched his fingertip to her lips. "Hush, Jenny. We have time. It gets better yet."

Standing up, he stripped off his own clothes. In the dim light, she glimpsed a tight abdomen bisected by a narrow line of soft black hair, lean waist and hips, strong thighs, unmistakable arousal.

She shivered. Not from cold—the room seemed overly warm. And warmer still when he came to lie beside her once more. Skin against skin, rough hair against smooth breasts. She didn't think she could feel more, and was astonished to learn she could. She struggled for sanity, for an anchor to keep her from spinning off the earth.

Theo's gentle laughter tickled her ear. "It's all right, Jenny. Let yourself go. I'll catch you."

Her skin flushed a rosy pink, exquisitely sensitive to the path he traced over her body. Desire coiled tightly inside her, begging for release. She clenched her fingers in his hair and groaned, trying to wrap her legs around him.

He wouldn't allow it. He stroked her softly, murmuring gentle words. "Slowly, Jenny. Slowly. We have all night."

But I don't, she wanted to cry out. *I want you now. I have to have you. Now.* "Please," she whispered.

"Please, what?" he asked, amused.

Her head tossed back and forth on the pillow. "I don't know. I need—"

"Yes, Jenny. A little more. I want to taste you. All of you."

He traced his hands and tongue around her hips, her belly, back to her thighs, up to her aching breasts. She felt as if she were burning, wet heat melting over his fingers.

Urgency gripped her. At the same time, perversely, she wanted to slow it down. She wanted to savor every nuance of pleasure, yet she couldn't stand to wait, couldn't stop the mad rush into passion.

"Jenny," he murmured, the softness of his voice belying the urgency with which he tore open the package and rolled on the condom. "You're so sweet, so hot. I want you, wrapped around me. I want to be inside you. Now."

He kissed her closed eyelids. She could feel him nudging her, hard and swollen, hot, wanting her. "Open your eyes. I want to see you when we make love."

Wonder filled her as she saw the emotion in his eyes, the sheen of tears. For an instant sanity returned, the urge to scream that this was false, a lie, that she had no right to make love with him as long as he didn't know what she'd done. Then all thought fled as he entered her, thick, hot, completing her.

"Theo," she whispered, despair in her heart. "Theo, please."

She was tight and he paused, searching her face. She'd stiffened a moment ago, and he'd seen a glimmer of pain in her eyes. Had he hurt her? He searched her face. No, her eyes were open, watching him, trusting, her features taut with an inner rapture that echoed within his own soul.

He moved against her, once, twice, profound elation burgeoning in him. She was his.

It was as if they had been lovers forever. He stroked her lightly, then more deeply, somehow knowing exactly how she loved to be touched. And was rewarded by her ecstatic smile and the beginning of a ripple that clenched him tightly within her. A flush marked by a fine gloss of perspiration spread over her breasts and up to her neck, delicate pink washing her cheeks.

He fought to hold onto his control. "Jenny," he gasped, sweat dripping from his tangled hair, tears burning his eyes. "Jenny, I—"

He couldn't speak as the strong pulsations gripping her body dragged him closer and closer to the center of the inferno that beckoned. As she convulsed around him with a cry of deepest pleasure, he hurled himself into the blaze, propelled by a rapture so powerful he felt it in the depths of his being. Nothing had ever been like this. No woman had ever made him feel this way.

Only Jenny.

He lay there, unwilling to analyze the feeling but knowing he'd never be the same again. No matter what happened she was part of him, inseparable. They were one.

He looked down at her closed eyes. Her chest moved gently as she slept. A wave of tenderness made his eyes sting, and his arms tightened around her.

He pulled up the quilt, turned off the light and fell into sleep.

JENNY WOKE with a start. The room was dark, and a warm, heavy weight lay over her stomach. The cat, she thought, pushing against it. Her hand froze. Instead of resilient fur, she encountered hard muscle and soft hair.

She closed her eyes, fighting panic. No, she hadn't, had she? *They* hadn't? She shifted her legs, brushing against his. They were both naked.

It was clear they had. She stifled an ironic laugh. She'd been in trouble before, but now she was sinking into quicksand. He'd never forgive her.

She edged over to the side of the bed but his arm pinned her. She tried to lift it but he murmured in his sleep and snuggled his face into her shoulder, his breath hot as he nuzzled her. Against her will, renewed desire awoke in her belly.

Rolling over, she squirmed away from him. "Jenny." His voice was rough with sleep. She stiffened, hoping he wasn't really awake.

No such luck. "Jenny, where are you going?"

"Bathroom," she muttered. Not very original but an excuse he couldn't argue with. He moved his arm, caressing her hip as he set her free.

Keeping her back to him, Jenny picked up her shirt and draped it over her shoulders. She went into the adjoining bathroom and sat down on the edge of the bathtub, the enamel cool against her bare bottom.

What could she do now? She sat there, her hands over her face, sunk in misery. She had to tell him. The sooner the better. And live with the consequences.

"Jenny," Theo called through the closed door. "Are you okay?"

Before she could answer, he opened the door and came in. To her relief, he'd pulled on his underwear. She tugged her shirt down over her knees, hunching them up to her chest.

He knelt beside her, taking her hands in his. The ten-

derness in his eyes made her want to cry. To scream.
"Jenny, what is it? Are you ill? Did I hurt you?"

"No, you didn't hurt me. But you're going to hate me."

He gave an incredulous laugh. "Hate you? Not a
chance. Even if you were an ax murderer in another life,
I couldn't hate you."

"Yes, you would. And it's worse than that. Much
worse."

She pulled her hands free and got up. The shirt barely
reached the top of her thighs but she hardly noticed. "We
have to talk."

"So talk. But we might as well be comfortable."

In bed? Too intimate, sheets still warm and scented with
her perfume and his soap. Too much a reminder of what
she'd never have again. But where else could she go? Too
dispirited to argue, she climbed back into bed, making no
protest when he lay down beside her.

She bunched the pillows behind her and pulled the quilt
up to her chin, wrapping her arms around her knees, deliberately making it impossible for him to hold her. He
gestured toward the lamp. "Do you want it off?"

She shrugged. "Doesn't matter."

He lay down, propping his head on his lifted palm, his
gaze on her, dark and puzzled. "Jenny, tell me."

She dragged in a long breath and swallowed to moisten
her dry throat. Her palms were sweating and she wiped
them on the sheet, twisting a corner of it into a tight knot.
She lifted her head to look at him, her eyes as dry as if
she'd been in a sandstorm. It hurt to blink. "Someone
wants to kill you," she said starkly.

He laughed, a harsh, humorless bark. "Tell me something I don't know. I've figured that out on my own."
His eyes narrowed, the anger glittered in them. "Or do
you know who and why? Is that what you're hiding?"

She shook her head. "I only wish I did."

"Then what?" He grabbed her hand, tearing it away from the sheet she was torturing. "Stop doing that."

She folded her hands on her knees, resting her forehead on them, welcoming the discomfort of digging her skin into bony knuckles. "I delivered the money to the person who is doing these things to you." The words came out in a rush and she braced herself for the explosion.

It never came. The silence stretched. Finally she lifted her head and met his eyes. Ice rushed through her veins. She'd seen that look before, on the face of a man who'd ended up in a shelter. A man whose wife had tried to kill him and their child.

Betrayal. The knowledge of giving love only to have it thrown back as if it were worthless garbage.

"Theo, I'm sorry." Her voice caught on a sob, but she swallowed to control it. "I'm so sorry."

He didn't move. "How?" he whispered, a mere movement of his lips, as if he couldn't trust himself to speak. His hands clenched the quilt, knuckles white, and his face was still and pale.

Fear welled up in her, nearly choking her. He had himself under rigid control but if he let it go... That quiet, dark side of his soul that she'd glimpsed at times—would it escape and run wild?

"How?" he said again.

She looked away, pleating the edge of the sheet with agitated fingers. "I picked up an envelope at a bank, and delivered it. I found out afterward it was money to pay someone to make life miserable for you."

"I see." She sneaked a sidelong glance at him. His expression had lightened marginally and a frown creased his brow. Good, the anger was under control and he was thinking. "Did you know what the envelope contained when you delivered it?"

She shook her head. "No, but most envelopes from banks contain money or important documents."

"How did you find out what it was for?"

"Some quirk in the phone lines." She quickly related the conversation she'd overheard.

"Had to be one of your lines. Someone in your office."

"There was no one in my office. No one at all. There was something wrong with the lines. I had the phone company check it a few days ago. They said the wiring is old and that sort of thing happens sometimes."

He waved aside the explanation, his expression intent. "And what did you do after you overheard this conversation?"

"I tried to get the envelope back, but Ms. Herrington had already delivered it."

"To someone in my office." The toneless quality of his voice was more frightening than anger would have been.

"She didn't know who. The person might also have picked it up from her desk without her noticing, if they were expecting it."

"And that's why you waylaid me in the hall outside the office last Tuesday afternoon."

"Yes." She ducked her head again, agony squeezing her heart. If she'd known then, one short week ago, how she would feel today, she would have blurted out the whole story and let him think what he wanted.

"Why didn't you tell me what you'd heard?" His voice was deceptively soft but she could hear the fury underlying it, smell it in the heat that radiated from his body.

"You would have thought I was crazy. I couldn't just walk up to you, a stranger, and say someone was trying to kill you."

"You could have called the police."

"They would have said I was a nut, that I'd misunderstood what I heard, or something. Especially since there seems to be no motive to hurt you." Her eyes searched his face. "Or is there?"

His mouth tightened, that mouth that had given her so

much pleasure. Her heart ached with the knowledge that it would never happen again, that she'd destroyed any chance at love they might have had.

"No," he said flatly. "But you had no right to make that judgment without knowing me. Maybe you were only trying to save your own hide, since you might have been considered an accomplice."

That stung, because of the truth in the accusation and the guilt she'd felt because of it. Whatever her motives, saving herself seemed the least noble. "Maybe there was that, too," she snapped, using anger to stop the despair she refused to give in to. "I had a business to run, people who need their jobs. I couldn't take any chances, could I?"

"No, you only took a chance with my life." He stood up and went to the door, his movements jerky, as if he'd forgotten how to walk. "I could have been on guard, damn it, all along. Instead you left me in the dark. And you managed to move into my house. Maybe you're behind it. How do I know?"

He flung the door open and went out. A moment later, his bedroom door slammed. She rolled over, her body aching as if she'd been beaten. Tucking her knees up to her chest, she rocked back and forth, too emotionally spent to cry. Even if she'd had any tears.

Footsteps in the hall roused her. Theo stood in the doorway, dressed in shorts, a T-shirt and running shoes. "I"m going out," he said in a biting tone.

"At two in the morning? Isn't that dangerous?"

"No more than keeping this from me for a week while I'm attacked by snakes, crates and bullets. Call Constable Baldwin. Tell him everything." A moment later the outside door slammed.

She lay on the bed, curled around herself, wishing she could cry but knowing if she did, she'd never stop. Once, in college, she'd thought herself in love, had made rosy plans for a wedding, children, a Volvo and a dog. He'd dumped her for some rich little girl whose daddy had dangled a tempting job offer. She'd cried then, walking around in a daze for a month before burying her grief in her books and acing her final exams. By the time summer was over, she'd been amazed to realize she could barely remember his face.

This was different. As she'd known it would be. Even though he hadn't said it, he probably wanted her to leave. She thought of the stricken look on his face when she'd told him the truth. He'd felt the same agony that gripped her.

She was staying. He'd torn out her heart and she wasn't going to leave without it.

Neither was she going to stand aside while somebody killed him.

Buoyed up with new determination, she rolled out of bed and got dressed. She went into the dining room where he had set up her computer, which they'd brought from her apartment since it looked to be several more days before the repairs were done.

There had to be something in his past that was now catching up to him. If she could find out what, maybe she could find a way to protect him.

Sitting in front of the computer, she thought back over the little she knew about him. He'd come from Montreal, four years ago. His wife had died the year before that. He hadn't mourned her; that was clear from his attitude. In fact, she'd gotten the impression he had lost any faith in women he might have once had. She paused with her fingers poised over the keyboard. Maybe that was one reason he'd reacted so strongly to her deception. He'd had this sort of experience before.

How had his wife died? And what had happened to make him leave an apparently successful career in Montreal to start over from nothing in Vancouver? Did any of it have a bearing on the threat to his life?

She was probably searching on the wrong planet but she had to start somewhere.

Unexpectedly tears flooded her eyes. Would he ever forgive her? Blinking to clear her blurred vision, she logged onto a computer network and typed in a request. Montreal newspapers, five years ago. His wife hadn't died of old age. That meant an accident or illness. It might have made the news, if not the general papers, then the society pages.

She tried the English language papers first, since her French was more than a little rusty. Luckily she could request a search by name. Her fingers slipped on the keys as sweat broke out on her hands. She typed Theo Zacharias.

A moment's wait. A headline appeared on the screen, dated the middle of May. It had made the front pages.

Black print screamed at her. "Prominent broker's wife dies in hit-and-run accident. Car removed from river." She scanned through the story. Lisa Zacharias, 26, had been killed after being rear-ended in a rainstorm at three in the morning. She had been alone in the car. The car had gone down a steep incline, into the river. Cause of death had not been drowning, however. She had not been wearing a seat belt and the impact of her head against the windshield had killed her instantly. She and her husband, Theo Zacharias, had been married six years, no children. The last paragraph of the story speculated as to the disposition of her family's fortune of which she had been the sole heiress.

For the next several days, the story continued, mostly reports of the police search for the hit-and-run driver. They had found the vehicle, which had collided with Lisa's, but that had proved a dead end since the car had been reported stolen earlier in the day.

A week after the accident, the story had again been promoted to the front page. "Autopsy shows traces of barbiturates and alcohol in Lisa Zacharias's body." Then, two days after that, the headline that startled Jenny: "Theo Zacharias questioned. See section two for an in-depth report."

Eyes widening, Jenny skimmed through the story, which related Theo and Lisa Zacharias's history, a mixture of fact and innuendo that skated on the edges of libel. The marriage, by all accounts, had been tumultuous.

Jenny punched the keys to print out the information on the screen. She returned to the previous stories and printed them as well.

She ordered a further search. The story had been followed up, but with little added information. Eventually it had died. She was about to abort the search as weeks went by with no reference to his name when it came up again. This story, in typical newspaper convention of putting the sensational on the front page and everything else progressively further back, appeared in a sidebar headed Local News. No charges were contemplated against Theo Zacharias. Lisa's bungling lawyers and her own ill-advised contributions to questionable charities had been responsible for her business setbacks. Theo was completely exonerated.

Jenny printed this also. She searched the rest of the year, and the following one, for good measure, but, sensation over, the media had ignored Theo Zacharias. Printouts in hand, she clicked the quit command and turned off the computer.

She went into the living room and slowly read through the news stories. Theo's wife had been extremely rich at the time of their marriage when she was twenty and he twenty-three. Jenny stopped to calculate. Six years of marriage, five years since, that made him thirty-four now.

Now why should that matter? she asked herself. Just

because he was the right age for her wasn't important, any more than the fact that his hair felt soft and crisp at the same time, curling around her fingers during the love-making she knew she had to forget. She rebuked the heat that surged through her veins. Hormones. Nothing but overactive hormones.

She was still lying to herself.

She pulled her attention resolutely back to the story. Theo and Lisa had met in college. A year after their big society wedding, Lisa had become richer still when her entrepreneur father died and left her his business empire. But after her death, it came out that the business was on the verge of bankruptcy. Lisa had liquidated most of her father's holdings, acting on the advice of her handsome new husband, it was thought.

At this point in the article, facts became opinions and speculations. Theo, in seclusion since his wife's fatal accident, had refused interviews but that hadn't even slowed down the reporter. He asked the question: Who else but her clever husband with his degree in business administration would advise a woman who had no financial experience beyond shopping and hosting business dinners and cocktail parties? And the speculations about Theo's perceived greed raged rampant among Lisa's friends. They were only too eager to give interviews, to bask in their moments of fame. Fingers were immediately pointed at Theo, accusing him of mismanaging his wife's affairs.

Which led to further uncharitable speculations, namely that he might have murdered his wife since the troubled stage of their marriage had deteriorated during the last year from cool sarcasm to public viciousness. There were those who wouldn't have held it against him.

It was also speculated that Theo might have killed her for her money, but when it became apparent that there was little left, the theory changed. He must have done it to cover up his ineptitude in managing her affairs.

Of course, in the end, Theo hadn't been arrested. His alibi, flimsy as it was, had stood up, largely due to witnesses who had placed Mrs. Zacharias, alone, at several club lounges during the evening. And he had ultimately been cleared of suspicions of financial wrongdoing in handling his wife's affairs.

But did a man ever regain a lost reputation? No wonder he had left Montreal. And no wonder he had developed that cynicism. He needed it to protect himself.

She scowled at the papers in her lap. Did any of this help her to identify his stalker? She turned off the light and sat down to wait for him to come back.

THEO RAN through the night, his breath puffing out in a white cloud. The night had turned cold, the temperature bordering on frost. The starlight was blocked by heavy clouds massing overhead. It would rain before morning.

The raw cold bit into his muscles, seared his lungs. He ran faster, ignoring the pain in his knee, the one he'd banged up in a car accident in high school.

How could he have fallen for her, suspecting she hadn't been honest with him? He swore pungently. Fool, driven by an overdose of testosterone. What he should have done as soon as he'd felt the attraction was turn to another woman he knew.

The chilling fact was that since he'd met Jenny, the thought of any other woman turned him off.

Twice a fool. First Lisa, gorgeous, but a liar, who had cheated on him before the honeymoon was over. Who had him pegged as little more than a boy toy, a man she could manipulate, who would give her respectability and convince her father she'd settled down. She'd used him.

And now, so had Jenny.

He ran up a long hill, his breath labored, his chest aching. A cold drizzle began to fall, rain running over his face, dripping off his chin.

She'd loved him with fire and passion, given him a satisfaction that went far beyond simple sex. And beneath the uncertainty in her eyes, he'd seen love.

He thought he had. Obviously he'd been mistaken.

Or had he? He paused and leaned against a cedar, gasping. When his breathing slowed, he sank onto the needle-strewn ground beneath the spreading boughs. It was dry but still cold. He sat there until his muscles cramped painfully.

Jumping up, he jogged in place to speed up his circulation. He ran down the road, blanking out all thought, concentrating on taking air into his lungs, letting it out, breathe in, breathe out.

He reached an intersection. If he went right, he would be home in half an hour. If he went left, he would reach the country store with its pay phones outside and he could phone Baldwin.

He turned right, and spent the hard run home asking himself why he was giving her another chance.

JENNY HEARD the front door open and close. Running shoe soles squeaked on the quarry tiles as he came into the dark living room. "You're still here." His voice was quiet, calm and unsurprised.

"How did you know?" she said out of the depths of the chair in which she sat.

"Your perfume."

"I'm not wearing any."

He shrugged. "Whatever, your shampoo or something. And your car is still in the garage."

Tiger, who had come in with him, sauntered over and

jumped into her lap. Theo scowled at the cat. "I might have known you'd be too stubborn to give up," he said.

He reached over and turned on the light. Jenny blinked in the sudden brightness. "I didn't call Baldwin."

"Didn't you? Still think you can fix it on your own?"

She drew a fortifying breath, her fingers clenching in the cat's fur. "Together, we can."

He walked up to the chair and stared down at her. His hair hung in wet points over his forehead, dripping on her. Her nostrils flared as she inhaled his scent, sharp, tangy, cedar resin. "You ran in the woods."

"No, on the road, but I stopped out of the rain under a tree." He crossed in front of her and sat down heavily on the sofa. Setting his elbows on his knees, he clasped his hands between them. "Why, Jenny? Why did you do it like this?"

She closed her eyes to shut out the pain in his. "I thought I could fix it."

"The police are paid to fix things like stalkers."

"They wouldn't have believed me," she said stubbornly. "And it was my fault."

"Pride then."

"So? I do have pride. In fact, at times, it's all I've got."

He was silent for so long that she finally looked at him. He sat with his head back against the sofa cushions. His eyes were closed. One hand restlessly kneaded his knee. "Jenny, why did it have to be like this? What I was beginning to feel for you—" He broke off.

Fresh agony shafted through her. She'd ruined it, for herself and for him. It was too late now. The words echoed through her like a funeral dirge.

"Why did you have to lie?"

His voice cut through the fog of pain. "I only lied because you wouldn't have believed the truth."

"It was still dishonest. You came on so innocent, all

big blue eyes as blank as the sea. I knew you were hiding something but I decided eventually you'd tell me, we'd laugh about it, and go on from there."

"We can go on," Jenny said, her voice wobbling only a little.

"How?" he asked starkly.

"We can find the person who's after you."

Chapter Eleven

Theo sat up straighter, his eyes narrowed. He lifted one foot onto his knee and began untying his shoe. "What makes you think I'd want to work with you? Is there any reason I should trust you?"

"Maybe not," Jenny said. "But I'm all you've got."

"There's always the police." The shoe hit the floor with a thud. A moment later the other followed.

She set the cat on the floor and walked across the room. Picking up the telephone, she thrust it into his hand. "Here, call Baldwin. And have him tell you they've got plenty of other cases and not enough manpower to put a twenty-four hour guard on you."

When he made no move to take it, she let the phone drop back onto its base. Standing over him, she folded her arms across her chest. "He knows someone shot at your tire but did he suggest a guard? No, he just told you to be careful. Do you think knowing what I did will change much?"

His chin set stubbornly. "Maybe it will."

She went back to the chair, picked up the papers that had slid down beside the cushion and shuffled them into order. "Theo, I've done some research. You were accused of some pretty rotten things after your wife died."

"What?" He reared up from the sofa and strode over

to her, snatching the printouts from her hand. "What's this?" The anger radiating from him seared her, and she took a step back. He glanced over the papers, eyes flashing as he fixed them on her again. "What gave you the right to snoop in my past?"

Her own temper flared. "I had to start somewhere. We can't sit around waiting for something else to happen, something that could be fatal. Since you say you don't have any present enemies, there must be something that occurred before, that made somebody want to get even."

He shook his head. "There's nothing." Was his denial a little too vehement, or was that her imagination looking for trouble?

"There has to be, Theo. Nobody stalks someone without a motive."

"Sometimes they do," he insisted.

"Yes, sometimes, but not often. I've worked with enough stalkers, men whose wives had left them, for example. They stalk and attack for revenge or to save their own necks. They don't go after strangers. I doubt if it's a stranger after you. The tone of the conversation I heard implied familiarity." She took the papers from his lax hand and leafed through them. "Is it possible that someone connected with your wife has chosen this late date to try to get even with you? Maybe they believed the innuendoes about you having a motive for her death."

"She had no relatives left. And her friends were the kind of superficial people who forgot her as soon as the funeral was over."

Theo shivered, his socks squelching on the tiled floor as he shifted from one foot to the other. Jenny saw the drawn lines of his face. His clothes were wet. She remembered the rain and noticed for the first time how cool it was in the room. "You're freezing. Go and take a hot shower while I make us some coffee."

To her relief, he went down the hall, leaving wet footprints in his wake. A moment later she heard the shower.

BY THE TIME he returned, wearing jeans and a sweatshirt, the coffee was ready, filling the kitchen with its fragrance. Jenny handed him a mug, laced with cream and sugar, just the way he liked it. Only four days of living together and she knew his habits.

He sank onto a chair at the table, taking a long swallow of the coffee. He set down the mug, keeping his hands wrapped around it. Jenny stood at the stove, turning ham in the frying pan and sticking bread into the toaster. Four eggs waited on the counter. Through the window he saw the sky begin to turn a light shade of gray. A gust of wind rattled the eaves. Raindrops peppered the glass.

Standing under the hot spray of the shower, he'd felt much of his anger wash down the drain along with the water. He'd mulled over what she said and realized it made sense. Someone in his past was after him. Had to be. But the fact remained, he had no enemies. The charges against Lisa's thieving lawyers had been settled out of court. No reason for any of them to come after him.

He drained his mug, and got up to pour another. Sat back down to eat the food she set before him. Across from him, Jenny forked food into her mouth, her face shuttered, closed. He hadn't thought it possible for her to hide her feelings so thoroughly when they were usually on display for all the world to see.

Faint misgivings again stirred to life within him. What did he know about her, after all? She might be the one stalking him for all he knew.

No, not likely. No motive, and his gut told him she wasn't the type for obsessions. Too open, too impulsive.

"Uh, Jenny," he said tentatively, "you can stay here until your apartment is repaired. I'm sure we can keep out of each other's way. We're adults, after all."

Recalling just how adult she'd been last night—was it only last night? Seemed like forever—made his body stir hopefully. He still wanted her. He could deny it all he wanted, tell himself she was a liar and whatever else, but he still wanted her.

"That's generous of you, Theo." Her voice was so low he couldn't tell if she were being sarcastic or not. "But I can always stay with Blossom. She lives in town."

He watched himself reach across and take her hand. After a moment's resistance she let it remain, cool and limp, under his. Pain at what he'd lost—actually never had, except for the fleeting moment when he'd been sure their souls had melded into a single entity—tore through his heart. She was lost to him now. He wondered how he would live with the pain.

"Jenny." His voice hitched and he had to clear his throat before he could go on. "Jenny, I'm sorry. No matter what, I'm not throwing you out on the street. Don't forget, someone attacked you, and the same person who called me made threatening phone calls to you as well. This person might be counting on the stress getting to us, so he can get each of us alone. We can't take any chances. I'd be happier knowing you're safe, here."

Life sparked back into her face. He could see she had forgotten the threats. The thought chilled him. No matter how clumsily she'd handled this, she was in danger, too. And most likely because of him. One corner of her mouth tilted up in a faint smile. "Then we'd better solve this," she said. "By working together."

A frown creased her brow. "There's one more thing I forgot to tell you. It's only supposed to go on until April 13. But they've apparently picked April 10 or earlier for me. Unless I leave you alone. I haven't, so they must be pretty upset by now."

"What?" he demanded, stunned. "Run that by me again."

She repeated the dates, relating the phone calls as well as she could remember. Theo sat back in his chair. "We should be able to figure some of this out."

"It's got to be someone in your office. Who is most likely to need money?" She balled her fist on the table. "Why am I even asking? All the people who work in your office are rich. So the motive isn't money."

"Stock markets have been pretty bad for the past year," Theo said. "Could be someone got in over their head, leveraging."

She frowned. "What's that?"

"Borrowing for investment purposes. It's something you have to be careful with. If the market drops, you still have to pay back the loan."

"Do you know of anyone who'd do that?"

"Lots of people, but no, not anyone who wouldn't be prepared to live with the risk."

"What about Ms. Herrington? She wears awfully expensive clothes. Can she afford them on what she makes?"

"She's very well paid, and I know she buys her clothes in wholesale outlets. It's not likely she's in financial trouble. I've given her advice, seen her portfolio. It's conservative but growing."

"So it's not money with her. What about the personal angle? How badly has she tried to date you?"

"I told you she's asked a couple of times, nothing too serious."

"Don't rule her out yet. Sometimes people hide obsession. But I still think it's more likely someone in your past. What about Doug Stevens? Has he ever lived in Montreal?"

"Yes, he did, once."

"Are you sure?"

"Yes, but we never met there." Theo smiled faintly. "Montreal's a large city."

"Yes," Jenny agreed, "but you are in the same business. You might have crossed paths."

He shook his head. "Not until I started at PRI."

"What do you know about him?"

"He likes parties. He's seeing Blossom but it's not serious. He dates other people, including Janice Herrington." He shrugged. "I don't know. He can be a pain in the neck but I don't think he's involved in anything illegal."

"Would you know?"

Theo stared at her. "I guess not. I don't know the guy that well."

She made a note on the back of one of the printouts. "So we'll check him out."

"Wouldn't it be better to let the police do it?"

Jenny shook her head. "They wouldn't have any grounds for digging into his life unless they suspect him of something. No, we'll have to do it ourselves. I'll talk to Blossom again."

She got up and took their plates to the sink, running water to rinse them. She opened the dishwasher and set them on the racks. "Are you going to work today?"

"Sure. Why wouldn't I?"

"Just asking, because if you're not, I'll take my car."

"You can ride with me, Jenny." What choice did he have? Like it or not, they were in this together.

He stood up and set his mug in the dishwasher, taking care not to brush against her. Even so, he couldn't escape the light sweet scent of her.

He looked out the window and saw a dark figure in the trees at the end of the lawn. Alarm rushed through him but dissolved when he remembered Baldwin was coming to look around that morning. A moment later, he saw him clearly, circling the lawn in his navy blue uniform.

"I'm going out to speak to Baldwin," he said, and opened the back door.

JENNY WAS DRESSED for work and waiting when he came out of his room later. She'd put out the cat and made sure the doors were locked. They went out through the side door into the garage, Theo pushing the control to open the large door as he went by. Jenny was relieved to see no nasty surprises outside.

Of course Baldwin would have checked it out but he'd been gone for an hour and you never knew. The stalker seemed to have their comings and goings pretty well monitored.

"What did you tell Baldwin?" she asked once they were clear of the garage and going down the road.

"I told him about the night you were attacked in your office building, and that you'd had a threatening phone call."

"Not about my delivering the money?"

"No." His tone was short, his face set in hard lines, as if he were fighting with himself over the wisdom of his action.

She waited until they were stuck in the traffic crawling across the bridge, a place he couldn't stop to dump her out of the car, before she asked the question burning inside her from early this morning. "What did your wife do to you to make you so bitter? Every time her name comes up, I can see how you change."

A muscle ticked in his jaw, and he tossed her a look that would have stripped paint. Her heart knocked erratically against her ribs. The traffic began to speed up on the down side of the bridge and he shifted into a higher gear. She sat back, swallowing her disappointment. He wasn't going to answer.

But he surprised her. "Jenny, I married Lisa because I was in love." He gave a short, derisive laugh. "In love with love, probably, or in lust masquerading as love. What does a kid of twenty-two know? We met in college, married the next year, big society wedding, the social event of the season, I think it was called.

"We flew to the Virgin Islands for our honeymoon." He laughed again. No humor in it. "Virgin, get the joke? I didn't expect her to be but I thought maybe she was, because she wouldn't let me make love to her all the time we were going together. She was so prim and proper I thought her reputation must have been wildly exaggerated."

"Her reputation?" Jenny nearly choked on the words.

"Yeah, all through high school she was in one scrape after another. Boys called her morning, noon and night. She was once nearly busted for drugs but apparently she hadn't been using, but others at the party she was at were. Her father fixed it up."

"How do you know this?" Jenny asked tonelessly.

"A couple of days before the wedding, her father called me into his study for a talk. He told me how happy he was that Lisa was marrying someone like me. She'd settled down. He was sure she would give him a flock of grandchildren before he was too old to enjoy them. Like the young, arrogant fool I was, I promised to do my best to make her happy. He told me about her past, said it wouldn't be honest to let me marry her without a complete disclosure. Turned out he didn't know the half of it."

"What happened?"

Theo's knuckles whitened as he gripped the steering wheel. "The first night at the hotel on our so-called honeymoon, I woke up and she was gone. I found her in the bar, coming on to some guy twice her age. She laughed when I asked her what she was doing. 'Having fun,' she said."

The traffic rolled to a stop around Cariboo. He ground the gears, downshifting, telling Jenny with more than words how upset he was. "Theo," she said gently. "You don't have to tell me anymore."

"No, I guess I don't." But he went on as if he couldn't help himself. "That's the way it went during our whole marriage. After a while, we moved into separate bedrooms. I didn't want to know what she was doing. And after her father died, she didn't even bother trying to cover anything up. I must have been the laughingstock of Montreal but I just threw myself into my work and pretended everything was okay. She finally consented to a divorce but then she died and that was that."

"Except for the slurs against you. Why didn't you sue the papers? Seems to me you had grounds."

Theo shrugged. "I just wanted to be rid of the whole miserable affair. As soon as I could, I got out of Montreal. And came here."

He glanced at her, and she winced at the pain in his eyes. "And I've brought you more trouble," she said.

"If you're not behind it, it's not your fault. If you are..." he let his voice trail off.

Hurt, she stared out the window at her side. He still didn't trust her.

THE FIRST THING she did upon reaching her office was to call Blossom at work. "Oh, Jenny, I didn't expect to hear from you so soon. Is something wrong?"

"Not really," she lied. After a long debate with herself, she had decided she couldn't tell Blossom the real reason behind her questions. After all, she couldn't be sure how close she and Doug were. Although Blossom had changed, the tough street kid still lived inside her, the kid who had lied more often than told the truth. "Blossom, what do you know about Doug Stevens? Is he really short of money, like you said the other day?"

"Why, does he owe you?" Blossom asked. Jenny could hear a smile in her voice. "Wouldn't surprise me if he did. He owes a lot of people and some of them aren't very nice."

Jenny's senses went on full alert. "What do you mean?"

"I mean gambling debts. He bets on the ponies, he goes down across the border to play at those Indian casinos, and he likes poker. That's why I don't hang around with him much anymore. These guys who collect debts can be mean and it has a way of hitting the bystanders if you're too close. You know what I mean?"

"Yes, Blossom, that's very wise of you." Her brain seething at this news, Jenny could barely force the words through stiff lips.

"Why are you asking about Doug?" Blossom said. "I thought you didn't like him much. Oh, oh, gotta go. There's another call. I'll call you, Jenny. We'll have lunch again and you can give me the lowdown. Bye."

She broke the connection before Jenny could reply.

"Was that Blossom?" Cindi asked from the doorway.

Jenny started. She'd expected to be alone in the office for another half hour. "You're early," she said as evenly as she could. "It's only eight-thirty."

Cindi lifted one shoulder and nibbled the edge of a nail. Bad habit, that. Jenny had mentioned it to her once or twice in the past. Cindi, the picture of efficiency in her red suit and white silk blouse, chewed her nails. "I thought I'd get caught up on the stuff I didn't finish yesterday since I left early. Girls'll be in soon. Want me to unlock the storage or will you do it?"

"I'll get it," Jenny said. She had to phone Theo as well. "I might have to go out for part of the day. I've got some business to take care of."

"Okay. I can take care of the office."

As soon as Cindi closed the door, Jenny dialled Theo's number, crossing her fingers that he would pick it up. Doug Stevens answered. "Could I speak to Theo Zacharias, please?" she asked formally, not letting on that she recognized his voice.

"Jenny, is that you?"

She stifled a groan.

"How are you?" Stevens went on with the exuberance of a puppy. "I'd still like to have dinner with you but I guess Theo's keeping you busy."

For a split second, she considered it. Over dinner she might discover more about him. But she discarded the idea as quickly as it formed. Theo would be better for this job. He knew the man and he could have a drink with him or challenge him to racquetball, some guy thing.

"Yes," she said noncommittally. "Could you put Theo on, please?"

"Sure, anything you say, babe." The phone clicked as he put her on hold.

"Yes, Jenny?" Theo sounded distracted.

"Doug isn't with you, is he?"

"No, he transferred the call. What's up?"

"I think I hit the jackpot. He owes a lot of money, Blossom says. He's a gambler."

"So he's worth checking out," Theo said. She heard the scepticism in his voice. "Although I wouldn't have thought he'd have enough imagination to do the things that have happened. And what possible motive would he have?"

"That's what we have to find out. As for imagination, it's clear someone else is paying him, if he's the one. The other person could be dreaming up the stuff."

"Yeah, I guess you're right." He still didn't sound convinced.

"It's worth a try," Jenny said. "Have a drink with him or something. Get him talking."

"Okay. He's not my idea of a fun date for lunch but I'll see what I can do."

"Good," she said enthusiastically. "I know you can do it."

THEO HUNG UP THE PHONE, a reluctant smile tugging at his lips. She landed on her feet, he had to say that for her. And she didn't give up. Which could make her a real pain in the neck, or a good ally.

Before he could have second thoughts, he walked into Doug Stevens's office. "How about lunch today, Doug? It's on me."

Surprise leaped into the man's face. He recovered quickly, however, his eyes narrowing in a calculating look. "Sure, Theo. It'll have to be a late one, though. I've got an appointment at noon. Meet me at the pub down the street, you know the place. That's where I'm meeting this guy but we'll be through at one."

"Great." Theo forced heartiness into his voice.

He cleared his desk and made sure he reached the pub by twelve-thirty. Entering the place, he shook his umbrella dry and used it as a partial shield while he scanned the dim interior for Doug. He spotted him right away, sitting at a booth in the back. Theo ducked behind a partition in case Doug turned his head and saw him. The man with Doug wore a distinctive plaid raincoat, which he'd kept on despite the steamy warmth in the pub.

The place was crowded. Theo went back outside into the rain, walking down the block, pretending he was window-shopping. He crossed the street and stared at a display of books, watching the reflection of the pub in the window. He killed a little time inside the shop, keeping an eye out for the plaid coat while he bought a book he didn't need and hadn't noted the title of.

Almost one. He went out and waited in a doorway next to the pub. The man came out, carrying a plain leather briefcase, apparently an ordinary businessman. Theo laughed to himself. What had he expected, some enforcer with a machine gun in a violin case?

His gaze sharpened when a long limousine with darkened windows glided up. The man in the plaid coat got in and the car slid off down the street. Very interesting, especially since the coat, which looked as if it came from Value Village, didn't seem the sort of garment someone who could afford a limo would wear.

Thoughtfully Theo entered the pub and rolled his umbrella. Doug waved at him from the booth at the back. Theo sat down, shrugging off his raincoat.

Doug held the menu in front of him. The laminated folder shook slightly. He put it down, signalling to the waitress. She came over and took their orders. "I'll have a screwdriver," Doug said. "How about you, Theo?"

"Ice water," Theo said, not taking a chance on muddling his head.

The waitress came back with the drinks. Doug grabbed his and gulped down half of it in one swallow. The ice cubes clinked as he set down the glass. He took out a handkerchief and wiped his forehead.

Theo filed away the information. The room was cool but Doug was sweating. "Bad deal?" he asked blandly.

"You might say that." Doug laughed humorlessly. "Nothing winning the lottery wouldn't fix."

So the man had been after money. "If you're in a bind…" Theo let the words trail off.

"No, no. I'll work it out. I may be coming into some money soon. I'll manage until then." He finished his drink and ordered another.

Theo picked up a corner of his club sandwich, chewing it slowly as he tried to figure out a way to get more information from Doug. "How's Blossom?" he asked with forced heartiness.

"She's fine." Doug pushed fries around his plate, his fork scraping on the heavy china. "Bank's been after me. My car payment was late this month. I'm selling it. The buyer's picking it up this afternoon."

That hadn't been a bank official in the limo, Theo

knew. Banks called you into their offices if there was a problem; they didn't go to see clients.

"I think I'll go to Vegas on the weekend," Doug volunteered. "Make some money."

"Or lose it," Theo said wryly. "Do you go often?"

"About once every couple of months. Take in a few shows." Doug stared morosely into his almost empty glass as if he were debating having another.

Theo pushed his plate aside. "Gotta get back." He signalled for the check, and took out his credit card. "Look, Doug, if you're really in a bind, come and talk to me about it."

Doug stared at him, then drained the glass. He laughed bitterly. "Thanks, Theo, but you're the last person I'd ask for a loan." He stood, and picked up his coat. He missed the sleeve on the first try but wrestled the garment into place. "Thanks for the lunch. We must do it again."

Theo watched him walk unsteadily across the room. The waitress returned with the receipt and he signed it. By the time he stepped out into the rain, Doug had disappeared.

In his own office, Theo looked up a number in an old address book he kept in his desk. He dialled it quickly, calculating that it must be nearly closing time in Montreal. The phone rang and was answered by a voice he still recognized. "Felix, how are you?"

"*Bien, monsieur.*" He switched to English. "Who is this? We're about to close."

"It's Theo."

"Theo! I thought you'd forgotten all your old friends. How are things on the rain coast?"

"Wet," Theo said, deadpan. "Look, can you do something for me? Check out the background on Doug Stevens." He gave what details he knew.

Felix, an old school friend, who'd quit the police force

to open a private detective agency, promised to get back to him in a couple of days. "Is that all?"

Check out Jenny. The thought jumped into his head. No, she'd been born and raised here. Nothing for Felix to find in Montreal. On the other hand, if she'd lied... "See if you have anything on a Jenny Gray. If there's nothing over at your end, don't worry about it."

"Great. I'll be in touch."

He hung up the phone. It rang again, under his hand. "Yes?"

"Theo, how did you make out with Doug?"

Jenny. The way his heart lurched disconcerted him. To cover it up, he said brusquely, "You could have waited until I digested my lunch."

"Never mind that," she said. "I followed the guy he met before you."

Oh, great! He buried his face in his palms. He knew he shouldn't have called her back this morning and told her where he was meeting Doug. He should have guessed she'd play amateur detective. "Who asked you to do that?" he asked furiously. "You could have gotten into big trouble."

"Why? I only followed the car."

"With what, one of your pink bikes?"

"As a matter of fact, yes," she said smugly. "In the traffic a bike goes faster than a car any day."

"Okay," he said, resignedly. "Where did he go?"

"Luckily not far. To a fancy new condominium complex on Cambie Street. He rang the penthouse. When he went in, I checked who it's listed to. David Jones."

David Jones. The name sounded familiar. Theo searched quickly through his memory.

"Isn't he the guy who was fined for insider trading last year?" Jenny asked.

Theo snapped his fingers. "Yes. And he owns a string of loan offices. I believe the Better Business Bureau doesn't recommend them. How did you know who he was?"

"I do read the financial pages once in a while. But everyone knows who he is. The insider trading thing made the front pages. You would have had to be a hermit in a cave not to know."

"So it looks as if Doug owes money to some heavy-duty people. But the two thousand you say he or somebody else is being paid wouldn't have much impact on a major debt."

"Maybe not, but the caller said there might be more later."

Theo rubbed his fingers over his chin. "Yeah, how much would they pay to kill me?"

Chapter Twelve

A chill passed over Jenny's body. Yes, the plan was to kill Theo. She was certain of it, much as she wanted to deny it.

"You didn't happen to get back in time to follow Doug when he left?" Theo asked.

"Actually I did, but the only place he went was into the Hyatt Regency lounge. He sat down and ordered another drink."

"In other words, don't expect him back this afternoon."

She was silent for a moment, wondering whether she could do it. Whether she should. "I could go there, pretend I just happened by. Maybe he'll tell me something."

"Forget that," Theo said flatly. "If he's capable of the things he's done, you're not safe with him."

"I'm not going to be alone with him. And he has asked me out to dinner."

"No, I don't want you to do that."

The forcefulness of his tone startled her. Was he jealous, in spite of last night? He sounded too emphatic for it to be simple male protectiveness. "I'll do what I want," she said, pushing him. "You can't stop me."

"Maybe I can't but it's dangerous." He dragged in a long breath. "Look, Jenny, I've called someone to check

him out. At least wait that long. Shouldn't be more than
a couple of days, unless he really has something to hide
and has managed to bury it too deep to find."

THEO AND JENNY rode home together in his car. Home.
After a few short days, she was beginning to think of his
house more as home than her own apartment. She chided
herself. Once her place was repaired, she wouldn't have
a reason to stay with him anymore. Depression settled
down on her like a month of rain.

Theo stopped the car in front of the garage doors. He
took her arm as they walked to the front door. Tiger lay
on the step, getting up and stretching sinuously when they
approached. "Looks as if no one's been here," Theo said.
He inserted his key into the lock. "Still, I'll take a look
around."

"Why, are you going somewhere?" Jenny asked.

He looked at her. "Oh, didn't I tell you? I've got a
meeting with a client close to Guildford. I'm afraid you're
on your own for dinner."

She could have gone out with Doug, she thought. Pre-
suming he was in any condition to drive or eat. Although
she saw the wisdom of Theo's warning, the fact that she'd
meekly heeded it stung.

Maybe it wasn't too late. Doug must have a cell phone
or a pager. She might be able to get hold of him.

"Okay, Theo," she said, smiling.

His eyes were suspicious as he fixed them on her.
"What are you planning, Jenny? Not some more detective
work, are you?"

"Who, me?" she said, her eyes wide and innocent.

"Yes, you." He clasped her shoulders. "Jenny, I realize I can't stop you from doing what you want, but be
careful."

He did care. Despite his anger last night, he did care.
"I will," she promised. "I'll be careful."

He let her go to walk into the living room and push the Replay button on the answering machine. A couple of hang ups, one of them filled with static, then a message from a telemarketer announcing a special on carpet cleaning. After that, Constable Baldwin's voice came on. "Mr. Zacharias, please call me when you can."

Another beep. Another blank hang up. The machine whispered scratchily as it rewound. Theo picked up the phone and punched out the number for the police station. Jenny realized he must have memorized it.

He asked for Baldwin, drumming his fingers on the table as he waited to be connected. "Zacharias, here."

He listened for several moments, making noncommittal replies. "Okay, thanks." He hung up and sat there, staring at the little, blinking light on the answering machine, as if it held the secrets of the universe. Apparently deciding it didn't, he stabbed his finger against it, resetting the machine.

"Well?" she said.

He looked up at her, his eyes momentarily blank. "He didn't find anything significant. Says it was probably kids fooling around. The shot was a twenty-two, but we already knew that. He says there's no reason to believe a connection with this and the dead raccoon."

"So he's not taking it very seriously."

Theo shrugged. "With nothing concrete, what can he do? They hardly have the manpower to post a guard."

"Then it's up to us."

"I guess." Theo stood up. "Will you be all right alone?"

"Sure." She tickled Tiger's good ear. "I'll have my attack cat for protection."

"Okay. But if you hear anything unusual, call 911. That was all Baldwin could suggest."

"I will." Her breath caught in her throat as she saw

his gaze fall on her lips. His mouth parted and she waited, in breathless anticipation. Was he going to kiss her?

She swallowed her disappointment when he turned and quickly walked out the front door, using his key to lock it behind him. The car growled to life. She reached the window in time to see it disappear down the curving driveway.

She laid her hand on the cool glass. "You have to trust me, Theo," she whispered. "I'm all you've got."

AFTER FEEDING THE CAT, she heated a tin of soup and made herself a grilled cheese sandwich. She ate at the kitchen table, listening to the silence of the house around her. Finally, to banish her disquieting thoughts, she turned on the radio sitting on the fridge, letting heavy metal music, which she ordinarily hated, beat around her.

She dumped the dishes into the sink and went into the living room, booting up the computer. If nothing else, she might be able to find something in the newspapers.

She called up the same Montreal newspaper as before, asking for a search on Douglas Stevens, going back ten years. The cat jumped on to her lap and settled down, a comforting weight on her thighs.

"Bingo," she murmured presently. Doug Stevens had made the papers, eight years ago. He'd been questioned in a bank embezzlement. The paper two days later had an update. Doug had been cleared when one of his co-workers had confessed, a woman he'd been dating. She admitted to planting evidence in his desk and home. Doug had been reinstated in his job but apparently hadn't stayed. That must be when he'd moved to Vancouver.

She asked for further references but nothing showed up.

She typed in another request. Theo Zacharias. Maybe he had some kind of trouble before his wife's death. She should have thought to check farther back the other night.

Words began to materialize on the screen but before

she could read them, the doorbell rang. Theo back already? No, he would use his key.

She turned her head toward the window. In the shadowed dusk she could see the yellow bells of daffodils nodding in the planter. Rain still fell, desultorily pattering the glass. She let the cat slide to the floor and got up and pulled the curtains closed.

The doorbell rang again, a long, insistent note that broke off into a burned-out buzz, as if the person out there knew she was home. Pushing her chair back, she glanced at the computer screen. The screen saver sent flying toasters across a midnight sky, little wings flapping.

Doug Stevens stood outside the door. His eyes were bloodshot and beard stubble emphasized the pallor of his skin. His wet, sandy hair flopped on his forehead, refusing to stay in place even when he raked it back with his hand. "Doug—" she said.

He sniffed, rain dripping from his face. "Yeah, I know. I look like hell."

"How did you get here?" She subtly moved to the center of the doorway, blocking it while she decided whether to let him in.

"Drove," he said, mopping his face with a ragged tissue.

"In that?" A battered white Rabbit stood near the corner of the garage, half hidden by the lilac bush. "What happened to your car? I'm sure Blossom said you've got a BMW."

"Sold it. I needed the money."

As well as the money to harass Theo? she wondered. Did she dare challenge him?

"Aren't you going to invite me in?" he asked, his voice taking on a whining note.

"Should I?" she asked. "Theo could be back anytime."

Doug's mouth turned down petulantly. "Yeah, and I

suppose he thinks he owns you. He's always been possessive about his women. I never could understand how he came to marry Lisa. He must have known what she was like."

A hollow, icy sensation invaded her stomach. "Did you know Theo and his wife in Montreal?"

He looked briefly startled. "Didn't Theo mention it? I knew Lisa, both before and after she married Theo."

Theo had lied. Fighting nausea, Jenny stepped back from the door. "I guess you might as well come in."

The wolfish smile that crossed his face almost made her change her mind. She took a step forward, but he gestured with his hand. "Don't worry, Jenny. I never wanted to hurt you."

"No," she said boldly. "You just wanted to hurt Theo."

His eyes narrowed craftily. "Why should I want to hurt Theo? Just because he married Lisa didn't make him my enemy."

He walked past her into the living room. Jenny closed the door. Her knees trembling, she followed him. He flopped down on the sofa, pulling at his loosened tie until the two ends hung over his wrinkled shirt. "You don't have a beer or something, do you?"

Jenny shook her head. "We're all out." By the looks of him, he didn't need any more to drink. She wondered again how he'd managed to drive there. It must be true that God takes care of fools and drunks. "I can get you a soda, if you want."

"Better than nothing."

She left him to get the drink from the fridge. When she returned he lay in the same position, his eyes closed. He jumped when she thrust the cold can into his hand. He sat up, fumbling with the tab before he could lift it to open the can. The top popped and fizzed. Doug raised the can to his mouth and drank deeply.

Lowering it, he stifled a belch. Disgusted, Jenny stared at him, questioning her recklessness in letting him in, questioning whether she should listen to what he had to say. If he was the man tormenting Theo and found out she suspected him, she was in big trouble. And Theo might not be back for hours.

Tiger padded out of the kitchen. He spotted the visitor and crouched down, tail lashing. He bared his teeth and hissed viciously. Doug recoiled, drawing his feet in their scuffed loafers up on the sofa. "Get that animal away from me."

"Why, are you allergic to cats?" Knowing she'd scored a point, Jenny didn't bother to keep the amusement out of her voice.

"Not allergic. I just don't like them, sneaky things always slinking around, like spies."

Jenny snapped her fingers. Tiger flicked his ear toward her, then reluctantly rose to his feet and stalked over to her chair. He sat down at her feet, alert green eyes fixed on Doug.

"He doesn't like strangers," Jenny explained.

Doug lowered his feet. "You're telling me." He lifted the can and drained it, dropping it with clatter onto the table. He stood up and wandered around the room, pausing at the entrance to the dining room. "Your computer?" he asked casually. "What are you doing, your taxes? I can give you some pointers if you want."

"Theo's promised to help me," Jenny said with a calm she didn't feel. If he showed signs of going over to the table and touching the mouse, deactivating the screen saver, she would have to stop him. She wasn't going to let him see what was on the screen even if she had to throw the cat at him.

Doug moved back into the living room, resting his hand on the mantel. "Look, Jenny, what do you really know about Theo? He was investigated once, in Montreal. I think he paid someone to cover it up."

"What about you?" Jenny said, figuring she had nothing to lose. After all, she could have found it out by calling the securities commission.

"I'm straight," he said, looking her right in the eye. If she hadn't seen his hand clench into a tense fist, she might even have believed him.

"Sure you are, Doug," she said soothingly. She stood up. "I'd like to get back to work, if you don't mind. So I'll have to ask you to leave."

"I wanted to talk to Theo."

Jenny headed toward the front door, holding it open in a manner he couldn't ignore. "You'll see him tomorrow. It can't be that urgent."

"Guess not." On the step, he turned back. "Watch yourself with Theo. He can be a hard man. He really got burned by Lisa."

"Thanks," she said dryly. "I'll keep it in mind. But you might as well know, I can take care of myself."

He grinned. "Yeah, I guess you can, at that." He touched his finger to his brow in an almost military salute. "I'll take a rain check on our dinner together. Good night."

Jenny closed the door and let her breath whoosh out. She listened to the rattle of the diesel engine as the Rabbit took off down the driveway. Now what had that been about?

She'd been so sure Doug had to be the one who'd received the money at PRI, but his visit awakened doubts. He hadn't acted guilty; he'd denied being investigated when she knew he had. Newspapers made all kinds of errors but not one of that magnitude, which could have invited a lawsuit for defamation of character.

The cat stropped himself against her legs, then walked

a little way toward the kitchen. "Just a minute, cat," Jenny said. "I have to think."

He meowed plaintively, came back and batted a sheathed paw at her ankle. "Okay, I'll let you out."

She opened the door for him and he bounded out. Into the rain? She noticed that it had stopped, and remembered that even when Doug left falling drops no longer dimpled the puddles on the driveway. The air smelled fresh, wet earth and the heady sweetness of hyacinths.

Closing the door, she crossed the kitchen, pausing at the sink to gulp down a glass of water. Why had Doug come to see her? Or Theo, as he'd said at the end? How much of what he said could she believe? He'd implied he'd known Lisa. Yet, Theo had said he'd never met Doug in Montreal. Which one of them was lying? Theo hadn't given her any reason not to trust him, and neither had Doug. If Theo said he hadn't known Doug, it must be true. He had no reason to lie.

Or did he? The chilling question hit her. If he and Doug were connected and he did know the reason behind the harassment and wanted to make sure she didn't find out what it was, he might lie.

The computer.

Going into the dining room, she shifted the mouse to get back the screen. Words materialized, black headlines. "Judge Arrested For Wife Battering."

She frowned, puzzled. What did the arrest of a judge have to do with Theo? She didn't wonder long. Farther down in the story, his name appeared, the neighbor who had called the police after hearing the disturbance in the house next door. Must have been quite a disturbance since the houses were set on large, secluded lots and not exactly close together.

She moved to the next day's paper, using the judge's name, Gustav Schulze, as a reference. A smaller story, not on the front page, indicated that Schulze had been released on bail, and that his wife was still in a coma.

Several months went by with no mention of the case. Then the headline: Judge Schulze Receives Seven Years. She scanned the story. The neighbor, not named in this story, but she assumed it was Theo, had testified to repeated sounds of violence from the house. The judge had maintained his innocence but the jury hadn't taken long to come to a guilty verdict. The sentence was seven years. Mrs. Schulze had been in the court, wearing a hat to conceal the uneven growth of hair on the half of her head, which had been shaved to repair her fractured skull.

The judge had spoken briefly to the milling press. He'd protested his innocence, citing that Zacharias had railroaded him because of a property dispute. He'd vowed to appeal his sentence and take Theo to court for maligning his character. The photo accompanying the story showed Theo in the background, looking grim.

Jenny checked the date of the story. Approximately one year before Theo's wife had died. No connection there, she figured, even if the judge had taken his anger with Theo out on Lisa. No matter how slow the courts were, the appeal wouldn't have taken that long, not with a powerful defendant like Schulze.

She scrolled through the next month, then the one after that. Yes, there it was. The appeal had been denied, the judge had been disbarred and warned that if he pursued the matter further, his sentence would be increased. He had been summarily sent to prison.

Jenny sat, chin in hand, in front of the computer. Was it possible the judge, even in prison, had taken revenge? No, it couldn't be. Too much of a coincidence. And no suggestion of anything other than misadventure, slippery road and an impaired driver, in Lisa's accident.

She mulled over the time span. Seven years in prison. With good behavior, he might have been released in three or four. And give him a little time to locate Theo who was not listed in the phone book as a financial planner. He only appeared in the white pages along with a lot of other Zachariases. Even if the judge had talked to Theo's former co-workers, they might not have known where Theo had gone. It would have taken time to track him down, even if Schulze knew he was in Vancouver.

The snick of a key in the front door lock brought her head up. "Theo, is that you?"

"Yes, I'm here," he said from the doorway. "Did you eat?"

"A long time ago," she said. "Did you?"

"Yeah, I had a hamburger." He stepped up next to her and focused on the computer screen. As he took in the words, she saw him stiffen. "It's not him, you know."

She gaped at him. "What makes you say that? I would've thought he was the perfect suspect. And he said he'd get you."

"He can't," Theo said flatly. "He's dead."

"Dead?" She couldn't believe that her conclusion would shatter with just two words. "How do you know?"

"The police in Montreal let me know. He was killed in a fight in prison."

So that was that. With a snap of her wrist, Jenny directed the mouse to the exit command. The screens dissolved into the okay to shut down the system. Reaching behind the machine, she clicked it off.

"Well, I tried."

Theo touched her shoulder. "Yes, you did, and I appreciate it. But I knew that was a dead end. I would have suggested it myself if I hadn't known it was impossible."

"What happened to his wife?"

"You mean, would she go after me? No, she's alive and fairly well although she still suffers some memory loss because of the skull fracture. She still sends me a card at Christmas."

That was a relief. During her tenure as a social worker, Jenny had found out that battered women often refused to press charges against their abusers, and sometimes even blamed those who had rescued them. It was one of the most frustrating aspects of her job, one reason she'd burned out.

"Then who is it?" she said, grinding her teeth in frustration. "Think. It has to be somebody."

Theo shook his head. "It must be a stranger. Even Doug has no reason to be my enemy, and this goes beyond professional jealousy. Besides, I've sort of given up on Doug as the guilty party. He needs money but he seems too inept to have done any of the things that have happened."

"Yeah, I'm beginning to think the same thing." Jenny bit her lip in indecision, then added, "He came by here tonight, said he wanted to see you."

"And you let him in, I suppose," Theo said in a resigned tone. "That's why there's an empty soda can on the coffee table."

"It could have been mine."

"You don't leave stuff lying around. You'd put it in the recycling box as soon as you'd finished it."

"Do you know that he sold his BMW and now he's driving a little beater?"

"Yeah, he mentioned it at lunch," Theo said.

"But are his money problems serious enough for him to moonlight as a hit man?"

"Knowing Doug, I can't see it."

Jenny got up and paced around the room, straightening a picture on the wall as she passed it. Behind her, Theo chuckled. "See why I knew you didn't leave the soda can? You tidy things, you don't leave messes."

She spun to face him. "Are you implying I'm uptight?"

Theo shook his head. "Not at all. You're too impulsive

in other circumstances. No, uptight you're not. Tell me what's mulling around in your head now. And don't say nothing is. I can tell when you're chewing on some problem.''

She crossed her arms across her chest and clasped her elbows in her palms. ''A couple of things don't add up.''

''Only a couple?''

She smiled faintly, her uneasiness after Doug's revelation dissipating in Theo's reassuring presence. ''Maybe more. But for starters, do you suppose there could be a connection between Doug and the judge?''

''I thought we'd decided Doug was innocent.''

''We've got no other suspects, have we? So let's prove his innocence before we let him off the hook.''

''If there is a connection, we'll know by tomorrow or the next day. I've got a detective looking into his past in Montreal.''

Jenny nodded. ''He was questioned in an embezzlement but someone else was arrested.''

Theo's brows rose. ''Oh?'' Jenny watched him closely but his surprise appeared genuine. ''How did you learn this?''

''Newspapers. Same as I found out about your wife's accident.'' She paused for a second, then blurted out, ''Doug says he knew Lisa.''

Theo groaned, closing his eyes. ''And I told you I'd never met him before. You think I lied.''

''I wondered.'' Jenny swallowed the lump in her throat. ''But I wanted to hear what you'd say about it.''

''I didn't lie, Jenny. I did not know Doug in Montreal. I found out after he left that he'd known Lisa. I believe they even dated for a time, in high school.''

''You didn't also go to the same high school?''

''No, I didn't. We didn't live in that neighborhood. Too rich for our blood. My parents were simple people who lived in the same area as many of the other Greek immigrants in Montreal.''

He walked into the kitchen, opened the refrigerator and contemplated the contents. Jenny followed him. He hadn't turned on the light and stood silhouetted against the fridge light.

"Do they still?"

He lifted his head, bumping it on the freezer compartment handle. "Ouch, damn it. Do they still what?" He rubbed his head, letting the fridge door fall closed.

"Your parents. Do they still live in the same neighborhood?"

He opened a cupboard, looked inside, closed it, opened another. "No, they don't. The area changed—they moved to the suburbs. But they still have the same deli." Slamming the cupboard door, he opened a third one.

Talking about his parents bothered him. Jenny had noticed it before. The estrangement must hurt him terribly. "Can I help you find something?" she said. "Before you damage the hinges."

"How would you know where anything is? I live here, remember?"

"Yes," she said sarcastically. "How could I forget? What's the matter, didn't your meeting go well?"

"It went fine but the hamburger I ate is giving me heartburn. I know there's some antacid tablets here somewhere."

"Maybe in the bathroom."

"Maybe," he agreed. "My cleaning lady must have moved them." He walked out of the room and a moment later she heard him banging cupboards and drawers in the nearest bathroom. He came back, chewing a tablet and grimacing at the chalky taste.

"Look, Jenny," he said. "I'm sorry I snapped at you. But this thing is getting to me, especially when we keep hitting dead ends. I appreciate what you're doing but I don't see how it can be anything in my past. I've had a pretty boring life.''

"Was Lisa boring, too?" Jenny couldn't resist asking.

Instead of anger, an ironic smile crept across his face. "No, but that kind of excitement I can do without, thank you."

"Have you thought of marrying again?"

She expected an offhand dismissal of the subject, but he stood there, frowning thoughtfully as he considered the question. "Maybe, if I found the right woman. Maybe when this is over."

With that cryptic remark he strode down the hall to his room. Jenny sighed and went into the guest bedroom, and read a book until her eyes burned like fried eggs.

She woke the next morning, feeling dull and logy, and dragged herself into the kitchen. Theo was already there. He took one look at her and poured her a cup of coffee. "Here, you'll feel better. It's not your responsibility to lie awake at night worrying about me. It'll work out."

"Yeah, when you're dead," she said dolefully.

All day Jenny had a sensation of holding her breath. The incidents had accelerated steadily to this point. Something even more disastrous was bound to happen soon.

To her surprise, nothing did.

"What's that, three days now that nothing's happened," Theo joked as they drove across the bridge on Friday evening. "Brace yourself in case my brakes fail."

Alarm rushed through her. "Why, do they feel mushy?"

Traffic ahead slowed down, and Theo put his foot gently on the brake pedal. The car slowed and came to a stop. "They feel fine."

Jenny aimed a fist at his shoulder. "Then don't joke about it. I doubt if they've given up after everything that's happened so far. Let's hope it's not something at the house."

They pulled into the driveway. Theo frowned as he saw
the car parked in front of the garage, a car Jenny had never
seen before. "That's funny. The car belongs to Edith, my
cleaning lady. She's usually gone by now."

Theo had barely shut off the engine when a small, gray-
haired woman ran out of the front door, waving a newspaper. As soon as she saw Theo getting out of the car,
she laid a shaking hand on her chest. "Mr. Zacharias,
you're all right. I was so worried."

"Worried? About what?" He grabbed her arm as she
swayed. "You look pale. Come inside and sit down and
tell me all about it."

Jenny followed them in, sniffing the air. Flowers.
"Jenny," Theo said, helping Edith to the sofa, "get her
a glass of water, please."

Jenny poured a glass from the bottle in the fridge,
bringing it back to the living room. The cloying perfume
of flowers filled the room, stealing the air. Too sweet. Her
stomach shifted uneasily. Several arrangements stood on
the hearth. Glancing into the dining room, she saw more
bouquets on the table. Where had they come from, these
precisely manicured florist's offerings?

Theo took the glass from her and held it while Edith
sipped a little. The small woman waved the glass away,
smiling wanly. "That's enough. I'm all right, but I was
so relieved to see you."

"Don't I always come home at this time?" Theo
sounded amused but Jenny saw that his eyes were as hard
as chips of ice.

For answer, Edith thrust the newspaper, folded to the
back pages, into his hand. "This. The paper always comes
on Friday afternoon and look what it says."

Jenny saw it was a small community paper, distributed
mostly for its advertising. Theo held it up, scanning the
column Edith had marked in red pen. He gasped, and
turned as white as the paper the words were printed on.

Chapter Thirteen

Jenny stepped up next to him and pulled the paper around so that she could see the marked paragraph. She gasped as she read: "Theo Zacharias passed away suddenly, aged thirty-four. Predeceased by his beloved wife, Lisa. No children." The obituary went on to eulogize a distinguished career. "Funeral arrangements to be announced."

The words blurred and the room spun around her. Jenny groped behind her and found a chair, sinking down as if the tendons of her legs had been severed. So they didn't have until the thirteenth. The date had been moved up.

Theo, a white line around his mouth, stared at the paper in his hand. "This is ridiculous." He managed a strangled laugh. "I'm afraid I have to agree with Mark Twain, that the reports of my death have been exaggerated."

"For which we're very grateful," Edith said, picking up the water glass and bringing it to Jenny. "Here, my dear, you look as if you need it more than I do."

Jenny gulped down the water, her hands shaking. She handed back the glass, murmuring her thanks as she struggled to focus her thoughts. "There's no dates," she suddenly exclaimed.

"What?" Theo said.

"No dates. I thought the final date was supposed to be the thirteenth, and this means it's been stepped up, but maybe it doesn't. Maybe it's just another piece of psychological torture."

"So I've either got no time, or I've got nearly two weeks," Theo said darkly.

Edith put her hand on his arm. "Please, Mr. Zacharias, don't joke about it. Who is the monster doing this?"

Theo wearily raked a hand through his hair. "If we knew that, we'd do something to stop it. Have there been any phone calls?"

"Yes, several," Edith said. "One of them was from a reporter. He asked if I'd be willing to do an interview. When I asked him what for, he told me about the obituary. I wouldn't have seen it otherwise."

"Well, the paper has wide circulation in the area but that doesn't mean everyone reads it. Most people probably use it to wrap yesterday's chicken bones."

The phone rang. Theo picked it up. He listened for a moment, frowning. "As you must have guessed by now, I'm very much alive. And I've got nothing to say. Goodbye."

"Another reporter?" Jenny asked.

"Yeah. He seemed disappointed that I wasn't dead."

The phone rang again. This time it was a worried client who at least seemed relieved to hear the report was wrong. Theo had just put the phone down when it rang once more. This time he snarled into it and hung up abruptly. He lifted the phone and turned the ring to low, then turned the sound off on the answering machine as well. The phone buzzed irritably. Someone else calling. They listened as the answering machine beeped. Theo turned it up a little. Another reporter.

He rolled his eyes up at the ceiling. "What is it, some kind of telepathic communication? Why are they calling this number? If I'm really dead, I wouldn't be here. I'd be lying in some funeral home."

Jenny shuddered at the image.

"Please, Mr. Zacharias," Edith said. "Maybe you should call the police."

"What for? They know I'm being threatened. There's not much they can do, with no suspects." He picked up Edith's purse and sweater and gently steered her toward the door. Pulling his wallet from his pocket, he added an extra twenty dollars to what he normally paid her. "Edith, don't worry about it. I can handle it. And the police know about the threats."

"Do you want me to come back next week as usual?"

He frowned. "Maybe you should let me call you. I'm beginning to wonder if it's safe for you to be coming here to an empty house. We don't know what kind of a deranged maniac is doing this."

"I've never been nervous in your house, Mr. Zacharias," Edith assured him, but the faint tremor in her voice showed that today's incident had shaken her.

Theo patted her shoulder. "I know, but I don't want to take any chances." He forced a smile. "By next week, the whole thing might be over." One way or the other, he thought with black irony. "I'll call you."

"You will be careful, though," Edith said worriedly, backing out the door.

"I will. I promise. I'll be in touch."

He stood at the door, watching while she turned her car and drove down the driveway. When she was out of sight, he let out the breath he was holding, and turned around.

Jenny stood behind him, the stubborn set of her chin telling him it was no use asking her to leave. She could; her own apartment had been repaired and cleaned. She'd told him that the building manager had called this afternoon to let her know it was ready for her to move back in.

With surprise, he admitted he'd gotten used to having her there, liked having her with him. He hadn't gotten close to a woman since Lisa, actually since long before his wife's death, even though her disregard for their marriage vows should have given him the freedom to take the same liberties. And after she was gone, he hadn't met anyone he'd wanted to be with.

Until Jenny. Jenny whom he had little reason to trust. Jenny who was beginning to seem an indispensable part of his life. Jenny who just didn't give up fighting for him.

"I'm not going away until this is over," she declared defiantly.

He laughed. "Does it look as if I'm kicking you out? Of course, I should, for your own protection."

"What about your protection? Two pairs of eyes are better than one. We can look out for each other."

He wrapped his fingers around hers, their palms mating as if they'd been meant to from eternity. "Come on, let's get some food. How about if we go out for a pizza? Then we won't have to ignore the phone ringing."

THEY SHOWERED and changed into casual shirts and jeans before going out to the car. Theo accelerated down the driveway, the engine purring like a satisfied cat. He glanced into the rearview mirror, then across at Jenny. She had her head turned away from him, looking over her shoulder at the house. "Do you have the feeling we're escaping?" she said.

"It's not the house. It's the idea that someone could be watching every move we make and we wouldn't know it."

At the end of the driveway, he nearly collided with a florist's van turning in. He pulled up alongside, and waited for the driver to roll down the window. "My condolences," the young man said before Theo could speak. "I've got flowers for the family."

Someone was going to an inordinate expense since all of the floral arrangements had come with the same, unsigned card, the same message: Soon This Will Be Real.

"No family, no flowers," Theo snarled. "I'm not dead."

The young man looked taken aback. "I'm sorry. Just a minute." He checked a clipboard at his side. "Yep, this is the address. What do you mean, you're not dead?"

"Do I look like a corpse? Take the flowers back. Give them to an old-age home or something, without the condolence card. And don't come here again."

"All right. Sorry."

The kid backed up slowly. Straightening the van, he put it into drive, and accelerated away, peeling rubber as if the hounds of hell nipped at his wheels.

Theo gunned the Saab's engine, coughing as the acrid smoke of abused tires swept in through the open window.

"So much for fresh spring air," Jenny said dryly.

Theo laughed bitterly, surprised that he still could. This had gone beyond ridiculous to ludicrous. If he were smart he'd hit some travel agency, buy a ticket to Hawaii or Tahiti and get away from here for a month, until it all blew over.

And he would take Jenny along. His face softened. Just the two of them on some tropical beach, sipping drinks with pieces of fruit in them. The kind he normally hated but they seemed acceptable, even necessary, in a fantasy. They would go for a walk and find a secluded cove and he would love her until they could barely stagger back to the hotel. Where he would love her some more, until he'd imprinted himself on her very soul.

He was a fool. How could he let his blood run hot and thick, wanting her, when he should be alert to the danger around them?

A THIN SLIVER of moon hung in an inky sky when they drove home. Jenny rested her head against the cool window at her side. She was tired and pleasantly relaxed; maybe tonight she would be able to sleep. She'd almost forgotten what it was to have a full night's sleep. Yet, she realized in surprise, it was less than two weeks since this madness started.

They'd eaten pizza, washed down with a pitcher of root beer. Afterward they'd gone to a video arcade, the only people over twenty in the place, and she had beaten Theo at several games. She'd laughed at his clumsy efforts, unable to believe he'd never played video games in his life. "Weren't you ever a kid?" she'd teased him.

"Sure I was but they didn't have these kinds of games where I was growing up. And I worked for my father when I was in high school. I didn't have the time nor the money to go out a lot. I was saving for college. What did you do, spend your childhood in arcades? I bet your mother loved that."

"She knew I was trying to help some of the kids who were thinking of dropping out of school."

"So you were a social worker when you were fifteen."

Jenny had pretended to scowl at him. "Not quite, but I knew what I wanted to do. The games came in handy later. Easy to get a kid's attention when you can beat him at arcade games."

As Theo turned into the driveway, an opossum ran across in front of the car, a pale furry ghost in the darkness. He braked, swerving to avoid the creature, and downshifted, coasting to a stop in front of the garage doors.

"Tiger," Jenny said suddenly. "Did you see Tiger this evening?"

Theo frowned, pushing the remote door opener. "No, can't say I have. But Edith was still here when we came. He doesn't like the commotion of cleaning. He's such a control freak, he hates it when anybody disturbs his domain. And the pine cleaner she uses makes him sneeze. Don't worry. He's probably on the back step right now, complaining about his missed dinner."

They went into the house through the inner garage door. In the kitchen, Theo flicked on the light and walked to the back door. He threw it open.

Jenny saw him go stiff. An odd sound came from his throat, as if someone were strangling him. "Theo," she cried, running across the room, "what is it?"

He put one hand to block the doorway, but she pushed against it, looking anyway. She clapped her hand over her mouth as the pizza threatened a return trip.

On the step lay a dead rat, spread-eagled and neatly eviscerated. A sheet of white paper hung on the door frame, held in place by a large chef's knife. Words sprawled across it, blotches of red ink.

Swallowing the bitter bile in her throat, Jenny blinked to clear her vision. "Next time it won't be a rat. It will be a cat." Night damp had made the letters run so that they resembled dripping blood.

"Call Baldwin," Theo said tonelessly.

Baldwin came within fifteen minutes, prompting Theo's question: "Don't you ever take a day off?"

"Of course I do, but this isn't one of them." A camera dangled from his hand. "Let's see what you've got here."

Baldwin snapped pictures, and gathered the evidence into plastic bags, sealed and labelled them. His methodical competence did much to calm Jenny's frazzled nerves. "Where is your cat?" Baldwin asked, glancing around the kitchen.

"We haven't seen him," Theo said. "But a dead rat that he didn't put there would be enough to spook him."

"I suppose so." Baldwin stared at the bloodstain on the concrete, his fingers stroking his chin. He straightened. "You can wash it down, if you want. I'm through."

He wrote up a report, pursing his lips when they showed him the obituary notice and told him about the nonevents of the past three days. "The peace truly exploded, didn't it?"

Theo's mouth turned down. "An understatement, if you ask me."

"Any ideas yet who might be behind this?" Baldwin asked.

Theo shook his head. "Nobody that we would want to accuse. I am running a check on someone but since I requested it, we've talked to him and sort of ruled him out."

"Mind telling me who it is?"

"*We-e-l-ll,* if he's innocent, I don't want him to get into trouble. Especially since he seems to have troubles of his own."

Baldwin set his pen on the table with a snap. "Mr. Zacharias, contrary to what you see on television, we don't charge around making accusations without foundation. Any inquiries I make would be very discreet. You can trust me."

"Okay. It's a colleague of mine who seems in dire need of money to pay off gambling debts."

"You mean Douglas Stevens." He smiled a little at Theo's startled look. "Yes, we've considered him, too. But he appears not to fit the pattern of the incidents. Not enough imagination. Of course someone else may be controlling him."

"Someone is," Jenny said. "If it's him. I'm inclined to think we're barking up the wrong tree, though. The simple need for money doesn't usually drive people to criminal actions. There generally has to be another, even stronger motive. And we can't find any in Doug."

"So far," Theo reminded her. He turned to Baldwin. "I've got a private investigator in Montreal looking into his background. I should hear from him anytime."

Baldwin closed his notebook and returned it to his pocket. "I'll just take a look around the house, make sure there's no other surprises."

He checked the basement last, coming up frowning,

with a subdued Tiger in his arms. "Here's your cat. I checked all the windows and can't find how he could have gotten in there except by this door. Could you have shut him in by accident?"

"I don't think so. We didn't have the basement door open this morning." Theo went to take the cat from the policeman's arms but Tiger ignored him, leaping to the floor. He sat there glaring at all of them, looking thoroughly disgruntled. "Do you remember, Jenny?"

She shook her head. "No, I'm sure we put him out this morning."

"Well, he got in somehow. What about your cleaning lady?"

Theo's face cleared. "That must be it. Edith let him in and while she was working, he got down in the basement and couldn't get out." He looked at Tiger as the cat sat down by the back door and scratched at the panel, meowing. "He wants to go out."

"Is it safe to let him out?" Jenny asked anxiously.

Theo laughed harshly. "Safe or not, he'll make our life a misery if we try to keep him in. Besides, he's a smart cat, too smart to get caught by a stranger."

"And if it's not a stranger?" Baldwin said ominously.

"He hasn't been friendly to anyone but Jenny since I've had him."

"He came to me, just now," Baldwin said.

"That was because he wanted to get out. He didn't go to you the other day, did he? Or didn't you see him?"

"I saw him," Baldwin confirmed. "And you're right. He hissed and spat at me, defending his territory."

"There you have it," Theo said. He opened the door. The cat sinuously strolled through it, pausing to sniff at the wet spot on the step before daintily pacing around it. He vanished between clumps of heather in the flower bed.

"I guess that's it for tonight." Baldwin picked up the evidence bags and his camera. "I'll get back to you. Let me know if you hear from your investigator, or if you think of anything else that might be helpful. In the meantime, I'll order the regular patrol to make a couple of extra runs past here overnight. Good night."

He left, going out the back door. Theo called for the cat, who, surprisingly, came at once. And appeared willing to stay inside for the night. He went to his seldom used bed in the corner of the kitchen, turned around several times, kneading the cushion with his paws, and settled down, front paws curled toward each other under his chin.

"Smart cat," Theo said approvingly. Tiger flicked his good ear back and forth, yawned and closed his eyes.

Theo found Jenny in the living room, lights off, standing in front of the window, her arms crossed around her waist. He walked up behind her, wrapping his arms around hers. She stiffened briefly, then leaned back, molding her back to him, resting her head against his shoulder. He drew in the sweet warm scent of her, woman and flowers mixed with the tartness of apples. "Jenny," he pleaded. "Stay with me tonight. I need you."

She turned her head. He could barely see her eyes in the darkness, the sheen of tears in them. "Yes," she said simply.

They went to his room, undressing on opposite sides of the bed, using only the dim night-light in the hall for illumination. He looked across at her, and it seemed as if she silently entreated him to come to her. He knelt on the turned-down bed and held out his hand. She took it, coming down next to him.

They lay for an endless space of time, breast to chest, belly to belly, thigh to thigh, only their lips meeting, mating, absorbing the essence of each other through their skin. Theo sighed. "Promise me you'll give me a chance after this is over."

She said nothing, merely pressing her mouth to his again, as if she were drinking in his taste. Her scent swam in his brain. He inhaled the essence of her as if it were life itself. If this turned out to be the last time he ever loved her, he had to store up the memory against the sterile future, so that he would be able to take it out and replay it again and again.

She ran her hands down his body, inciting fire in every cell, exploring him so boldly he gasped and squirmed. He gritted his teeth, poised on the edge of explosion. Her mouth followed her hands. Wet heat enveloped him, flames licking along all the nerves in his body. He was losing it, but then she paused, smiling at him, and he grabbed onto the last shred of control. Giving himself up to the ecstasy, he began to count from a hundred backward.

He only made it to ninety-four. He pulled her beside him and leaned over her, kissing her deeply. She reached between them, wrapping her fingers around him and guiding him to her. He paused, gazing down at her, seeing the soft light in her eyes, the high flush on her cheeks that told him how close she was to climax. Truth or lies, she completed him, made him whole.

He joined with her softly, stroking her gently, savoring the delicious scent of her, the rapid beat of her heart against his. When she finally tensed against him for the final plunge into ecstasy, he was ready, leaping into space with her.

I love you. The words echoed in his head but he couldn't make his tangled tongue utter them. Not until he was sure they weren't a lie. Not until he knew there were no lies between them.

Tomorrow.

"WE NEED GROCERIES," Jenny said the next morning as she dragged herself out of Theo's arms.

"We could stay here forever," he said lazily, tightening them around her.

She squirmed against him, pausing to smile saucily when she felt his reaction. "Down, boy," she said. "You had plenty last night." She yawned luxuriously. "I haven't slept that well in ages."

"Neither have I," Theo said. "So why don't we sleep some more? Maybe we can outlast the creep if we never go out again."

"We'd starve," Jenny declared, finally freeing herself. She groped for her underwear and her shirt, holding them in front of her while she walked around the bed toward the bathroom.

Theo lay propped up against the pillows, as content as Tiger after a feed of tuna. "You don't have to be shy with me, Jenny. I've seen it all." His voice dropped to a seductive purr. "I've tasted it all."

She couldn't stop the blush that heated her skin, but she pulled the clothes away, spreading her arms wide for an instant before sticking out her tongue at him and whirling into the bathroom.

Theo stifled the urge to follow her. She was right. There was work to be done. He picked up the phone and punched in the numbers of the Montreal agency. Saturday morning, afternoon in Montreal, but that hardly mattered. The call would be transferred to Felix's house.

His friend picked it up on the second ring. "Theo, you finally called back."

Theo frowned. "What do you mean?"

"I left a message on your machine. Yesterday."

"Sorry. A lot happened here and I didn't check the machine. I thought the tape was full of crank calls."

"Okay, doesn't matter." Theo heard papers rustling. "Douglas Stevens, C.F.P., F.C.S.I., born and raised in Montreal. Attended university in Ottawa. Do you want to hear all this?"

"Just get to the good stuff," Theo said. "I know he and Lisa went to high school together. I know he was accused of embezzlement once but cleared. There's nothing against him here, although he's come close a few times. He's a gambler and in debt to what I gather are some rather nasty people.''

Felix whistled softly. ''Maybe you should consider changing your line of work, Theo. You're better at my job than I am.'' The papers rustled again. ''I checked out his gambling at your end, as well. That's why this took somewhat longer than it should have. Yes, he's in debt. In deep trouble. My man talked to some of his friends, and Stevens is thinking of leaving the country but he lacks the funds to do so.''

''He sold his BMW.''

''It didn't bring him much. He had to pay the outstanding loan on it so he only realized a couple of thousand. Not enough to bail him out. But wait for this.'' Felix paused.

''Come on, Felix. Give. What did you find out?''

''Your friend Doug was once friendly with Frances Schulze.''

''Frances Schulze?'' Theo thought for a moment. Suddenly the missing pieces fell into place.

Sort of.

''Francie Schulze,'' he repeated. ''Our neighbor.''

''*Oui.* That Frances Schulze. Whose husband, the judge, you sent to prison. Surprised?''

''Frankly, yes. Does this have something to do with her, after all? I thought the judge died in prison.''

''He did.'' He paused. ''Yes, I've got it here. He died on April 13, so it's almost two years ago. I talked to Frances. She's well and happy, about to be married again. She's relieved it's all over and asked me to thank you again.''

The puzzle pieces scattered again. Theo ground his teeth in frustration. ''Wherever we go in this, we hit a dead end. Unless Doug has some twisted motive we're not seeing. When did he know Francie and under what circumstances?"

"He dated her before she married the judge. They broke it off several years before Doug left Montreal. Amicably it seems."

"No motives there, then. And I didn't know any of them at the time. She and the judge were only married two or three years before he went to prison. There was quite an age gap between them, as I recall."

"Twenty years, at least," Felix confirmed.

"I wonder why she married him?"

Theo could practically hear Felix's shrug. "Prestige, maybe. The judge looked like a surefire appointment to the Supreme Court or the Senate. Until you exposed him for what he really was, a sadistic bastard who nearly killed his wife."

"Did Doug have anything to do with the judge and Francie after they were married?"

"Not that I could find out."

Disappointed, Theo sighed. "So he's in the clear. I guess we have to start over."

"Maybe not," Felix said. "I figured there had to be some kind of connection. It was just too convenient that his name came up with both Lisa and Francie Schulze. Seems the judge was married once before. He had a daughter about Francie's age. Stevens dated the daughter after Francie married the judge."

Dread gathered coldly in Theo's stomach. All his early suspicions of Jenny rushed back like a marauding horde. "What was her name?" He could hardly force out the words.

"Cynthia Schulze. At least I think that's still her last name."

Cynthia Schulze, not Jenny Gray. She couldn't be the daughter. The realization sent euphoria bubbling through his veins.

"I'm trying to track her present whereabouts," Felix was saying. "It appears she's not in Montreal anymore, either."

"Montreal must be almost empty, so many people have left," Theo said, knowing he sounded ridiculous but not caring. Jenny could be trusted. She wasn't behind the incidents. He felt like dancing around the room. Instead he nuzzled his face into the pillow next to him and breathed in her scent. The shower was running. If he could get rid of Felix—

"I'm trying to track this Cynthia down," Felix was saying. "Theo, are you still there?"

"I'm here." He almost laughed aloud.

"You wouldn't happen to know if Doug is dating anyone by that name, would you? Sometimes these things are easy."

"Not that easy, this time," Theo said. "Doug's seeing a young woman named Blossom but she's always lived in Vancouver. So has Janice, another woman he occasionally dates. I don't know about anyone else. What makes you think Cynthia might be here?"

"One of her friends I interviewed. Said Cynthia was thinking of going to the coast. Of course, it could be the East Coast but most people mean Vancouver when they talk about the coast. So I'm looking there first. Thought you could save me some time but since the name doesn't ring a bell, I guess I'll have to slog on." He shuffled the papers again. "About your Jenny Gray—"

Yes, his Jenny Gray, Theo thought smugly. He was never going to let her go.

"Gray is clean. Father took off when she was just a baby. Brought up by her mother. Scholarships helped her through college. Worked for the B.C. government as a social worker. Quit and started a bicycle messenger service. Barely making ends meet."

"Don't I know it?"

Something in his voice must have alerted his friend.
Felix laughed. "What, have you finally gotten over Lisa,
Theo? About time, I'd say. Is this woman the one? Let
me know. I want to dance at your wedding."

Theo laughed. "We'll see. I haven't asked her yet. And
if you'd get off the phone, maybe I can go work at it."

"Okay, *mon ami*. I'm gone. I'll call you."

Grinning, Theo headed for the bathroom where the
shower had just stopped.

IT WAS EARLY AFTERNOON before they headed for the
shopping center, taking both cars. Theo needed a service
on his. If it couldn't be done immediately, he didn't want
to leave Jenny waiting around when she wanted to go
grocery shopping.

She turned off the street into the supermarket lot. Theo
gave her a thumbs-up signal and drove to the garage two
blocks away.

Jenny cruised the parking lot, looking for a vacant spot.
She finally spotted one, next to an evergreen hedge at the
back of the lot. She got out of the car and locked it. Not
much activity at this end of the mall. Must be the employees' parking area, she thought as she hiked toward
the buggy corral.

She had her quarter ready for the shopping cart when
a hand fell on her arm. Startled, she whirled, coming up
against a solid chest.

"Doug, what are you doing here?"

Chapter Fourteen

He didn't smile. Tension lined his face. She shivered, un-
accountably nervous at the way he was looking at her.
Oddly, for such a warm day, he was wearing thin, black
leather gloves. "Doug, is something wrong?"

"Where's Theo?"

"He went to get his car serviced. Oil change, you
know. He should be here any minute." The wild look in
Doug's eyes frightened her. Had one of their speculations
about him been correct? Was he on drugs?

She stepped aside to move around him, smiling
brightly. "It was nice to see you, Doug. I've got to get
the shopping done."

"Not so fast. I want you to take me to Theo."

"Why?"

"Because I need both of you," Doug said. Sweat stood
out on his forehead.

A hard metal object poked her in the side. She looked
down. A gun. Disbelief rushed through her even as her
blood chilled. A gun. Where would Doug get a gun? And
why?

The deep breath she hauled in to steady herself died in
her throat. His cologne. An image of a dark hall and a
hard arm around her throat leaped into her mind.

"It was...you, wasn't it?"

"Me? What are you talking about?"

"In my building, last week. You attacked me."

He laughed harshly. "Only to scare you, dear heart. You had no business interfering. And now you'll have to pay."

He jabbed the gun barrel painfully into her ribs. "Come on. Back to your car. We'll pick him up."

"Pick who up?"

As she heard Theo's voice, a fatalistic dread made Jenny go numb inside. If only he'd stayed away a little longer. Once she was in the car, she could have bought more time by pretending she didn't know where Theo was. Theo would have realized she wasn't in the store and called the police.

But now that he was here, she had to warn him. She turned slowly, not wanting to make Doug more nervous than he was. The gun drilled into her side.

"Hi, Doug. A bit far from home, aren't you?"

A false cheerfulness in his voice alerted Jenny that he knew something was wrong. She hoped he wouldn't try any heroics, that he would casually walk away and call Baldwin. Did he see the gun?

The bigger question was, would Doug use it, or was he all show and no action? She thought of the eviscerated rat lying on the doorstep last night, and shuddered. No, he used actions if he needed to. She couldn't underestimate him.

"Haven't you started shopping yet, Jenny?" Theo said, again with the heartiness she didn't believe.

"I couldn't find a parking spot." Her voice shook only a little.

"Why don't we quit the charade and get back to your car?" Doug cut in. He moved his hand away from his body, revealing the gun to Theo. "Do exactly as I say or she gets it first."

Theo's expression didn't alter. He spread his hands, shrugging. "I'm cool. What do you want, Doug?"

Jenny's mouth was dry but her palms were sweating. She wiped them down the sides of her jeans. The gun poked into her ribs again. "Ouch, that hurt. I'll go with you. Just don't shoot."

She put a whimpering note in her voice, not that she needed to fake it. Her knees were shaking and she was scared out of her mind. But she hadn't lost the ability to think. To plan.

Doug was nervous. Nervous people made mistakes. She could get him to underestimate her. And if Theo would play along, not try to jump Doug until they had a good opening, they might get away yet.

Doug grabbed her arm, keeping the gun hidden against her sweater. No one came along. As she had guessed, this area of the parking lot, near the back of the mall, was little used. She deliberately dragged her feet and let her body hang limply against him as Doug herded them back to her car.

"In the back seat, Theo." Doug waited as Theo flipped the seat forward and crawled into the back of the little, two-door car. "You drive, Jenny." As he hesitated, she could tell he was calculating how to get into the car without taking his eyes or his gun off her. And watch Theo at the same time. Too bad this wasn't Theo's four-door Saab. They would have been able to jump Doug by now, unless he'd tied them up.

He slammed the driver's door, waving the gun at Theo for good measure. On the passenger side, he grabbed the keys from her and unlocked the door. He pushed her in ahead of him, leaning forward with the gun extended while she scrambled awkwardly over the gear lever. Then he sat down, pulling the seat belt around and snapping it into place.

"A law-abiding citizen, I see," Theo said sarcastically

from the back seat. Jenny glanced in the rearview mirror. Despite the grim lines of his face, he winked at her. Glancing surreptitiously at Doug, she blinked her left eye to show Theo she was on his wavelength. Any opening, they'd take it. They might as well go down fighting.

Doug turned his head and spoke quickly into a cellular phone he took from his pocket. He set it on the seat between his thighs and handed her the keys. "Okay, start the car."

Jenny put the key into the ignition. Don't start. Don't start, she chanted in her head. The ignition relay was worn, and the starter sometimes refused to engage.

The angel in charge of car technology wasn't listening. The engine, still warm from the drive to the mall, turned over immediately. She backed out of the space, debating whether to ram another parked car. Not a good idea. Not here, where there was no one around, and the sudden impact might jar Doug's tense fingers into tightening around the trigger. She would wait.

"Where to?" she asked, shoulders slumped. She made her hand tremble on the gear lever, pretending her foot slipped on the clutch. Doug nearly jumped out of his skin when the gears meshed with a horrible grinding noise.

"Don't you know how to drive?" he snarled, prodding her with the gun again.

She flinched away, aware of Theo clenching his fists and leaning forward. "Keep that gun out of my face," she said in a shaky voice. "You're making me nervous."

He pulled back the gun. "Just drive east down the Fraser Highway. I'll tell you where to turn."

She joined the line of traffic pulling up to the light at the intersection, keeping her eyes strained for the sight of a police car. Naturally they were never around when you wanted one.

She squealed her tires making the left turn, hoping to attract attention, but only a couple of guys in a rusty Camaro gave her a thumbs-up. She pointed with her left hand toward Doug, but the guys just waved and peeled off ahead of her.

"Look, Doug," Theo said. "This is stupid. I know it's about money but surely a few gambling debts can be cleared up without killing anyone."

"A few debts?" Doug snorted. "I'm in hock about half a million dollars and they want it yesterday. You don't have that kind of money, at least not where you can get your hands on it."

"And how much are you being paid for this?"

"Not enough, probably, but once you're dead, I'll get the rest of ten thousand dollars. It'll be enough to get out of here and make a new start somewhere else. I'm thinking of Mexico. It's still pretty cheap to live there, and I can always get a new name and set up a business. Lots of opportunity."

"And who's going to pay you this money?"

Doug let out a rough laugh. "Wouldn't you like to know? It's partly a favor for a friend." He pointed the gun between the seats. "Shut up, Theo. If you think this is like Perry Mason and that I'm going to spill my guts because you're dying anyway, think again. It's not going to happen."

"A favor for a friend, huh?" Theo said sardonically. "Some friends you've got."

"Did you hide Theo's files and try to blame poor Eddie?" Jenny asked.

"Eddie?" His brow furrowed. "Oh, you mean the janitor. Yeah, why not? He was new and I didn't want it to look like an inside job. Stupid kid, he didn't want to make some extra money."

"Why didn't you get help before you got in so deep?" Theo said. "There are organizations that help gamblers. And the police could have taken care of the people you owed."

"Fat chance," Doug said.

"Did you get a charge out of killing those animals and leaving them on my steps?" Theo said nastily.

"Not me." Doug shook his head emphatically. "I didn't kill anything. That must have been my partner. Now shut up. I don't want to talk about it."

They had passed Aldergrove before Doug told Jenny to turn south on a narrow country road. She glanced into the rearview mirror at Theo but he just shook his head. She interpreted that to mean "wait." A moment later she felt his left hand at her waist, squeezing gently. Reassuring.

Doug must have noticed the gesture. He lifted the gun and held it against Jenny's temple. "Keep your hands to yourself, Theo. I wouldn't like to blast her brains all over you."

"If I were you," Theo drawled with deceptive mildness, "I wouldn't mess with the driver. Your life depends on her, too."

The terrain became increasingly barren. In all the years she'd lived in the Lower Mainland, Jenny had never been in this area. Gravel pits dotted the landscape, scars next to green meadows where cows and horses grazed. The few houses visible were set well back from the road.

Doug lifted the cell phone and spoke briefly into it. Jenny could only make out the words gravel pit and a street name she didn't catch. She hadn't noticed what the number of this road was, something she was sure to regret, she thought. But maybe Theo had seen the sign.

"Okay, you'll see a driveway just ahead, with a chain-link fence," Doug said. "Turn there."

She did so, braking in front of a sagging, rusty gate. Inside the compound she saw a large pit, full of water from the winter rains. "Kill the engine."

She turned the key. Doug snatched it out of the ignition, shoving it into his pocket. He adjusted his hold on the gun and grabbed her arm. "Come along. I have to open the gate but I'm not taking any chances on you and Theo cooking up some plan." He glanced into the back seat, at the silently glaring Theo. "And don't try to get out of the car. If I see you moving, I'll kill her. I don't much care how I do it."

Jenny again went into her act of the terrified woman, forcing him to half carry her. Swearing profusely, his shirt soaked with sweat under the arms, Doug managed to get her up to the padlocked gate. How was he going to get it open?

Jenny didn't have to wait long. In one smooth movement, he flipped the heavy chain over the post. It fell to the ground with a clank. He'd prepared it ahead of time, she realized. He pulled her with him as he dragged the gate along the dusty ground. Toward her car.

Jenny bit her lip to keep the groan of frustration inside. If it had opened inward, they would have been farther from the car. Theo might have had a chance to either rush Doug or run for help. Knowing Theo, the first was most likely. He wouldn't leave her behind, at the mercy of this bastard pulling her arm practically out of the socket and waving the gun under her nose with his sweating, shaking hands. Any moment now it would go off and she'd be dead.

She wiped the back of her hand across her forehead, and let her knees sag. Doug jerked her upright. "Oh, no, you don't. Just get back in the car."

He gave her the keys. She restarted the car and drove into the compound, tires crunching on the gravel. He directed her to the back end of the pit, where a steep bank hung high over the still water.

"Okay, now we wait." He pulled out the cell phone, punched in a number and spoke into it. "Where are you?" Pause. "Good. About ten minutes, then."

Ten minutes to live? Jenny met Theo's bleak gaze in the rearview mirror. They couldn't just sit there, waiting for Doug's accomplice. The two of them against Doug, even with a gun to fortify his position, was better odds than two against two. They couldn't afford to wait. The other person might also have a gun, making the odds impossible.

Ten minutes. She searched her mind for an excuse to get out of the car. "I have to go to the bathroom. There isn't one in those old buildings, is there?"

Doug shifted uncomfortably. "Do you have to? It won't be long now."

It would be if she had anything to say about it. She fully intended to live to a ripe old age. With Theo. She put a note of desperation in her voice. "I really have to go. I always have to go to the bathroom when I'm nervous."

She could have sworn Doug blushed. "Okay," he said. "Drive down there."

She slowly backed the car away from the edge of the bluff, praying the ground wasn't as unstable as it looked. Next to the rusting trailers, which had once served as offices, she stopped the car. Doug opened the door and backed out, gesturing for Jenny to follow him. "You, too, Theo."

Theo looked at Jenny as he rose to his full height beside the car. She nodded faintly. They walked around the trailer. Half hidden in a small clump of alders, Jenny could see a blue plastic cubicle. A portable toilet no one had bothered to remove when the pit closed down.

She walked quickly, making the men hurry to keep up. If she could just get Doug off his guard for an instant—

Bees buzzed around her, flitting among the dandelions, which grew thickly along the barely defined path. She glanced up at the faded blue cubicle. More bees, flying in and out of the half-open door.

She smiled grimly. Her desperate prayers were about to be answered. Reaching the little building, she pretended to trip, letting herself fall with a thud against the hard plastic. The toilet rocked, almost toppling before it steadied. "Watch it," Doug said, his voice rising to a high squeak. The hand holding the gun twitched. He batted his other hand at a bee flying past his face.

"Shouldn't wear so much cologne, Doug," Theo said with a grin. He winked at Jenny, still half lying on the ground, and her spirits rose.

She scrambled to her feet, slamming her hand against the cubicle. The buzz of the bees rose to an angry pitch. She glanced back, gauging how close Doug was. Close enough. She stumbled backward, swatting her hand at the bees, which were pouring out of the cubicle.

They flew past her, heading for Doug and she nearly laughed. Theo was right; Doug's cologne was attracting them. He waved his arm in a desperate attempt to ward off the swarm of bees circling his head. He slapped his neck, the gun dangling loosely from his hand. "Ouch, damn it. I've been stung."

Jenny launched herself at Doug, putting all her weight into the lunge. Already off balance, he tried to push her back, but Theo was ready. He snatched up a rock and whacked Doug behind the ear. A solid blow would have knocked him out but Doug jerked his head to avoid more of the bees bearing down on him. The rock glanced off the back of his head.

Still, he fell to his knees, shaking his head and dropping the gun.

But the bees seemed determined that he was a threat to their territory. Another stung him, and another. Doug screamed, flailing his arms. He scrambled to his feet and ran toward the gate.

The sound of a car engine froze Jenny and Theo in their tracks. Doug burst out from behind the trailer just as the car turned into the driveway. The driver jerked the steering wheel around. Gravel spraying out from its wheels, the car spun in a new direction.

Straight toward Doug.

"Look out!" Jenny yelled.

He was blinded either by panic or bee stings. He appeared to throw himself directly into the path of the car. The bumper struck him below the knees and he flew over the hood, landing on the ground with a heavy thud. He lay in the settling dust, as limp as a rag doll.

Jenny and Theo ran toward him. The car's engine revved to a scream. Jenny slammed her hand over her mouth in horror. The car reversed and ran over Doug's body, lurching as if it were going over a speed bump.

Jenny and Theo slid to a stop on the driveway. The car stood facing them. "Get ready to run," Theo muttered. "I think we're next."

The driver revved the engine, wheels spraying gravel. The car spun toward them. Fortunately the poor traction slowed it down. Theo grabbed Jenny's arm and yanked her behind the trailers.

The car swung around the corner, metal shrieking as the fender scraped against the building. "Come on," Theo said. "It's too flat here. There's no cover, and we don't have time to check if any of the doors are unlocked."

They ran up the slope toward the high side of the quarry. Jenny gasped for breath, her throat burning as if she were being barbecued by a blow torch. Beside her, Theo wrapped his arm around her waist to drag her up the last, steep mound of earth.

The car couldn't follow them up there. Could it? Jenny looked back. It was climbing after them, fishtailing in the loose sand, then steadying in the weedy grass. The driver let up on the gas, shifted to a lower gear. The engine lugged valiantly, the tires scrabbling to find traction. A moment later it shot up to the top of the embankment.

"Run along the edge," Theo said urgently, giving

Jenny a push. "He won't go that close. The ground's too soft."

Jenny ran, a stitch in her side stabbing her. Her legs felt numb. Where was Theo? The blood roared in her ears, making her almost deaf but she should have heard his footsteps.

She glanced over her shoulder and her heart stopped. He was running away from the pit, drawing the car toward him. Terror arced through her, bitter and corrosive. *Theo, don't. No!* She wanted to scream but fear paralyzed her vocal cords.

Sweat dripped into her eyes. She wiped it away with the back of her hand. Through a shimmering veil, she saw the car.

It had veered away from its pursuit of Theo and was coming straight toward her. She ducked her head and ran, her breath rasping in her aching chest. Her legs felt mired in wet cement. She knew it was hopeless.

The car was so close she could feel the heat of the engine, smell the burnt coffee odor of a cooked radiator. Steam drifted over the hood. New hope surged into her exhausted mind. If she could just hold out a little longer, run a little farther, the engine would seize and they would be safe.

She ran close to the quarry's edge, sand and gravel shifting under her feet. Her leg gave way as she tripped in a pothole. She fell to her knees. Gravel rained down into the water below her.

The car was upon her. She clawed the ground, bracing herself to jump. But it slowed, then stopped, inches from her, the engine throbbing like a hungry lion savoring the moment before the kill.

Jenny gathered her legs under her. The car leaped forward. She rolled to the side, away from the edge. At the last second, the driver realized his mistake and swung the steering wheel. The worst thing he could have done. The car skidded on the loose gravel, fishtailing violently, out of control. Jenny lay on the ground, watching as it tilted and fell over the bank, nose first toward the water.

She crawled to the edge. The car hit with a great splash, then settled level in the water. Because of the rolled up windows, it didn't sink immediately.

Theo's hand fell on her shoulder. "Are you all right?"

Trembling all over, fighting nausea, she nodded.

He squeezed her arm and took off running down the slope. "We've got to get him out before the car goes down," he called back over his shoulder. "Get Doug's phone and call 911."

Coughing as she breathed in the dust hanging over the quarry, Jenny ran over to Doug. A dark stain seeped into the ground beneath his body, and she swallowed as her stomach heaved. Acid seared her throat. She crouched down beside him, gasping in disbelief when she saw he was still breathing.

She lifted his head, brushing back his hair. Pink bubbles fluttered over his lips with every labored breath.

He opened his eyes. "Can't collect now, can they?" A thin smile played over his blood-flecked lips. "Forgive me. Sin—" His eyes rolled back, glazed and unseeing. The shallow motion of his chest stilled.

Jenny expelled her own breath, willing her heartbeat to slow. She had to be strong, to think. She couldn't fall apart now. She reached into his pocket, grimacing at the sticky feel of blood soaking his clothes. She pulled out the cell phone and punched out 911.

"Your location, please."

Her eyes skittered around the site. "South of Aldergrove. Not sure what street." Her gaze fell on the faded lettering on the trailer. "A & B Excavating." She could hardly force the words out. "Looks like they've been closed for years. We need the police and an ambulance here as soon as possible."

A brief pause and then the operator's voice again. "I have your location. I'm relaying the message now."

Jenny put the phone in her own pocket. She glanced around, looking for something to cover Doug. It seemed obscene to leave his body out in the open with nothing to protect it.

Her car. It stood nearby. She opened the trunk and dragged out the blanket she carried for winter emergencies, and draped it over him.

She jogged back toward the quarry, anxiety knotting in her chest. Was Theo all right? She didn't hear a sound except the buzzing of the bees, and the almost hysterical chirp of a robin perched on one of the young alders.

She gulped in relief as she saw Theo wading to the edge of the pond, dragging the Rabbit's driver by a tight grip on the back of his jacket. She could only see a slender body, head covered by a black, knitted toque. A kid. He looked like a kid. Wraparound sunglasses hid his face.

Theo lifted the kid, hoisting him over his shoulder in a fireman's carry. "I don't know who it is," he said.

"Is he dead?" Jenny asked, amazed at the steadiness of her voice. She felt as if her emotions, having gone into overdrive for the past ten minutes, had now shut down in self-defense. Would she ever feel again?

"Just knocked out. Hit the steering wheel, I think, when the car went down. But there's not even any blood. Only a goose egg on his forehead. He'll be all right."

Theo laid him down on the grass near Doug's body. He bent and lifted the blanket Jenny had pulled over his face.

"Too late, poor bastard," Theo said softly, his mouth set grimly. He turned toward his captive, who was beginning to groan. "Let's have a look at who we've got here."

He yanked off the toque. An icy chill washed over Jenny. The sunny day turned gray, then black, and she swayed. She would have fallen if Theo hadn't noticed her sudden pallor and caught her against him. "What is it, Jenny? Not a kid after all, I see. Do you know her?"

She dragged herself back together, opening her eyes and squinting in the brightness. "It's...Cindi," she said in a strangled whisper.

Theo gaped at her. "Cindi? You mean the Cindi who transfers my calls to your office?"

Jenny nodded, her stomach a cold, empty hollow. She hugged her arms around herself, thinking she'd never be warm again. "Yes, that Cindi."

Suddenly angry, she threw herself down in the grass and grabbed the front of Cindi's black jacket, yanking her up. "Cindi, how could you? We were friends."

Cindi's hair stood in spikes all over her head. She opened her eyes, blinking slowly. The pupils were dilated, and they had a peculiar glassy sheen.

"Why, Cindi?" Jenny demanded, her voice rising. "I thought you were my friend."

"I was, but you went to Zacharias. How did you find out?"

Jenny opened her fingers to release Cindi's jacket. She flexed them, realizing she'd had the fabric in a death grip. Cindi lay inert, her arm across her eyes. "I heard you on the telephone, planning it," Jenny said. "Of course I didn't know it was you but you made the call from the lunch room, didn't you? It wasn't crossed wires after all. And when I went in there, you'd already gone out the door. How did you get away so fast?"

"Down the fire stairs."

Jenny nodded. She hadn't thought to check them that day. "And what did you use to disguise your voice?"

Cindi laughed hoarsely. "A scrambling device. I did my research. My only mistake was thinking Doug had the guts to go through with this. But he kept screwing up and I had to do practically everything. This wasn't supposed to happen today, either. But he was too chicken to wait..."

Her voice went up a decibel, to a shrill screech. "That idiot didn't even load his gun."

"What?"

Theo picked Doug's gun up from the ground where it had fallen when he and Jenny had run from the Rabbit. He released the clip and swore as he saw it was empty.

"So Doug held us hostage with an unloaded gun," he said in disgust.

"He kept wimping out on the tough stuff," Cindi snarled. "He even tried to pay some kid to do what I hired him for."

"Eddie," Jenny said.

"Yeah, Eddie. Even punks are wimps these days."

Jenny bristled. "Eddie's no punk. He's got a job and a future."

Cindi turned her head and spat out dust. "You got to him, did you, Ms. Do-gooder Social Worker? I might have known. So Doug struck out there, too. I had to get the gun myself. By then Doug said he needed the money so badly he'd do it. But he screwed up again. He felt sorry for you, Jenny. Wanted to save you. Probably thought you'd go for him if he killed Theo."

"Not likely," Theo said explosively. "Besides, he was planning to leave, go to Mexico."

"I wouldn't have let him get away. He knew too much." Cindi fixed her gaze on Jenny, hatred in the harsh lines that made her look older than her age. Jenny crouched in the weeds, wondering how Cindi could have fooled her for a year. Of course Jenny hadn't been the target all this time, but some latent evil should have been visible.

"How can adults be such fools for love?" Cindi said. "You really fell for Theo the minute you saw him, didn't you, Jenny? It just made me sick to see you mooning around over a man like that." She snorted derisively. "I thought you were so smart, and here you go and fall for a bastard like him."

Jenny settled back on her heels, frowning. "I don't understand. What did Theo ever do to you? He didn't even know you."

"I knew her father," Theo said quietly. "Didn't I, Cynthia Schulze?"

Cindi's eyes widened. Her mouth twisted into an ugly grimace. "You killed him."

"He nearly killed his wife. Was his life more valuable than hers?"

"To me, it was. She was never my mother. We were doing fine until she got her claws in him. She took him away from me." Cindi spat out the words. "When he died in prison, I swore I'd get even. It took a while to track you down, but I did it. And then I had to make you suffer, like he did, in that prison, with the criminals. Do you have any idea what it's like for a judge to be among animals like that? They saw him as the reason they were prisoners. They made his life a misery. I had to make you suffer the same way."

"So that was it," Theo said. "April 13. Your father died on that day so you wanted to take me out on the anniversary."

Cindi shrugged. "It seemed appropriate."

"And I suppose it was you who stole the bike and attacked Theo with it?" Jenny asked, smarting under the lash of betrayal.

"Of course. Since you gave me breaks whenever I wanted them, you played right into my hands."

She turned to Theo, letting out the weird, cackling laugh Jenny had heard on the phone the first day. "I hope you enjoyed my little offerings on your doorstep."

Theo said nothing. He stood there, looking down at her, his eyes empty of all but pity, while sirens wailed in the distance. "Here's the troops," he said tonelessly.

Two police cars rolled to a dusty stop, followed by an ambulance. Theo jerked Cindi to her feet and pushed her toward the officer stepping out of one of the cruisers. "This woman is responsible for that man's death," he said, dusting his hands as the officer took over.

He handcuffed Cindi and led her to the car. Cindi turned her head and screamed, "I'll get you yet, Theo Zacharias. You won't get away with it."

"Don't worry, sir," the other policeman said. "We'll take care of her. Now, tell me what happened here."

The ambulance crews examined Doug's body, shaking their heads. They covered him with a black plastic sheet and transferred him to a stretcher. They loaded it, and after a short conference with the police, drove off.

The two officers walked over to the quarry, staring at the white Rabbit, settled in the water with only its roof visible above the surface. They came back, measuring the skid marks on the gravel road, making notes.

Jenny, her knees as weak as overstretched rubber, sat down on a patch of grass with her back against a rusty trailer. After giving Doug's gun to the police, Theo joined her.

He took her hand in his, turning it over and kissing the grimy palm. The smile he offered her was strained. Lines radiated from the corners of his eyes and he looked as exhausted as she felt.

"You will marry me when this is over, won't you, Jenny?"

Shock rendered her speechless. "I—I—" she stammered.

His smile became more natural. "It's a simple question. Only needs a simple answer."

"Why?" she said, feeling like a fool as soon as the word burst out. "Only a few days ago, you didn't trust me. You were still equating me with Lisa. We've never talked about it."

He shrugged. "Do we need to? Lisa's in the past. This is now. I did trust you, Jenny, a long time ago, but I wouldn't admit it. But this whole thing has shown you're a woman I can depend on. No matter how rough it got, especially today, when anyone would have been panicking and screaming her head off, you stayed cool and got us out."

"We got out together." She grinned, unable to suppress the elation rising in her. "Yes, I'll marry you, Theo. I'd be honored."

He looked at her, a smile spreading over his face. "My parents will love you. I think it's time I made it up with them."

He leaned toward her. She waited, breathless, for his kiss but before he could join their mouths, he saw the policemen approaching. "Oh-oh, here comes the interrogation squad. And since we're out of Baldwin's jurisdiction, we'll have to go through the whole story from the beginning."

"IF WE HURRY," Theo said outside the Langley police station several hours later, "we'll be able to pick up my car. Otherwise it's in the garage until Monday."

"Okay." Jenny rubbed her temples. Her head ached from the hours of going over every detail of the stalking. The Langley police had contacted Baldwin's unit but since he was off duty until seven this evening, they hadn't spoken to him directly. Which meant Jenny and Theo had had to answer innumerable questions. She hoped the cops enjoyed writing up the lengthy reports.

She handed her car keys to Theo. "Why don't you drive?"

The garage was just closing when they pulled up. The mechanic handed Theo his keys and directed him to the office. "I'd about given up on you." He ran his gaze up and down their rumpled, dusty clothes. "Looks like you were in a war."

Jenny and Theo exchanged glances and burst out laughing. "Something like that," Theo said when he could talk. "Congratulate us. We're getting married."

"I wish you well." The mechanic went back into the garage, shaking his head and muttering about crazy people who must have had too much sun for this early in the spring.

"Just go on home, Jenny," Theo said. "I'll be right behind you."

The house appeared undisturbed. For once Jenny didn't have a sensation that someone might be watching them. Theo pulled up in front of the garage and got out of his car, slamming the door. Tiger, his tail raised in a graceful arc, strolled out of the bushes, purring.

Theo unlocked the front door. He scooped Jenny up in his arms, carrying her inside and pushing the door shut with his heel. He let her slide down his body and covered her mouth in a kiss that sent ripples of heat all the way to her toes. "Have I told you I love you?" he said when he came up for air.

Jenny grinned, her breathing quick and unsteady. "No, I think you forgot that part. But it's okay. I love you, too."

She tangled her fingers in his hair and brought his face down to hers, kissing him deeply. Tiger took one look at them and stalked off to the kitchen in disgust.

The phone rang, startling them. For an instant, Jenny felt the hot surge of adrenaline that had been her too-frequent companion in the past two weeks. Then she laughed, forcing herself to relax. It was over. No one was stalking them now.

"Are you going to answer that?" she asked.

"Naw, let the machine get it."

She barely heard the outgoing message as he began to

kiss her again, one hand delving beneath her sweater, warmly circling her breast.

"I've tracked down Cynthia Schulze," said a male voice Jenny didn't recognize.

"Felix," Theo said. "My investigator."

"She's moved to Vancouver," Felix went on. "I'm working on an address. But it seems she got married somewhere along the line although hubby's long gone. But she kept his name. These days, she calls herself Cindi Brown."

Jenny's eyes met Theo's and she groaned. "If only I'd known."

Theo grinned and whirled her around. "Then I would never have met you. So I'm grateful to her."

Caught in his arms, Jenny gazed down into his face. "Then so am I. So am I."

Ring in the New Year with babies, families and romance!

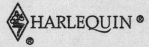

HARLEQUIN®

I N T R I G U E®

In steamy New Orleans, three women witnessed the same crime, testified against the same man and were then swept into the Witness Protection Program. But now, there's new evidence. These three women are about to come out of hiding—and find both danger and desire....

eye WITNESS

Start your new year right with all the books in the exciting EYEWITNESS miniseries:

#399 A CHRISTMAS KISS
by Caroline Burnes (December)

#402 A NEW YEAR'S CONVICTION
by Cassie Miles (January)

#406 A VALENTINE HOSTAGE
by Dawn Stewardson (February)

Don't miss these three books—or miss out on all the passion and drama of the crime of the century!

Look us up on-line at: http://www.romance.net   EYE1

Harlequin and Silhouette celebrate
Black History Month with seven terrific titles,
featuring the all-new *Fever Rising*
by Maggie Ferguson
(Harlequin Intrigue #408) and
A Family Wedding by Angela Benson
(Silhouette Special Edition #1085)!

Also available are:
Looks Are Deceiving by Maggie Ferguson
Crime of Passion by Maggie Ferguson
Adam and Eva by Sandra Kitt
Unforgivable by Joyce McGill
Blood Sympathy by Reginald Hill

On sale in January at your favorite
Harlequin and Silhouette retail outlet.

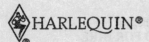 

Look us up on-line at: http://www.romance.net   BHM297